'But I am no g...

There was a ... ...ice
which made ...

'No, that mu... ...y,
and when he ... ...ed
up the bar of ... ...ed it at him. Her
aim was good and it struck him on the side of
the head, bounced off his shoulder and slithered to the floor. 'Get out!' she yelled.

He laughed and retrieved it, weighing it in his
hand as if considering whether to throw it
back. 'I could do with a bath too. How about
sharing it with me?'

Dear Reader

This month we offer you EMPIRE OF THE HEART from Jasmine Cresswell, where Lucy forcibly spends two years in Afghanistan before being rescued by 'Rashid', but on her return to London she finds that a certain Lord Ridgeholm bears a striking resemblance to the trader! This book offers a marvellous insight into the Victorian Empire, as well as a crackling romance. In THE PRICE OF HONOUR, Mary Nichols gives us Olivia, who foolishly defied her father to marry her sweetheart, and so found herself at the centre of heartstopping adventures in the Peninsular War! Two fast-paced and moving romances for you to enjoy.

The Editor

Born in Singapore, **Mary Nichols** came to England when she was three, and has spent most of her life in different parts of East Anglia. She has been a radiographer, school secretary, information officer and industrial editor, as well as a writer. She has three grown up children, and four grandchildren.

Recent titles by the same author:

THE DANBURY SCANDALS
DEAR REBEL

THE PRICE OF HONOUR

Mary Nichols

All the characters in this book have no existence outside the imagination of the Author, and have no relation whatsoever to anyone bearing the same name or names. They are not even distantly inspired by any individual known or unknown to the Author, and all the incidents are pure invention.

All Rights Reserved. The text of this publication or any part thereof may not be reproduced or transmitted in any form or by any means, electronic or mechanical, including photocopying, recording, storage in an information retrieval system, or otherwise, without the written permission of the publisher.

This book is sold subject to the condition that it shall not, by way of trade or otherwise, be lent, resold, hired out or otherwise circulated without the prior consent of the publisher in any form of binding or cover other than that in which it is published and without a similar condition including this condition being imposed on the subsequent purchaser.

First published in Great Britain 1993
by Mills & Boon Limited

© Mary Nichols 1993

Australian copyright 1993
Philippine copyright 1993
This edition 1993

ISBN 0 263 78057 0

Masquerade is a trademark published by
Mills & Boon Limited, Eton House,
18–24 Paradise Road, Richmond, Surrey, TW9 1SR.

Set in 10 on 10½ pt Linotron Times
04-9307-84539

Typeset in Great Britain by Centracet, Cambridge
Made and printed in Great Britain

PROLOGUE

'You have done *what*?'

'We have cashiered him, my lord, for unofficerlike and ungentlemanlike behaviour — after a proper court-martial, of course. In Lisbon.'

The heat in the room was intense and made no cooler by the temper of the commander-in-chief of the British forces, whose names included Hooknose, Nosey, the Peer and the Leopard, a name given to him by Napoleon, to which he had added the epithet 'hideous'. It did not bother the newly created Viscount Wellington in the slightest; he had adopted it with some amusement and was often heard to refer to his men as 'my leopards'.

For six months hardly a shot had been fired by either side and the inaction was causing boredom among the troops, not to mention impatience at Westminster. But now the enemy was on the move. Across the Pyrenees they had come, the hordes of Napoleon, eighty thousand strong, marching down through Salamanca towards the Portuguese frontier, mile upon mile of blue and white uniforms, led by Marshal André Masséna and accompanied by heavy cavalry and light horsemen, their coloured plumes moving up and down with the rhythm of their mounts; cuirassiers, whose breastplates glinted in the glaring heat of a Spanish summer; heavy guns on limbers pulled by teams of huge horses, baggage wagons by the thousand, kicking up the dust, advertising their presence to the bands of *guerrilleros* who watched from their mountain hide-outs, ready to pick off stragglers and raid the supply wagons.

They were still a long way from Celerico Da Beira

5

where the British commander-in-chief had his head-quarters, and he showed no sign of going out to meet them. While they waited, the officers filled their time with horse racing and shooting matches and the rank and file went fishing and whoring. There were times when the colonel wished the French would hurry their advance and mount an attack, just to give the men something gainful to do, but even if they did it would not happen here. Between them and the enemy front line stood General Craufurd and his Light Division. The colonel envied the dashing general who had found something better to do than keep discipline and worry about supplies.

'Dammit, he is one of my best scouts.' Wellington's voice broke in on his thoughts.

'Yes, my lord, but you did issue an order that there was to be no looting, and he was caught red-handed. No exceptions, you said, and the officers must set a good example.' The colonel stood his ground. He had only carried out orders, and how was he to know his lordship would ask for the man specifically? As far as he had been aware, there was nothing out of the ordinary about the fellow.

'To be sure I did.' The angry tone of the commander's voice softened as he realised the justice of what the colonel was saying. 'Looting, you say?'

'Yes, my lord.'

'Of all the ignoble things to be cashiered for,' his lordship mused. 'If he had to fall foul of regulations, why could it not be for duelling? At least that has something gentlemanly about it. I could forgive him for that.'

'Yes, my lord.'

'Where is he now?'

'I do not know, my lord. He left.'

'Has he returned to England, do you think?'

'I doubt it, my lord; he would not want to face his father, the viscount, and the public disgrace.'

'Then find him. Find him and bring him to me.'

There was no arguing with Wellington in his present mood; the colonel inclined his head and left the villa which was his regiment's temporary headquarters. The heat, as he stooped below the lintel and stepped outside, rose to meet him from the baked earth and the strong midday sun almost blinded him. Clapping his cocked hat on his head, he marched across what had once been a field but which now resembled a parade ground as a group of English drill sergeants endeavoured to make soldiers of the untidy riff-raff which made up the Portuguese army. There was a good deal of ribald comment from the red-coated British troops but the untested Portuguese *cacadores* took it all in good part. They were, after all, going to fight in defence of their homeland and were perhaps the only ones to be glad of the long period of inactivity, in which to train.

Where was Robert Lynmount? the colonel asked himself. Where was the one-time captain of Hussars, hero of the battle of Talavera and now disgraced? And how, in the middle of a war, when he had better things to do, was he going to find him and bring him back? And, what was more, how was he going to reverse the verdict of a properly convened court-martial when there was no doubt about the fellow's guilt? He swore loudly and sent a trooper in search of Captain Rufus Whitely.

CHAPTER ONE

SHE would go home, Olivia decided, back to England, to cool green glades and soft summer rain, to winter fires and roast beef, even to the censure of her friends and Papa's anger. Papa. If he could see her now, he would most decidedly tell her 'I told you so'; that was if he even recognised her as the daughter who had stood in his library three years before and rebelliously stamped her foot at him. She had, she remembered, been dressed in a becoming blue gown of watered silk, which had cost him a pretty penny, but then he had always been the most generous of papas — until she'd defied him.

Now she was wearing an old uniform jacket of Philippe's over a white blouse and green skirt which had certainly seen better days. On her feet were a pair of French infantry boots, nothing like as good as those worn by the British forces but certainly more serviceable than ladies' shoes, and on her head was a large straw hat tied down with a scarf. Her face, she had no doubt, was suntanned and dirty, and she was painfully thin. No, he would hardly recognise her.

She smiled to herself as she strode along the narrow pot-holed road, empty except for a bearded brown goat which had wandered down from the mountainside to crop the wayside grass, and a buzzard which tore savagely at the remains of a hare, anxious to have its dinner done before it was interrupted. It looked up as she approached, a juicy morsel hanging from its bloodied beak, but, deciding she was no threat, it resumed its meal.

It was funny how easy it was to lose the knack of thinking constructively, especially when all her thoughts kept coming back to the same thing—it was her own fault she was in the mess she was in; she could blame no one but herself. She would go home and face the music. Would the fact that she had been widowed twice in as many years elicit any sympathy from her father? But was it sympathy she wanted? She had never been one to feel sorry for herself, so why should she expect others to be sorry for her?

Tom Beeston was not a suitable husband for her, Papa had said; he was a nobody and she was rich enough to marry a title; he wanted her to marry a title. Besides, they were both too young to know their own minds on the subject. If she married Tom, she could expect no help from him if things went wrong. Young she had been, but she had also been determined and accustomed to having her own way, and this unexpected opposition had taken her by surprise and strengthened her determination. Married they were. Tom, she discovered within a month of the wedding, was a gambler, and before long was so deep in debt that she was in despair. But he had not been prepared for her to be equally stubborn about refusing to ask her father for help.

At his wits' end, he had fallen victim to the blandishments of a recruiting sergeant, so what else could she have done, she asked herself, but to stick by him and follow the colours? Not for a moment had she anticipated being lucky in the ballot which would allow her to accompany him abroad a few months later. They had hardly set foot in Portugal when the army, under the command of Sir Arthur Wellesley, had marched to free Oporto from the occupying French, and two days after that she was a widow for the first time.

It was the usual practice for women in her position to marry one of her late husband's comrades and carry on as before, but there was no one she liked well enough and she had had enough of the army. In the torrential rain which followed the battle and hampered

the British advance, she had tried to make her way
back to Oporto, hoping to find a ship's captain soft-
hearted enough to carry her back to England. Instead
she had blundered into the rearguard of the fleeing
French troops. They had seen in her an easy target and
would have taken their anger and humiliation out on
her if Philippe had not arrived to stop them. Not that
she had given in without a struggle; she had seized one
of their muskets and turned it on them before they had
overpowered her, laughing at her furious kicking and
scratching.

It was his sense of fair play and his admiration for
her courage that made him defend her in the first place,
he had told her, but within days he had declared he
loved her to distraction and no one would harm her
while he was at hand to protect her. He was a lieutenant and very young, lonely too, she suspected, and
highly susceptible. She had liked him enough to agree
to marry him when the alternative was too horrible to
contemplate, but she did not think she had ever been
in love with him, any more than she had, on reflection,
been in love with Tom.

That had been over a year ago, and since then she
had followed the French camp in much the same way
as she had followed the British with Tom, living each
day as it came and refusing to think of the future. It
had been the same the night before; her only thought
had to been to escape from the band of *guerrilleros*
who had killed Philippe, not what she would do afterwards. But with the coming of day she knew she had
decisions to make.

The land on either side of the road was parched, the
grass dried to the colour of ripe wheat which shim-
mered in a heat haze that made it look as if it were on
fire. Behind her the mountain rose to a craggy peak; to
her left the ground fell sharply away so that she was
looking down on the tops of the pines which covered
the lower slopes and partially hid the village in the

valley. It was set on either side of a small river which reflected the cobalt-blue of the sky and looked cool and inviting. Should she make her way down there? Would it be safe? The problem was that she did not know if she was in Spain or Portugal, nor whether the area was in French or allied hands.

To the French with whom she had lived for the past year she was English, and without Philippe to protect her she had no idea how they would view her reappearance, even supposing she could find them again. The British would, she was almost sure, look on her as a traitor, and she had no idea what punishment would be meted out for that, but whatever it was she would have to face it. It might be mitigated by the fact that she did have something to tell them. She knew the dispositions and the strength of the French army in the north and that it was unlikely that Marshal Soult, comfortably ensconced in the south, would come to their aid; Philippe had been more than a little indiscreet. But she would say nothing of that until she could speak to the right person, Viscount Wellington himself, if necessary.

The goat made for the hills again as she neared it and the buzzard, replete, soared into the sky. She stopped to watch it go, shading her eyes with her hand, but, alerted by the sound of the clip-clop of a horse behind her, she turned, poised for flight, though there was nowhere to hide. But the rider seemed in no hurry, certainly not as if he was pursuing a fugitive. He came slowly into view over the rise behind her and she stood to one side to allow him to pass. The black stallion, she noticed, was beautiful — in much better shape than its owner.

He wore a dusty red uniform jacket without braid or buttons to denote his rank, if rank he had, though he held his back straight and his head up as if he was used to command. His dark breeches and riding boots, though of good quality, were covered in the grime of many days' travel. His hair, beneath his shako, was cut

very short, and his face, though tanned, was unlined.
He could not have been more than thirty, but there
was about him an air of detachment, almost as if he
cared not whether she was a helpless female or a well-
armed enemy soldier. He might have been out for a
quiet hack in the English countryside, though a new
rifle slung on his saddle struck a jarring note. He
seemed indifferent to her, or too exhausted even to bid
her good day.

She watched him pass, his hands relaxed on the reins
as the horse took him down the steep slope and round
the next hairpin bend.

Why had she not hailed him? He might have been
able to tell her exactly where she was, how far she was
from the allied lines. He might even have offered to
take her up. Long gone were the days when she would
have been horrified at the very thought of sharing a
horse with a complete stranger. But his whole demeanour had discouraged her from speaking, and a British
coat meant nothing; it could have been stolen from a
body on a battlefield. He could have been a deserter
and going away from the British lines, not towards
them. She wondered what would happen if he ran into
the *guerrilleros* she had fled from during the night. He
would need to be more convincing than Philippe had
been.

Poor Philippe! He had been badly wounded at
Talavera and they had spent the winter at his home in
France while he recovered. His parents had tried to be
kind to her for his sake, but she was only too aware
that they thought of her as the enemy and she could
hardly blame them. Although she had been more than
grateful for Philippe's protection in those terrible days
after Tom had died, she had never truly changed sides.
Philippe himself had been restless and keen to return
to the war, even though his regiment had been all but
wiped out and the survivors had been posted to other
units. They had arrived back in Spain in July 1810, just

in time to be with Napoleon's army when it took the Spanish border post of Ciudad Rodrigo. The French troops had poured into the town, only to find it bereft of food and supplies.

Foraging parties had been sent out immediately and as the army was unlikely to continue its advance until it had been fed and provisioned—as always by the inhabitants of the surrounding countryside—Philippe had suggested a day out in the hills with a gun; they would shoot themselves a meal, he had said, and it would make a pleasant day out, just the two of them, away from everyone. The idea cost him his life and very nearly hers. And she was not sure yet if she was out of danger.

She blinked hard in an effort to erase the gruesome image of Philippe swinging from the branches of a cork oak, his legs kicking frantically as the life was choked from him. She had not wanted to watch, but her head had been jerked back by the leader of her captors. 'Too much for you, is it? You watch, *madame*, you watch and learn.' He had spoken in French and yet he'd looked no different from the rest of his band. All had been bearded and roughly dressed in goatskin coats and woolly hats and armed to the teeth with knives, swords and stolen muskets. 'That's one Frenchman who won't pull the tail of the leopard, though I could wish it were not his tail being presented to our enemies. It is his teeth we need to see.' He had moved round to face her. 'Now what shall we do with *madame*?'

She had recoiled as he'd advanced on her, which made him laugh. 'You are afraid of me?'

She had nodded. Ever since she and Philippe had been brought into the camp, she had been struck dumb and had not uttered a word, neither plea nor protest. Had she become so hardened to life in the raw, she asked herself, or was it simply a numbness, which crept

over her as kind of self-protection, a notion that if she
kept a tight hold of herself she could endure anything?

'We don't make war on women.' He had laughed
loudly while his men had looked from one to the other
and grinned, though she was sure they had not understood. 'Women we make love to.'

'Why do you speak in French?' she had asked in
English, and watched with satisfaction the look of
surprise on his swarthy face. 'That is the language of
your enemy.' She had paused, praying that Philippe
would forgive her, then added, 'And mine.'

'You are English?' The lecherous look had left his
face as he sat down beside her and leaned against the
tree to which she had been tied.

'Yes. And I thank you for my deliverance from
that. . .' She had made herself jerk her head towards
Philippe, whose futile kicking had ceased. His body
hung limp, spiralling slowly as the rope untwisted. 'I
was his prisoner.'

'When did that happen?' He had changed to speaking English. 'And how?'

Better not say Oporto, she had decided, that was too
long ago and might arouse his suspicion; better make it
more recent. 'A skirmish,' she said. 'A week ago.'

'You are a camp follower?'

She had drawn herself up and looked into his face
with all the dignity she could muster. 'I am a soldier's
wife.'

'What regiment?'

Where was Tom's regiment now? She was not sure,
but then the *guerrilleros* might not know that either.
'The Twenty-ninth.'

'Hmm, we shall see.'

'Perhaps you would be kind enough to take me to
the British lines?'

'You think we have time to spare to escort women
about the countryside? No, madam, you must wait on

our convenience. Besides, how do we know you are telling the truth?'

'Would I ask to be taken to the British if I were not?'

'To save your hide perhaps?'

'Am I in danger?' she asked sweetly, wishing they would take Philippe's body down and bury it decently. 'You said you did not wage war on women; I ask you to show that chivalry for which Spanish men are renowned and take me to my friends.'

He laughed at her flattery although not taken in by it. 'Perhaps you are a spy, sent to find out where the troublesome flea is that keeps biting the backside of the French cur. We could not let you take that information back to them.'

'Why should I do that?'

'It is not unknown for women to do such work.'

'Not I.'

'We shall see.'

'What are you going to do with me?'

'Keep you here while we find out where you have come from.' He paused and grinned. 'Do not worry, madam, we will not touch a hair of your head until we know the truth, but if you are lying. . .' He nodded towards Philippe. 'We will not hesitate to carry out the same punishment. You understand?'

She understood all too well. Could they prove she had lied? She was very much afraid that they could, and then what? She inclined her head in acquiescence. 'I will wait.'

'Good. Now you will eat.' He untied her hands and beckoned to another of the band and issued orders. Olivia, who had been in the Peninsula long enough to pick up a little Spanish and Portuguese, though she found speaking the latter difficult, understood he was ordering food and wine and a blanket for her. That meant they intended to spend the night in the camp, high up in the rugged mountains somewhere on the border between Spain and Portugal.

By the time the food was brought, they had taken
Philippe's body down and carried it off, presumably to
bury it, or perhaps to send it back to the occupiers of
Ciudad Rodrigo as a lesson to any who strayed outside
the perimeter of the town. Whichever it was, she forced
herself to pretend indifference, though she was glad
when she no longer had to see it.

The food was good and the blanket welcome and she
spent the rest of the evening pretending she was
pleased to be among friends. Only after they had all
settled down on the hard ground to sleep did she decide
to test whether they had posted sentries. Stealthily she
crept away, but before she had gone far a man stepped
out of the shadows and barred her way. 'I must relieve
myself,' she whispered, clutching at her abdomen and
grimacing. 'I have a pain.'

He waved her on. She walked slowly at first, even
going so far as to pause and pretend to be squatting
down, but when he moved over to the other side of the
camp she started to run and did not stop until she was
sure they were not pursuing her. By the time the sun
had risen above the distant mountains and felt warm
on her back, she estimated she had put several miles
between herself and her husband's murderers.

It was strange that they had not come after her, but
then perhaps they did not think she was worth the
effort. Now she had to make up her mind whether to
go into the village in the valley, which might contain
the homes of those same partisans, or keep to the high
ground and try to find her own way.

She had become so used to the distant rumble of
guns that she ignored the sound, but when the wind
blew suddenly chill and the sky became overcast she
realised it was not guns but thunder which reverberated
round the mountains. At the same moment she became
aware of huge spots of rain splashing on to the road.
She began to run.

The road dipped into the tree-covered lower slopes

and she noticed an iron gate with a crest on top, guarding a long drive. There was bound to be a house at the end of it, and a house meant shelter. The gate creaked noisily as she pushed it open but no one came out of the nearby gatehouse to ask her business. She ran up the drive, pulling Philippe's coat up over her head, and arrived, panting, on the steps of a considerable mansion.

She pounded on the door, but there was no response. She ran round to the back, found a door unlocked and let herself in. It had once been a luxurious home, she decided, as she moved through the kitchen quarters into the main hall with its grand staircase and beautifully tiled floor. Shouting in Spanish and then Portuguese, 'Is anyone at home?' produced no reply. She took off her wet coat and threw it over a chair, then made her way up the stairs and checked every room. The house was completely deserted. The few pieces of furniture which remained were of good quality, and those curtains which still hung at the windows were sumptuous, though covered in thick dust. She found a huge bedchamber with a carved and gilded four-poster and in the next room a hip-bath. She looked in the cupboards and discovered soap and towels and, thrown in the back of a wardrobe, a quilted dressing-gown. It was unclear whether the owners had had time to pack before leaving or whether the clothes and more easily carried furniture had been looted. She began a more systematic search and discovered a few more garments which, apart from the dust, were infinitely better than the skirt and blouse she had been wearing for the past week. They would have to be cleaned before she could wear them but that could be done later.

She had become so accustomed to watching French soldiers looting for their needs that she had no compunction about appropriating what she found for her own use. Here was luxury she had not seen since

leaving her father's home. It was heaven. She dashed
down the stairs again to look for food. There was
nothing to be found in any of the storerooms except a
few large onions, but outside there were thick-stalked
cabbages growing in the vegetable garden; she could
make herself *caldo verde*, a rich green cabbage soup
which seemed to be the staple diet of the Portuguese.

In no time she had a fire lit in the kitchen stove and
set a cauldron of water on it. Hungry as she was, a
bath came before food. She dragged the bath down the
stairs and set it before the kitchen fire, then went out
to gather the cabbage leaves. By the time she had
sliced the onions, set them on to boil and shredded the
cabbage finely, the water in the pan was hot enough to
add to the cold water she had already poured into the
tub. She smiled to herself as she threw off her clothes
and climbed into it. Once upon a time she had had a
maid to fill her bath, help her dress and see to her hair.
Her clothes had been clean and pressed and were
always ready to put on. As soon as the slightest sign of
wear or a tear had appeared, they had been discarded.
She looked across at the peasant skirt and blouse she
had been wearing for weeks and smiled; they were fit
for nothing but the bonfire.

She slid down among the soap bubbles and imagined
herself back at home. Her bath would be in her
bedroom, where a fire would be blazing and all her
clean clothes laid out on the bed. Jane would be fussing
round her, soaping her back and helping to wash her
red-gold hair. It had been long in those days but that
had become impractical while she was following the
colours, not only because she had no one to dress it for
her, but because of the difficulty of keeping it clean
and free from vermin. She had cut it very short and
been surprised when it sprang into curls all over her
head. She soaped it now and ducked beneath the water
to rinse it, then came up laughing.

She was free! Gloriously and happily free! She felt

no guilt because she had always done her very best for
both Tom and Philippe, sharing the hardships of the
march, scavenging for food, cooking in almost impossible conditions, cleaning their uniforms and even, on
occasion, carrying their packs, when they were utterly
exhausted. She had taken both for better or worse and
now it was all over. Over!

Never again! She had had her fill of marriage. From
now on she would keep her independence. She still had
to find her way back to England, still had to face up to
her father, but that was nothing compared with what
she had endured in the last two years. Two years. Two
years wasted. No, she decided, not entirely wasted; she
had learned a great deal about herself, not all of it
good, but she had emerged, she hoped, a little wiser.
She began to sing as she soaped herself and the bath
filled with bubbles.

> 'The noble Duke of York,
> He had ten thousand men,
> He marched them up to the top of the hill,
> And he marched them down again.'

'*Madame* is in good spirits,' said a voice in English.

She froze. Slowly she reached out for a towel and
held it to cover her breasts, then turned her head
towards the door. The man who had come in from the
rain and was standing on the doormat knocking the
water from his shako was the rider she had seen earlier.
He was carrying a rifle and a dead hare. Was this his
home? Was she the intruder or was he? She decided to
attack first.

'Is it not the custom where you come from to knock
before entering?'

'I did. You were making so much noise you did not
hear.'

'Noise, sir?' She dared not move for fear of disturbing the bubbles which enveloped her. 'Some have said
I have a passably good voice.'

He smiled and walked over to the stove to sniff appreciatively at the pot; it brought him round to her front. 'Is your mistress at home?'

'My mistress?' she repeated, then, realising he thought she was a servant, laughed. 'I call no one mistress.'

'You are surely not the lady of the house?'

'No. I have never met her.'

He laughed aloud. 'Oh, I see. An opportunist like myself. Are you alone?'

She hesitated, but there was no point in denying it; he would soon discover the truth. 'Yes.'

He indicated the pot with a jerk of his head. 'That smells good.'

'The least a gentleman would do is leave a lady to finish her *toilette* in privacy.'

'But I am no gentleman.' There was a hint of bitterness in his voice which made her look up into his face. There were tiny lines etched around his eyes which could have been laughter-lines but could equally have been caused by long hours squinting into the sun. His mouth was firm and his teeth were strong and white; a handsome man, she decided, but refreshingly unaware of it.

'No, that much is evident,' she said crisply, and when he made no move to go picked up the bar of soap and hurled it at him. Her aim was good and it struck him on the side of the head, bounced off his shoulder and slithered to the floor. 'Get out!' she yelled.

He laughed and retrieved it, weighing it in his hand as if considering whether to throw it back. 'Out?' he asked mildly, appraising what he could see of her—a mane of red-gold hair, which lay against freckled cheeks in wet tendrils, a long neck and sloping white shoulders which disappeared behind the towel she was holding against herself. The vision was spoiled to some extent by hardened brown hands which were obviously accustomed to work. 'But it is pouring with rain. And besides, I am hungry. Now if you were to share the pot with me I could provide something to improve its flavour.' He waved the hare at her.

'Go away and leave me in peace. I do not want or need your company.' There was nothing else at hand to throw except the towel and she was loath to let go of that, and he showed no sign of doing as she asked. With nothing in her hand to defend herself, she was obliged to change her belligerent attitude to one of reasonableness; and the idea of meat made the saliva run in her mouth. 'Can't you see I am in no position to do anything about the soup or the meat with you hovering over me? And this water is becoming cold and I want to dress.'

He grinned. 'I could do with a bath too. How about sharing it with me?'

'If you go and leave me to dress, I will cook the hare and heat up some more water for you.'

'That sounds like a fair bargain to me.' He paused and pointed to the door into the rest of the house. 'Have you been through there?'

'Yes. It is empty, nothing to steal, I am afraid.'

'What a disappointment for you.'

She was about to say she was referring to him and that *she* was not a thief when she remembered the clothes she had found and intended to keep. Instead she said, 'Go and wait in the hall if you want any dinner.'

He made an ostentatious leg and left the room. As soon as she was sure he had really gone, she scrambled out and dried herself quickly, then dressed in her own underclothes and topped them with the dressing-gown she had found. She went to the door and called to him. 'If you want a bath, you had better empty this one and draw more water.'

She went to stir the pot and skin the hare and did not know he had come back into the room until he spoke. 'Where is the owner of this?'

She turned towards him. He was standing just inside the door holding Philippe's coat at arm's length. 'Dead,' she said flatly, returning to her task.

'Who was he?'

'My husband.'

'Your *husband*?'

'Yes. Lieutenant Philippe Santerre.'

'A Frenchman?'

'Yes.' She looked at him boldly. 'Does that change your mind?'

'About what?'

'About sharing a meal.'

'No, why should it?' He began dragging the bath towards the door. She watched as he opened the door, tipped it up and emptied its contents into the yard where the soapy bubbles dispersed in the puddles already there. He brought it back and stood it on end against the wall. 'Is there anyone in the house at all?'

'No. Unless they are hiding in a cupboard. There is a cellar, but the door is locked, I couldn't open it.'

'Best be sure.' He picked up his rifle and left her. She could hear him moving about the house, doing as she had done earlier and searching every cranny. She was stirring the pot and humming quietly to herself when she was startled by a shot. She ran into the hall, half expecting to see him lying dead at the feet of the rightful owner of the house, but there was no one about and all was quiet. A moment later he appeared clutching two bottles of wine. 'Had to shoot the lock off,' he said. 'But there was no one there. They probably evacuated when they heard your people were advancing.'

'My people?'

'Johnny Bluecoats.'

'They are not my people.'

'One of them was. You said so.'

'I am English, just as you are.'

'Ah.' He smiled wryly, taking the bottles into the

kitchen and setting them on the table. 'How can you be sure that I am?'

'You are dressed in a British uniform and you speak English as well as I do.'

'Neither of which is proof positive. No, if I were you, I would want to know a great deal more than that.'

'Why? It is of little consequence; our paths are unlikely to cross again.'

'Now that would be a pity,' he said. 'I thought my luck had changed at last.'

'You are impertinent, sir.'

He stood squarely and gave her a cool look of appraisal from her bare feet — army boots were hardly a suitable accessory for a blue silk dressing-gown — up over her five feet seven — she had the figure of an angel, he decided — to an oval face in which the green eyes flashed at him with a confusing mixture of humour and anger. He laughed. 'Pretending to be affronted by what was, after all, meant as a compliment, doesn't fool me, Madame Santerre. You are no drawing-room miss and, I'll wager, never have been. A camp follower, that's what you are, and, it seems, not particular as to the camp. Tell me, is it true that Frenchman are more romantically inclined than Englishmen?'

She picked up the kitchen knife she had used to cut up the hare and raised it as if she meant to throw it but, deciding that it would be very unwise and probably dangerous, she turned back to her cooking. 'Are you going to bath before we eat or afterwards? The water is hardly hot yet.'

'It will do me. I'll take it upstairs.' He picked up the cauldron of hot water with little effort, though it was extremely heavy, grabbed the handle of the bath and disappeared with them into the hall, carrying the one and dragging the other.

She went to the door and shouted after him, 'Not the room with the four-poster. I saw it first.'

Half an hour later he returned, looking much more presentable, though he had been obliged to put the buttonless uniform on again. 'There are no men's clothes at all,' he said. 'Perhaps the owner was a lady who lived alone. It would account for her leaving in the face of an army, don't you think?'

'Perhaps.' She filled two bowls to the brim with the hot stew and set them on the table, together with cutlery and glasses which she had found in the back of a kitchen cupboard. They were obviously not the family silver; that had gone, either with its owner or, after her departure, to marauding soldiers. 'Would you like me to sew your buttons back on?'

'No.' He spoked sharply. 'I like things as they are.'

'Do you? How whimsical.' She sat down opposite him and picked up her spoon. 'I should have thought you would be glad to be able to close your coat again. The wind and rain in the mountains are cold, even in summer.'

'I do not feel the cold.'

'No? Not outside perhaps, but inside?' She did not know why she said that, except that he looked like a man who kept his inner self very much to himself.

'What do you mean?'

She answered his question with another. 'Why are you alone, so far from the British lines?'

'Why should the British lines be of interest to me? I told you, you should not make assumptions from appearances.'

'Are you saying you are not an English soldier?'

'I am not.'

'But you were?'

'That is neither here nor there.'

She guessed that he had been cashiered and it made her curious. In times of war when every available soldier was needed they would not discharge a man unless there was a very compelling reason. What crime had he committed? Ought she to be afraid of him? She supposed if she persisted in asking questions he might become dangerous, but at the moment he seemed more concerned with tucking into his dinner; he was obviously not going to be drawn on the subject. 'No,' she agreed. 'It is no concern of mine. I only asked because I want to go back to the British lines myself and I thought you might take me with you.'

'No!' It was almost a shout. 'My business is not in that direction at all. Now, if you don't mind, we will change the subject.' He lowered his voice and smiled. 'Now, tell me how you came to be out on the mountain alone. It was you I saw earlier on the road, was it not?'

'Yes, but I did not think you had noticed me, you seemed so preoccupied.'

'I have been trained to notice things, but I must admit the filthy peasant I saw on the road bears very little resemblance to the beautiful young lady I found naked in a bath. If it had not been for the uniform coat, I might not have been so quick to realise they were one and the same.'

'Careless of me,' she said. 'I suppose if I want to get back to the British lines I had better dispose of it.'

'Why were you wearing it?'

'It is warmer than nothing and nights on the mountains can be cold.' She paused to sip her wine; it was a full-bodied red and made her feel sensuous and relaxed. She ought to beware of it. 'Why are you still wearing yours?'

He gave a cracked laugh. 'As you say, it is warmer than nothing.'

'We could exchange them. I'll have yours and you have mine.'

His head snapped up and he looked at her angrily. 'Now why should you imagine that I would lower myself to wear a French uniform? I. . .' He stopped suddenly as an idea came to him. 'Tell me about yourself. Where did you meet your husband?'

'Philippe, you mean? At Oporto, or more accurately a little to the north; I am not sure exactly where.'

'Is Oporto your home?'

'Of course not. I told you, I am English.'

'There is no "of course" about it. There is quite a colony of English in Oporto, wine merchants most of them. Why do you think the government at home was so anxious to free it? Port is one of their favourite drinks.'

'How cynical you are.'

'Perhaps I have reason to be.' He paused. 'Tell me about Philippe.'

'Why should I?'

'I am interested and it will while away the evening.' He leaned forward. 'Unless you can think of something more exciting to do?'

The implication was clear and it infuriated her. 'You do not have to spend the evening with me at all. You will find what you want in the village, I have no doubt.'

'What I want? How can you know what I want? You do not know me.'

'No. You have not even troubled to introduce yourself. Perhaps you are ashamed to do so.'

'You want my name? Of what importance is that? It might just as well be Philippe Santerre.'

'Philippe was an honourable man.'

'You think I am not?' He picked up his glass and drained it quickly, then refilled it. 'You may well be right, Madame Santerre, for who decides such things — a man's friends or his enemies. . .?'

'You are talking in riddles.'

'My apologies, ma'am.' He inclined his head and then lapsed into silence.

She watched him for a moment or two then stood up to clear the table. 'What are you going to do now? Get drunk?'

He laughed. 'It would take more than a couple of bottles of red wine to do that. Besides, I need a clear head.' He caught her hand as she passed him. 'Sit down and tell me about yourself.'

'It is a very long story.'

'But a fascinating one, I am sure. You speak like a lady, look like a tramp and behave like a hoyden, so how can I be other than intrigued?'

She laughed and sat down again. 'My aunt always said Papa had brought me up like a boy.'

'Impossible!' he said, laughing. 'You do not look in the least like a boy. In fact. . .' he smiled '. . .I could envy Philippe his good fortune.'

'I shouldn't do that,' she said quietly. 'He was hanged by the *guerrilleros*.'

'When?'

'Yesterday. We were out shooting hares and they captured us.'

'I am sorry.'

'I told them I was the wife of an English soldier and Philippe had taken me against my will. . .'

'Was that true?'

'Not exactly.'

'Tell me exactly.'

'I was married to an English soldier, but he was killed in the chase after the battle for Oporto.' She did not know why she answered, but it was a relief to have someone to talk to in English, and if he could be made to appreciate her plight he might be prepared to help her.

'Another husband! How many have you had?'

'Two.'

'And still only. . .how old?'

'It is no business of yours.'

'Twenty-two, twenty-three?' he queried. 'And already widowed twice?'

'You are a cynic, aren't you? Haven't you ever been in love?'

'Oh, yes,' he said, his face twisting in a wry smile. 'And little good it did me. But go on with your story,

we can come to mine later. Presumably you were at
the tail of the British advance with the baggage?'

'I was, until a courier who had come back with
dispatches told me Tom had been wounded. Then I
left it and went forward to look for him.'

'As any good wife would do.'

'As any good wife would do,' she repeated.

'You crossed the river?'

'Yes.'

'How?'

'If you are English, you know the whole army
crossed in small boats.' She paused and looked up at
him. 'Or are you testing me?'

He laughed, poured more wine and settled back in
his chair. 'Tell me, did you find him?'

'Yes, but he died very quickly. I tried to get back
but I lost my way and ran into a company of French
infantrymen.'

'And in the blink of an eye you had changed sides
and become a French soldier's wife. . .'

'It wasn't like that at all,' she protested. 'You don't
understand. And if that is all you have to say, then I
shall leave you and go to bed.'

'Bed. Now, there's a thought!' There was amusement
in his voice. 'Have you a mind to change sides again? I
might be able to accommodate you.'

She picked up her glass and threw it at him. It caught
his chin and shattered, scattering shards all over his
coat, the table and the floor. He calmly stood up and
brushed himself down, ignoring the tiny trickle of blood
on his chin. 'I shall take that as a negative answer,
which means you are still French, still the enemy. . .'

'And who are you to talk?' she demanded. 'You are
not so lily-white yourself, are you? Unless I miss my
guess, you are in disgrace, so what right have you to
censure me? I am going to bed. And I mean to
barricade the door. And I shall be obliged if you have
taken yourself off before I come down in the morning.'

He reached out to catch her wrist. She tried to pull herself out of his grasp, but the more she struggled, the tighter he gripped her. She circled round, pulling him round with her, so that she could reach the rifle he had left leaning against the wall. With all the strength she could muster, she twisted herself free and grabbed the weapon. 'Now!' she said, pointing it at him. 'Do not think I don't know how to use this because I promise you I do.'

He laughed and put up both hands in surrender. 'Lord preserve me from a gun in the hands of a woman! You may rest easy, *madame*, I was only going to suggest a truce. We could help each other.'

'How?' she asked warily, still aiming the gun.

'You want to go back to the British lines, do you not?'

'Yes. Will you take me?'

'Perhaps. If you do something for me first.'

'It depends.'

'You take me to Ciudad Rodrigo and get me through the French lines and later I will take you home — all the way to England, if you like.'

She lowered the gun to look at him, dumbfounded. 'You are mad,' she said at last. 'They'll kill you.'

'Not if you vouch for me.'

'Vouch for you!' Her voice was almost a squeak. 'I can hardly vouch for myself. They do not know me. Philippe and I had only just arrived when the town was taken. We had spent the winter in France while Philippe's wounds healed and were joining a new regiment. . .'

'You mean that no one in the town knew Philippe either?'

'I don't think so.'

'Better and better,' he said. 'I shall be Lieutenant Philippe Santerre.'

'For heaven's sake, why? Are you tired of living?'

He laughed, but the sound was not a cheerful one. 'Perhaps.'

'What happened to make you so bitter?'

'That is my business. Now, will you take me back to Ciudad Rodrigo or not?'

'Can you speak French like a native?'

'No, but I can understand it well enough, and, remember, I have just been hanged and my throat is sore. Why did they hang him, by the way? Why not just shoot him, so much quicker and cleaner?'

She shrugged. 'A rope is cheaper than a bullet and, besides, a shot echoes a long way in these mountains; I suspect they did not want their hide-out found.'

'One man's bad fortune is another's luck. I think my voice has been permanently affected by the ordeal.'

'You will never get away with it.'

'I will if you stay with me to be my guide and do the talking.'

'You must be crazy if you think I would agree to that.' She looked hard at him, trying to make up her mind if he was making some macabre joke at her expense, but his expression was perfectly serious and the light in his hazel eyes was not one of levity. He looked deadly serious, almost as if he was pleading with her. 'Why do you want to do this? Do you want to change sides? If so, there are easier ways of doing it; you could simply say you had deserted—some do, you know.'

'I could do that, of course, but this way seems the more interesting prospect, certainly more exciting than being a prisoner of war.'

'And if I refuse?'

'I'll do it anyway.'

'Then you will die in the attempt.'

He shrugged. 'Then so be it.'

He sat down at the table again with an empty glass in front of him and stared out of the window into the darkness beyond it, as if he could see something, or someone, who haunted his thoughts and dictated his actions. For a brief moment she felt sorry for him, and reached out to lay a hand on his arm. 'Sleep on it,' he said, without turning towards her. 'Sleep on it. I shall not disturb you.'

She left him reaching for the bottle to refill his glass and made her way up to the huge four-poster. It was all part of a macabre dream; he did not exist, the *guerrilleros* did not exist, Philippe had not been hanged. She was in bed at home and soon Jane would wake her with her breakfast on a tray. Home! How badly did she want to go home? How much was she prepared to pay for it?

CHAPTER TWO

OLIVIA was awoken before dawn by the sound of a horse's hoofs on the gravel of the drive, and she sprang up to look out of the window. He was riding away in the blustering wind which had followed the rain, walking his horse in the same slow, deliberate way she had seen him riding the day before. Had he had second thoughts about his preposterous idea or had he decided to go alone after all? If that were so, he would never succeed in passing the guard at the gates of Ciudad Rodrigo, let alone impersonating Philippe. It was true he was about the same height and build, and in a poor light his hair might look as dark as Philippe's, but in the glare of day, in the face of questioning. . . She shuddered at the risk he would be taking. Even with her it would be bad, but at least she could give him Philippe's uniform coat and take him to their lodgings where she could hand over her dead husband's papers and belongings. As long as he did not speak and met no one who had known Philippe, he stood a chance, if only a slim one.

She pulled herself up short. Why should she concern herself with a disgraced English officer? Why should she care what happened to him? And why, in heaven's name, should she delay her own return to the British lines to help him? She did not even know why he wanted to do it. She laughed suddenly. She did not even know his name. And there were other puzzling things about him — his demeanour, his speech and the way he sat his horse indicated that he had been an officer, but officers did not usually carry rifles. And the Baker rifle he had with him was only issued to the élite Rifle Brigade and their uniform coat was green, not red. Tom had often said that if he had known about the Rifles before he signed on he would have enlisted in the Ninety-fifth. Poor Tom.

She pulled on the robe and went downstairs determined to put the man from her mind; there were more important things to think of. First, she would clean the clothes she had stolen; she would have liked to say 'borrowed', but as she could not see how she could return them, nor pay for them, 'stolen' was the only appropriate word. Then she would leave the kitchen and the bedroom tidy; that at least she owed the owner of the house for her unwitting hospitality. After that, she would set off again. The coast of Portugal was to the west, so if she walked with the rising sun at her back she ought, sooner or later, to come across the British lines, or the sea. Obstacles in the form of rivers or mountains, or hostile people, she would deal with as she met them. It was simple.

True, she would rather have had an escort, someone to keep her company and help her overcome the difficulties whatever they might be, but she had learned in the past two years to be resilient and self-sufficient, and when there was nothing else for it, what was the good of wishing otherwise? The *guerrilleros* would not help her and perhaps that was just as well; friend or foe, they were terrifying.

And as for the Englishman, he was too wrapped up in his own problems to concern himself with hers. But she could not stop herself thinking about him, wondering about him. Why was he in the mountains alone? Why had he been cashiered, if, indeed, he had? She shrugged her thoughts from her as she put on a cotton dress she had found in a cupboard; it had a brown background and was decorated with poppy heads in large red splashes of colour, a servant's dress, she decided. The old boots and the straw hat completed her ensemble. Her preparations complete, she picked up the bundle she had gathered together and left by the door she had entered, carefully shutting it behind her. It was none of her business what he was up to.

She stopped when she saw him riding back up the drive, leading a mule. He was smiling.

'If you think that bringing that will make me change my mind,' she said, without bothering to give him good morning, 'you are mistaken. I will have nothing to do with your hare-brained schemes. You are mad.'

'But it is the mad ideas which have the best chance of success, don't you agree?' he queried amiably. 'And I thrive on a challenge.'

'You will not thrive on this one.'

'With you at my side, I could succeed.'

'Succeed in doing what?' she demanded.

He laughed. 'Do you know, I am not at all sure? I will put my mind to it as we ride.'

'I will not ride with you.'

'No? Would you rather the *guerrilleros* finished off what they started?'

She looked up at him defiantly but the tone of his voice suggested that she had not left the partisans as far behind as she thought. 'They are not interested in me.'

'On the contrary, Madame Santerre, they are very interested in you.'

'How do you know?'

'I know.'

'Where are they?'

'I saw them riding down the mountainside, about twenty of them, armed to the teeth.'

'They are coming here?'

He shrugged.

'I do not believe you.' But even as she spoke she realised he was telling the truth. 'Why would they send twenty armed men after one woman?' She paused. 'Unless they are after you too.'

'Whichever it is, *madame*, you and I are destined to spend some time together, so why not accept the inevitable? I will make a bargain with you. When we reach the main road from Ciudad Rodrigo into Portugal, you can go your way and I will go mine.'

'Is that a promise?'

'If that is what you want. Come now, we are wasting time. Mount up and let us be on our way; the sooner we start, the sooner you will be rid of me.'

She would have liked to defy him, to refuse to do anything he asked, but the thought of riding instead of walking, and having some protection against the blood-thirsty Spanish partisans, was a powerful persuader. Olivia tied her bundle behind the saddle of the mule and, using the doorstep as a mounting block, hitched up her skirt and threw her leg over the animal's back, aware as she did so that he was smiling. 'Do you think I have not ridden astride before?' she demanded.

'No, it is evident that you are quite accustomed to it.' He turned his horse and led the way, not back up the drive to the gates, but along a rough path that led from the side of the house, round an empty stable block and through an olive grove which went steeply downhill towards the distant river. 'Better than taking the road,' he said over his shoulder.

She did not answer but concentrated on watching where the mule was going, thankful for its sure-footedness as it picked its way over loose stones and the roots of ancient olives which clung to any tiny crevice where there was soil. When the path broadened out, he reined in for her to come abreast of him.

'Tell me about Ciudad Rodrigo,' he commanded. 'All you know.'

'I know very little. We had only been there one day, just long enough to find lodgings.'

'Describe the place, the streets, the buildings, the defences, anything you can think of. How are the inhabitants behaving towards the occupying forces? Do the French have trouble with them? Is there any resistance?'

'I would not think so. The town surrendered, after all. The resistance is in the hills.'

'To be sure.'

'And if I knew anything, would I be so foolish as to tell you, sir? I do not know you or why you are here, do I? You may be a spy. In fact, I think that is just what you are.'

'*Touché, madame.*' He smiled as if at some secret joke. 'Did you learn anything of the intentions of the *guerrilleros* while you were with them?'

'I do not trust them either; they are a bloodthirsty lot.'

'So they are, but not without reason. If someone had invaded England and pillaged your home town, raped the women and killed the men for nothing except keeping back food to feed their children, you would be bloodthirsty.' He turned to look at her. He seemed far less formidable than he had in the poor light of the evening before and yet, behind the hazel eyes, there was an alertness which was not immediately evident from his languid pose. 'The Spanish are hopeless when it comes to fighting in the disciplined way of the British army, but in small bands, in the hills where they can remain hidden until the time comes to strike, there are none better. The Peer knows that and he encourages them.'

'I think they are barbaric. They did not have to kill Philippe; he could not have harmed them.'

'He could have given away their position.'

'We were blindfolded when we were taken to their camp.'

'And yet you found your way out.'

'That was simple good luck.'

'They would not view it so. You could lead a French patrol back there.'

She looked startled. 'Why should I do that? I told them I was English.'

'And did they believe you? Did they even understand you?'

'Their leader did. He looked as uncouth as the rest of his band, but he spoke excellent French and very good English. He was — is — an educated man.'

'Don Miguel Santandos,' he murmured, almost to himself.

'You know him?'

'I know of him. He is one of the fiercest and bravest fighters in all Spain, but he is also ruthless. He will let nothing stand in his way; he would certainly not think twice about killing a woman. If he thinks you are likely to betray him, he will come after you; nothing is more certain.'

She laughed. 'If you are saying that to persuade me to go with you, you are wasting your time. I do not want to return to Ciudad Rodrigo, I intend to go home to England, and the sooner the better.'

'You may do as you please,' he said laconically. 'But before you can do that we have to cross the river and find the road.'

She rode silently for a moment or two, but curiosity drove her to speak again. 'What will you do in Ciudad Rodrigo, always supposing you manage to enter the town at all? You will have to remain silent, you know, so how will you make yourself understood?'

'A man who has been hanged and survived is still able to write, and my French is good enough for that.'

'You will never convince anyone you have been hanged. There would be a very nasty mark on your neck if you had.'

'I shall have to wear a bandage.'

'They are not fools, you know.'

'Neither am I.'

She could not believe he really meant to do it. It was a silly game he was playing with her, though what his reasons were she could not even guess. Unless he was testing her loyalty? Why? She had told him the truth, if not the whole truth, so what more could he possibly want? 'You have not even told me your name,' she said. 'What shall I call you?'

'Anything that takes your fancy, *madame*.'

'Have you something to hide?'

He laughed harshly. 'There is little that can be hidden behind a coat with no buttons. I am as you see me.'

'Cashiered,' she said. 'Dishonourably discharged.'

'My honour is my own affair,' he said stiffly.

'So it is; I have no interest in it. After all, we part at the crossroads and I do not expect to see you again. You will undoubtedly be shot by the French for spying — or by the English.'

'Better that than. . .' He stopped suddenly and sat forward in his saddle, holding his hand up to stop her. 'Be silent!'

She reined in and craned her neck to look past him. The village lay below them, nestling on the far side of a swiftly moving river which had cut a deep gorge through the mountain rock. There was a lone villa standing at the end of an ancient bridge. She watched, fascinated, as a group of men scrambled up from the rocks among the pillars of the bridge and ran into the villa. A moment later a huge explosion filled the air, flinging debris high into the sky. When the dust had settled, there was no longer a bridge.

'If we had been two minutes earlier, we would have been on it.' He chuckled. 'Thank heaven for an argumentative woman.'

'And if we had used the road we might have been even earlier and on the other side by now,' she retorted. 'Now, what do we do? Could we find a boat?'

He laughed. 'Do you think that after taking the trouble to blow up the bridge the *guerrilleros* are going to be so careless as to leave boats about? Besides, the banks are too steep for anyone but a mountain goat to get down to the water.'

'Why did they do it? It is hardly an important bridge. It looks to me as though it is only used by the villagers to reach their olive groves.'

'They want to stop someone from using it; that much is plain. Perhaps they are expecting company.' He turned his horse to face her. 'Or perhaps they want to keep a certain person on this side of it.'

'You?' she queried. Then, startled, 'Me?'

'Who's to say what is in the mind of Don Santandos? But I think we would be wise to move on.'

'Where?'

'North, towards the head of the river, there might be another bridge or, if not, a place to cross.'

'Why not south?'

'You may go south if you wish,' he said laconically. 'But I go north and then east.'

'You would not leave me here alone?'

'I thought that was what you most desired.'

'That was before. . .'

'Before?' He laughed. 'I am the lesser of two evils, is that it?'

'I am not even sure of that,' she retorted. 'Danger comes in many guises. Just because you look a little more civilised than that Spaniard does not mean you are less dangerous. In fact, I think you are possibly the more deadly of the two. Don Santandos said he would keep me safe until he had checked my story, while you. . .'

'And would he have been able to check your story? Are you sure you told him the whole truth?'

She did not answer and he turned his horse towards the mountain peaks and set off back along the path through the olive groves, leaving her fuming in her saddle. She looked behind her at the ruins of the bridge. The partisans were streaming out of the villa and up the hill towards them. She dug her heels into the mule's flanks and set off after the Englishman.

'I shall call you Mr Leopard,' she said, then laughed.

'Until such time as we meet someone who can effect a proper introduction.'

'Why Leopard?'

'Isn't that what Napoleon calls Viscount Wellington—a hideous leopard?'

'The comparison flatters me, ma'am. Did you know the leopard cannot sheath its claws?'

'No, I didn't.'

'I have none to sheath.'

'That I beg leave to doubt.' She paused. 'Are we going back to the villa?'

'No. We will turn off in the olive grove and find the path that follows the course of the river.'

'If there is one.'

They rode on in silence until he found the track he wanted and turned his horse northwards. Olivia followed because there was nothing else she could do. The ground became rougher and the hill steeper. She glanced behind her every now and again, but there was no sign of the *guerrilleros* and she began to think he had been wrong or trying to frighten her. 'Do you really think the bridge was blown to trap me?' she asked at last. 'Surely they would not inconvenience a whole village just to punish one woman?'

'It depends what they think you know.'

'I know nothing. If we were to wait and face them, could we not convince them of it?'

'I doubt it.'

'I begin to think it is not me but you they want. You are their enemy.'

'You may think what you please.'

'Are you going to ride all day without stopping?'

'If I have to.'

'I have some food in my pack.'

'Good.'

'You are not very talkative, are you?'

'No need to be; you do enough talking for both of us.'

'You wish me to be silent?'

'It might help.'

'Help you to think?'

'And help me to hear. Good heavens, woman, you would be useless on patrol.'

'I am not a soldier.'

'No, thank heaven. Listen!' He reined in and stood in the stirrups. 'The river is over there.' He started off again towards the sound of running water.

When they arrived on the top of the rise they had been climbing they could see the river, hundreds of feet below them, cut into a gorge whose cliffs were unscaleable. Olivia's heart sank. 'I said we should go south,' she said. 'Are you going to turn back?'

'Certainly not! Come on.'

She looked up at the distant mountain; the source of the river was almost certainly high up in those peaks. 'We can't go up there.'

'We may not need to.'

She was reluctant to start moving again, but he did not wait for her and she clicked her tongue at the mule and set off in his wake.

The sun climbed to its zenith, but they were so high in the wind-swept mountains that they could not feel its warmth. Olivia stopped to fetch Philippe's jacket out of her pack and put it on. She was not sure, but she thought he had slowed his pace a little to wait for her. It pleased her out of all proportion and she decided to test it by lingering longer than she needed, just to see if he would turn back. But he did not even turn his head; he simply walked his horse slowly until she caught up with him again.

'Do not do that again,' he said. 'Not without telling me. I could have gone on and left you behind. Anything could have happened to you.'

'I was cold. And I am hungry and thirsty. When are we going to stop?'

'When we reach that outcrop.' He lifted his hand to

point at a group of boulders poised on the skyline as if
some giant hand had taken great pains to set them
there, finely balanced and yet immovable. 'It will afford
some shelter from the wind and a fine view as well.
You shall have your picnic there.'

His tone annoyed her; it was as if he thought she was
a frivolous, empty-headed female who behaved as if
she were at home in England. Would that she were!
'Even I know that an army marches on its stomach,'
she retorted. 'We will go the better for having rested a
few minutes. And besides, what is the hurry? I cannot
see us being on the other side of the river before
nightfall however hard we press on.'

'You may be right.'

'I begin to wonder where you are leading me; we are
moving away from the river now.'

'If you had not been so busy refining upon this and
that, you would have noticed the river was taking a
wide curve; we are simply cutting across the bend.
When we reach the top of the hill, we shall see it
again.'

You seem to know your way very well. Have you,
perhaps, been here before?'

'I am a soldier, trained to be observant.'

'So you said before.'

'Did you learn nothing from either of your
husbands?'

'I learned a great deal, but as one was no more than
a private and the other a mere lieutenant tactics did
not come into it. Poor Tom was drilled to obey without
question, and Philippe. . .'

'Philippe was what?'

'A dreamer, a romantic. He came from a noble
family and he never took war seriously. Even when he
was wounded he laughed and said it was just bad luck.'

'Were you never exhausted and hungry?'

'Philippe always had money for food and a good bed,
but many of the ordinary troops suffer badly; you must

know the French commissary always relies on what the country can offer. . .'

'Offer! That is hardly accurate. If I know the Spaniards, they offer nothing.'

She smiled. 'You are right, which is why supplying the army is such a problem to the French command.'

'It is the same in any army, but forethought and planning and money to pay make the difference. Did Philippe not feel guilty, using his wealth to fare better than his men?'

'I do not think so. Sometimes he bought food for his troop as well.'

'Very magnanimous of him. He sounds exceedingly pompous to me.'

'He was nothing of the sort. How you think you can impersonate him when you have no idea what he was like I do not know.'

'But you said no one else in Ciudad Rodrigo knew him either, so it hardly matters.'

'You never know, someone might come along, an old friend, a fellow officer, someone who fought with him at Talavera. . .'

'That is a chance I will have to take.'

'I still say you are mad. Even madder to attempt it without me.'

'You will come, then?'

'No,' she said sharply.

His complacent smile annoyed her, but she was angrier with herself for even suggesting she ought to go with him. That was not her intention at all. She fell silent, concentrating on the group of rocks which were their goal and which seemed as far away as ever.

It was the middle of the afternoon when they reached them. He dismounted and left his horse to graze on the sparse vegetation and turned to help her down. She felt herself being lifted clean out of the saddle as if she had no more weight than a feather. And yet she was over average height and well built, if over-thin. As he set her down, keeping his hands about her waist for a breathless moment longer than he needed to, she realised how tall he was; that, unlike many men, he towered over her. Slowly she looked up into his face, wondering whether to speak or remain silent, to scold him for manhandling her or to thank him for his courtesy, but what she saw there silenced her. Behind the hazel eyes was a look of anguish, of a pain too deep for speech. Someone, or something, had hurt him very badly.

'Now, where is this feast?' he said lightly, turning towards the pack on the back of the mule's saddle.

She took out cold hare and a bottle of wine and from the depths of his saddle-bag he found bread.

'You did not have that last night,' she said, pointing at it.

'I did not have a mule either.'

'Where did you get them?'

He laughed and the hurt look left his eyes and was replaced by a twinkle of humour. 'Better not ask, *madame*.'

'My name is Olivia,' she said. 'And I do not like the French form of address.'

'Not even when it is correct? But as I have taken on the mantle of your dead husband, then it would be better to use your given name, I agree.'

'You surely do not intend to go through with that wild scheme of yours?'

'More than ever.'

'What have you to gain?'

'A new set of claws.'

'Is that all?'

'All? To me it is everything.'

'Tell me about it.'

'Not now. It is neither the time nor the place; we have to finish our meal and go on if we intend to find a river crossing by dark.'

She was wise enough to desist from prying and they ate in silence. When food and wine were both con-

sumed, they set off again. 'That was dinner,' she said
with a laugh which sounded hollow. 'What shall we
have for supper?'

He smiled. '"Sufficient unto the day. . ."'

'Oh, very droll. If we had turned south, we would
have found some habitation, somewhere where we
could buy food and drink and a bed for the night. Up
here in the mountains. . .'

'The mountains are teeming with life—hares, goats,
boars, maybe a mountain lion or two.'

She laughed. 'Leopards with claws.'

'I sincerely hope not.' His answer was clipped and
stopped her jesting. She did not know how to take
him; he was cheerful, almost boyish one minute and
morose and short-tempered the next, and neither her
teasing nor her anger seemed to change that. She
should remain silent, allow him to brood on his own if
he wanted to, but it was not in her nature to let things
lie. He needed taking out of himself and then he might
be prepared to confide in her. If he did that, and he
had some very compelling reason for wanting to go to
Ciudad Rodrigo, she might consider helping him. She
brought herself up short. Was she weakening? No, she
told herself, she would leave him at the first opportunity. Would he come after her? Riding a mule, she
had no chance of outpacing him.

'What's his name?' she asked, looking at the beautiful black stallion.

'Thor.'

'The god of thunder,' she said. 'Is he thunderous?'

'He is more than you can handle.'

'Indeed?'

The mischievous note in her voice made him turn to
look at her; her green eyes were laughing at him in a
way which made his pulses quicken. 'Indeed,' he
repeated firmly.

It was dusk when the track turned away from the
gorse-clad slopes and entered a pine wood. Once in the

shelter of the trees, he stopped and dismounted. '*Madame* desires a good hotel,' he said, eyes twinkling. 'This is the very best the region has to offer. The beds are soft and cleaner than most.' He pointed to heaps of brown pine needles. 'Supper will arrive in due course. Make yourself comfortable.'

'Where are you going?'

'To find our supper.'

'Another hare.'

'I had my thoughts on something a little tastier. I caught a glimpse of a herd of goats.'

'But they belong to the people. And in any case, what would we do with a whole goat?'

'Not a goat, a kid.'

'No!' Her voice was sharp. 'That would be cruel and unnecessary.'

'You may go hungry, if you prefer that,' he said. 'But I intend to eat.' He picked up his rifle, pouch and ammunition and set off through the trees, leaving her to make herself comfortable on the pine needles. She had eaten kid many times before, but then she had not seen it newly slaughtered, nor had a hand in the skinning of it; that had been done by someone in Philippe's troop. Half the time she had not known what she was eating anyway; hunger had made her less than fastidious.

She smiled to herself; she was deliberately trying the patience of the Englishman—the leopard without claws—just to see how far she could go before he lost his composure. It was a dangerous game to play. Supposing he left her and supposing the *guerrilleros* were really after her and not him? Supposing she lost her way? Supposing she was attacked by wolves or wild boars? She ought to be thankful for his protection. She sat down and leant her back against one of the trees. She ought to start a fire or, at least, gather the firewood; he would return soon and she had done nothing but dream.

He was coming back now; she could hear him walking through the pine needles. She smiled; he had grumbled at her for making a noise, but he sounded like an army on the march. She would tell him so. She turned and opened her mouth to speak as the undergrowth parted, but it was not her companion who faced her but a huge boar with tusks a foot long. She stood frozen for a second which seemed like an hour as they faced each other and then, galvanised into action, she scrambled up the tree she had been leaning against, leaving the animal in possession of their belongings.

It rooted around for a time and flung her bundle about with its snout but there was nothing edible in it. 'Go away, you stupid brute,' she hissed down at it from her perch. 'There's nothing there. Oh, go away, do, I feel such a fool.'

The horse and mule, both tethered near by, set up a neighing and braying as the frustrated boar began snuffling round the campsite. If only she had a gun! She began pelting the animal with pine cones but it did not even feel them. Where was Mr Leopard? Why didn't he come back? No, she did not want him to find her in this ignominious position, but neither did she want to stay up the tree all night. She took off her boot and flung it at the boar's head. It landed on its snout. It looked up at her, as if surprised at her temerity. 'Get out!' she said, determined not to raise her voice. 'Don't you know you are not welcome?'

She was startled by a chuckle close at hand and turned her head to see the Englishman standing not ten feet away, carrying a dead hare. 'Oh, I might have known you would think it funny,' she said. 'Now would you kindly get rid of that animal and help me down?'

She expected him to shoot it, but instead he advanced on the boar and raised the butt of his rifle as if he intended to club it to death. 'You fool!' she said. 'It'll kill you. Shoot it, for God's sake!'

The boar faced the Englishman, lowered its head as

if to charge and then turned and disappeared into the undergrowth. Olivia, who had not realised she had been holding her breath, let it out in a great sigh of relief. Her rescuer turned and held out his arms. 'Jump!'

She eased herself off the branch and dropped into his arms. It was only when she was safe on the ground, with his arm round her and his heart beating steadily against hers, that she realised she was shaking. She hid her head in the rough material of his coat, wishing she had the strength or even the will to pull herself away. 'It is all right now,' he said gently, making no move to release her. 'It won't come back.' He thought she was afraid! Well, she had been, just a little, but what was so annoying was that he had witnessed her helplessness. How could she boast that she could manage without him, when clearly she could not?

She moved away from him and began gathering up pine cones for fuel. 'You've brought supper, I see,' she said, to cover her confusion. 'I did not hear a shot.'

'I did not shoot it.'

'No, I suppose you caught it and strangled it with your bare hands. Why must you lie?'

'I always tell the truth. Now, how about a fire, while I skin and clean it? I take it you have no aversion to eating it?'

'No.'

'Double standards,' he muttered to himself as he took a knife from his saddle-bag and set to work on the animal. 'What is the difference between eating hare and eating kid?'

'The hares do not belong to anyone.'

'Of course it has nothing to do with the fact that kids are soft, adorable creatures who love their mothers.'

'Not at all.'

He laughed and began to hum a marching song as he worked.

'Why didn't you shoot it?' she asked. 'Why didn't you shoot the boar?'

'Why waste a bullet when it is unnecessary? Besides, the *guerrilleros* might hear a shot. You said yourself that sound carries a long way in the mountains.' He turned to face her. 'And you had best put a shelter round that fire; that might be seen too.'

'Do you know where the Spaniards are?'

'Not far away.'

She did as he suggested and moved quietly about her tasks, and when their meal was over she wrapped herself in Philippe's coat and settled down to sleep. He sat down with his back to a tree, his rifle across his knee and stared into the dying fire as if he could see pictures in its embers. What could he see, she wondered, things past or things yet to come? Were his thoughts on things he had done or those he had left undone? Was he even aware of her as a woman? She brought herself up short, reminding herself of her determination to remain free. Her apparent dependence on him tonight was just a momentary lapse and best forgotten.

He was still sitting in the same position when a new day showed itself in a lighter sky above the tree-tops and woke her.

'Have you been awake all night?' she demanded.

'No, I slept. Come now, we must be on our way.'

She rose drowsily. There was no opportunity for a *toilette* but she wished she had water to wash. Almost as if he could read her mind, he produced yesterday's wine bottle now filled with fresh water. 'Where did you get that?'

He laughed. 'The same place as I found the hare. Drink a little and use the rest to wash. With luck we shall be back in civilisation before we need more.'

She accepted it gratefully and five minutes later they set off again through the trees, picking their way along an ill-defined path and then out on to an open hillside where the sound of rushing water told them they had found the river again. He had been right about cutting off the bend. Why did he have to be right about everything? Her musing was brought to an abrupt halt by the sound of gunfire. He stopped just ahead of her and she drew alongside him. 'What is it?'

'I don't know. Stay here.' He moved off ahead of her towards the sound. She waited a moment or two and then curiosity drove her to disobey and follow him.

They could see the river again, narrower than it was but cut even deeper into the mountain rock, so that it lay at the bottom of a precipitous gorge. Straddling it, high above the foaming water, was a narrow wooden bridge. On the other side of the bridge, its walls continuing the face of the cliff as if it were part of it, was a monastery, guarding the bridge and the approach road. On the road was a French supply train, which had halted just short of the monastery.

They watched from their vantage-point on the other side of the river as the escort to the wagons exchanged fire with unseen protagonists hidden in the rocks and trees of the mountainside.

'*Guerrilleros*,' Olivia said.

'I told you to stay back.'

She ignored his censure. 'They got ahead of us.'

'It's hardly surprising; they know the terrain like their own backyards.'

'But what is a supply train doing so high up in the mountains?'

He smiled. 'Like us, they have been driven up here by the blowing of the lower bridge. Now Don Santandos has them where he wants them. Anyone holding the monastery holds the pass. Nothing can get through.'

He seemed to be right, because the murderous gunfire had killed most of the French troops and the rest had thrown down their arms and surrendered. The partisans poured out of their hiding places and surrounded them. Olivia could see Don Santandos giving orders to his men to drag the wagons into the monastery and then he turned to his prisoners. She cried out in horror when she saw him deliberately shoot them as they knelt on the ground.

'Monster!' she cried. 'Barbaric monster. They had surrendered.'

'I told you he was ruthless. Perhaps you will believe me now.'

'Oh, I believe you. And will you admit I was right and we should have turned south?'

'I admit nothing.'

'No, because you are pigheaded.'

He laughed aloud. 'I must be a very strange animal; a leopard with a pig's head. Perhaps if I have no claws I might be permitted to have tusks.'

'It is no laughing matter. What are we going to do?'

'Wait until dark. Then I will go down and look.'

'Not without me, you don't.'

'You will stay behind even if I have to tie you up, do you hear? Good God, woman, you don't know how to keep silent and I mean to go as close as I dare.'

'To what purpose?'

'We have to cross the bridge.'

'Right under their noses. I suppose you have a plan to make us invisible?'

He did not consider the question worth answering but turned and made his way slowly along the top of the cliff, looking for somewhere to shelter. She followed, very aware that they were exposed to the view of anyone who might happen to glance across the river. Luckily the Spaniards seemed more concerned with taking the wagons into the courtyard of the monastery than in posting look-outs. The path grew very narrow and they were obliged to dismount and lead the animals. 'I hope you know where you are going,' she whispered fiercely. 'I do not fancy a cold bath, even supposing I survive the fall.'

His answer was to lead the way into a cave. 'This will do. Now we wait.'

They settled down in the mouth of the cave, with their mounts safely behind them, and in minutes he was sound asleep, which convinced her he had stayed awake all the previous night, in spite of what he had told her. She sat there looking at him. In sleep he looked young. Perhaps he was young, but there was nothing like a war for ageing a man. Tom had been immature and gullible when he'd enlisted, but within months, if not weeks, he had grown up, had become hardened, like well-worn leather, brown and creased, but tough. The soldier who had died was not the young lad who had fallen victim to the recruiting sergeant's patter. And she was not the girl who had left home so consumed by love, so full of defiance, so confident she knew what she wanted. The confidence she had now was confidence of a different sort. It was all to do with self-preservation, the will to survive, the conviction that you never knew what you could endure until you put it to the test.

She smiled. If her contemporaries at home could see her now, they would be shocked to the core. Yet, looking back, it was an experience she would not have missed, but one she did not want to repeat. Home was her goal.

When the light began to go from the sky, the Englishman stirred and sat up. 'Better eat,' he said, going to his saddle-bag and fetching out the last of the hare. 'Then it will be time to go.'

'You are surely not going to leave me here alone?'

'Most decidedly I am.' He looked up from dividing the food. 'If you are afraid, I will leave the rifle.'

'Won't you need it?'

'No. This is purely reconnaissance.' He bolted his meat and fetched the gun. 'Here. It is loaded, so take care what you do with it. If you need me, fire into the air. Take hold of it so and point it upwards and pull the trigger. It will rebound, so be prepared.'

'Very well,' she said meekly.

He took Thor's reins and led him out on to the path. 'Don't fire unless you really must.'

He paused, as if reluctant to leave her, or pehaps reluctant to leave the weapon. 'How long must I wait?' she asked. 'If you do not come back.'

'Until dawn, but I shall be back long before that.'

She listened as his footsteps and the clop of hoofs died away, then sat down to wait. But Olivia was not a passive person; waiting was something she had never learned to do. She decided to make her way back along the path towards the track which led to the bridge, to see if she could see him going over. And if he managed to cross safely, why then should she not follow? It would save him having to come back for her. She had no sooner convinced herself of the sense of that than she was leading the mule back along the path, feeling her way carefully in the failing light.

She did not see him, though her eyes ached with trying to make out his form among the shadows. She jumped at every sound — the bleat of a goat, the hoot of an owl. As she drew nearer to the bridge, she could hear sounds of revelry coming from the monastery. There was a guard on the far side of the bridge outside the entrance to the building, pacing up and down, watching the road from the east. He did not seem to be interested in the path from the mountains. Had Mr Leopard evaded him? Could she pass him too? The sound of the water was loud enough to muffle the sound of her footsteps, but to take the mule as well would be too risky. She left it with reins trailing and set off across the bridge, darting from shadow to shadow until she was on the far side and very close to the sentry.

And there she froze. Two partisans appeared and called cheerfully to the guard, who answered and then

turned towards the bridge. He went down a few steps
and peered downwards towards the water as if expecting trouble from that direction. Olivia noticed the
rough path down the cliff as she moved lightly out and
across the road while his back was turned. By the time
he had returned to his post, she was in the shadow of
the monastery gate. Now what to do? she asked herself.

The sentry was coming back. There was only one
way to go and that was into the courtyard. She darted
across to hide behind the nearest of the French wagons
which stood just inside the gate. Here she stopped to
peer out at the *guerrilleros* who stood in a circle, facing
inwards. In their centre the Englishman sat on his
horse with his hands tied behind him. Around his neck
was another rope and the end of this had been thrown
over a branch of a gnarled cork oak.

'Thieves we hang,' Don Santandos said, addressing
his prisoner. 'And it matters not whether they be
French, English or Spanish.'

'You are not thieves, then?' Mr Leopard said, lev-
elly. 'You have stolen nothing.'

'Nothing that was not ours to begin with. Now you
will die unless you can prove who you are and why you
are spying.'

'I was not spying.'

'But you were thieving?'

There was no answer and Don Santandos walked
round the horse, stroking its haunch. A good thump
would set it off and leave the Englishman hanging.
'Oh, not again!' Olivia whispered. 'Not again.'

'Where is the woman?'

'I do not know what you are talking about.'

Olivia held her breath. Surely he would not rather
die than reveal her whereabouts? It did not matter; she
was not where he supposed her to be. Tell him, you
fool, she pleaded silently. Tell him what he wants to
know.

But he remained silent and Don Santandos was

losing patience. 'Englishmen are fools when it comes to women,' he said. 'Perhaps you want to die. Then I give you your wish.' He raised his hand and brought it down sharply on the rump of the horse, leaving the Englishman swinging.

'Oh, no,' Olivia whispered. 'No, you do not do this to me twice.'

Slowly, achingly slowly, she raised the rifle, rested it on the tailboard of the wagon and carefully took aim.

CHAPTER THREE

FOR one infinitesimal moment after the shot was fired, no one moved, except the Englishman, whose body fell to the ground with a thump and lay still. Olivia, from her hiding place, smiled in triumph and patted the butt of the heavy Baker rifle which had made it possible. But then all was commotion as some of the *guerrilleros* ran for guns which had been stacked against the wall and others turned towards the wagon where the difting gunsmoke betrayed her position. Now she had to keep the initiative and there was no time to reload. She darted out from her hiding place and ran to where the Leopard lay. Still startled, the men did nothing to stop her.

'You imbeciles!' she shouted. 'You could have killed him!'

Don Santandos was the first to recover. 'That, *madame*, was our intention,' he said. 'And but for your lucky shot he would be dead by now.'

She bit off the retort that it had not been luck but marksmanship, and concentrated on playing the distraught female. In a way she *was* distraught; without Mr Leopard, she was lost; reluctantly she had to admit it. 'He is my husband,' she said. 'He is the one who will tell you I am who I say I am. Oh, if he dies. . .'

The partisans were watching, doing nothing, but she could not expect them to remain inactive for long; she had to convince them. 'Darling! Darling, speak to me,' she cried, as she worked to loosen the rope around their victim's neck. She put her ear to his chest. His heart was beating like a hammer on an anvil. 'You are my husband,' she whispered, bending low over him so that her face was against his ear. 'Tell me your name.'

When he did not reply, she lifted her head to look at him, wondering if he had heard her, or even if he could speak. His eyes were closed and there was an angry red weal round his neck where the rope had been.

'Oh, do not die on me, my love!' she cried, with more anguish than ever for the benefit of the onlookers. 'I love you. I need you.'

She was not sure, but she thought she detected a slight grin on his face and hoped fervently no one else had seen it. To make sure of that, she bent and kissed him on the mouth and was completely taken aback when he put his arm round her neck so that her head was imprisoned and kissed her back. Where he found the strength to hold her so firmly after what he had been through she did not know. She was acutely aware of their audience as the kiss lengthened and became something more than a mere meeting of lips.

Then he moved his mouth, oh, so slowly, round to her ear, making her shiver. 'Robert,' he croaked. 'Robert Lynmount.'

'Come now, *madame*,' Don Santandos said. 'Enough is enough. Such antics are best left to the bedroom and prove nothing.'

She looked up at the Spaniards who stood round grinning and covered her confusion with a show of anger. 'You may think yourselves lucky that my husband is not dead, for Viscount Wellington would certainly have had something to say about it, I can tell you. Robert Lynmount is one of his most valued officers.'

Don Santandos laughed. 'I would say his value is less than a dozen buttons and a metre of braid.'

She chose to ignore this reference to the Englishman's mutilated uniform. 'Now, will you please help him to a bed where he can recover?' She prayed her authoritative manner would have the desired effect, because they had no hope of fighting their way out, even if she still held the gun and could reload.

'You have courage, *madame*, I'll grant you,' Don Santandos said. 'It has earned you both a reprieve, albeit a temporary one.' He turned to give orders to two of his men who went to pick the Englishman up, one at his head and the other at his feet, but before they could do so he sat up and pushed them away. They stood back and watched as he forced himself to his feet. He stood, swaying a little before finding his balance, but Olivia knew better than to try to help him. He was an exceptionally strong man and he was also proud.

Don Santandos smiled. 'Good. Come with me.' He turned to lead the way into the building.

Olivia, tagging along behind, realised it had been a long time since the monastery had been used for the purpose for which it had been built. It was a small fortress; every window was a gun embrasure, with weapons and ammunition at the ready. There was food stacked in the room which had once been the monks' kitchens and truckle-beds and straw paliasses were scattered about. They were obviously preparing for a siege. If they thought she and Philippe had been aware of their preparations when they captured them, it was no wonder they had been so anxious that they should not return to Ciudad Rodrigo and the French army.

'You look surprised, *madame*,' Don Santandos said in French. 'Why should that be?'

'Please do not call me *madame*. I am not French; I have told you so a dozen times. My name is Mrs Lynmount. And yes, I am surprised to find so much preparation for war in a place like this.'

'Because it is a monastery? They were built to withstand sieges, Mrs Lynmount.'

She was glad that he had changed to English; perhaps he was ready to be convinced, after all. 'Not just that, but because it is so far from the main road. I can't imagine an army deciding to come this way. The ground is too rough and the way too narrow.'

'It would come if there was no alternative. What we have done for a small force, we can do for a greater. Now I have said enough.' He opened the door to one of the monks' cells. 'You will be comfortable in here until we decide what to do with you.'

As soon as they had gone, Robert collapsed on to the narrow bed which stood against the wall, and shut his eyes. His hand strayed to his throat and he tried to swallow.

She knelt beside him. 'Is there anything I can do to ease it? A bandage perhaps?'

'I must. . .thank you for. . .my deliverance.'

'I was angry.'

He grinned, but it was more a grimace of pain. 'Angry enough to attempt. . .the impossible. . . The luck of the. . .gods must have been with you.'

'Luck didn't come into it,' she said, busily tearing the hem off her petticoat to make a bandage. 'I have been a crack shot ever since I was big enough to lift a pistol.'

His disbelief was obvious, but she let it pass; she was used to it. 'Even a rifleman. . .would consider that a. . .shot in a thousand,' he said. 'And you must have known. . .that even if it succeeded. . .you would be taken prisoner.'

'It was you who said "sufficient unto the day". And they had no right to do what they did. After all, they are supposed to be our allies.' Her touch was gentle as she wound the makeshift bandage round his neck; it belied the sharpness of her tongue. 'And you would do better not to try and talk.'

'It was. . .a brave thing to do.' His voice was becoming stronger as the effects of his ordeal wore off. 'Especially as you are not sure of my. . .loyalty to my country.'

'It does not matter what I think; it is the *guerrilleros* you have to convince. I told them when they first captured me that I was Philippe's prisoner and that I was married to an English soldier. You must be that soldier. You went absent without leave to look for me. You must make them believe it. Persuade them to let us go back to our own lines.'

'Us? Does that mean you are throwing in your lot with mine, after all?'

'Only until we are out of this scrape.'

'You would not be in a scrape if you had done as you were bidden and waited on the other side of the gorge for me.'

She had got herself into this mess, it was true, but it had started long before she met him. She smiled. 'I would have had a long wait.'

'Better than dying with me.'

'I do not intend to die.' She leaned back to look at her handiwork. 'Why were they trying to hang you? What were you supposed to have stolen?'

'A mule.'

'For me?' Her obvious surprise made him smile crookedly.

'How else could I have persuaded you to come with me?'

'And the bread?'

'I don't think they have missed that even now.'

She was beginning to look at him in a new light; he was certainly resourceful as well as brave and strong. 'The hare too? And the water?'

'Why not?'

'You fool! And all for nothing.'

'Nothing, my dear Olivia? How can you say that when Dame Fortune has smiled on our endeavours and given us a sure sign we are meant to go on?'

'Whatever are you talking about?'

He touched his neck gingerly. 'Now I don't have to pretend, I can be a silent Philippe and be convincing.'

'Oh, you are impossible! It is out of the question, and if the *guerrilleros* hear that you intend to go to the French they will make sure we do not escape. They may decide that hanging is too good for us and try torture. Besides, if the French are sending supply wagons as far forward as this, they must have left Ciudad Rodrigo to continue their advance.'

'Do you know how far forward we are?'

'No, and I doubt the *guerrilleros* will tell us.'

He sat up suddenly, swung his legs over the edge of the bed and pulled her up beside him as footsteps sounded on the stone floor outside their cell. When the door opened he was holding her in a tight embrace and his lips were on hers. To have tried to resist would have made the man who stood in the doorway suspicious and yet she did not want the Englishman to think that kissing strange men was something she made a habit of and he could do it with impunity. She had had two husbands before but neither had kissed her like this. His strength and determination went into that kiss, but it was more than that; it hinted at a latent passion which promised all manner of delight if only she would submit and return fire with fire.

But she would not; he was taking advantage of their situation and it just would not do. But even as the thought crossed her mind she was weakening; his mouth, exploring hers, overwhelmed her senses and made her whole traitorous body melt against his. She forgot everything—her surroundings, her widowhood, even the man who stood in the doorway, as she succumbed to a need she had never before acknowledged.

Robert lifted his head at last and looked over her shoulder at the newcomer. 'Go away; can't you see I am busy?'

The spell had been broken and she took the opportunity to pull herself away and sit up, now acutely aware of the smiling Spaniard. 'The chief sent me to fetch you to join him for supper. Come, follow me.'

Reluctantly Robert rose to obey and Olivia, struck dumb, could do nothing but follow as their guide conducted them to the refectory, where almost the whole band of partisans were sitting around a table laden with food and bottles of wine.

'Sit down, my friends,' Don Santandos said, waving a chicken leg at them. 'Eat heartily. Let it not be said Don Santandos does not know how to treat his prisoners.' He looked up at Robert. 'I trust your neck is not too uncomfortable for you to swallow?' He pointed at two empty spaces on the bench next to him and waited until they had taken their seats and food had been set before them. Then he filled their glasses. 'You were lucky, you know,' he said, addressing Robert. 'So lucky it is almost unbelievable, and because of that I am inclined to take it as a sign that you are not meant to die — not yet.' He smiled. 'We might have other uses for you.'

Robert, who was reluctant to put food into his mouth in case he could not swallow it, picked up his glass and held it up in salute to Don Santandos. 'Be assured, Don Santandos, if I can be of service, I shall deem it an honour. After all, one good turn deserves another.' He sipped the wine. Olivia, watching, noticed the almost imperceptible wince of pain as he swallowed it.

The Spaniard laughed. 'It is a good turn to be half strangled?'

'No, *señor*, I was referring to the fact that you had done me the service of killing the man who took my wife, and saved me the trouble.'

'Ahh.' He looked at Robert's untouched plate. 'Would you rather have soup, my friend? It will go down more easily.' He clicked his fingers and one of his men hurried to the kitchens. 'We shall, of course, have to have proof of your story. You have no papers, nothing on your uniform to tell us which regiment you came from, nor your rank. And there are no British troops this side of the Coa.'

'You are wrong.'

'You mean Craufurd's Light Division?'

'You know that, do you?'

'It is hardly a secret.' Don Santandos paused to swallow his glass of wine in one gulp. 'For someone who is supposed to be covering a retreat, he is being particularly aggressive. Is that where you came from?'

'No.'

'Why are you alone?'

'He came looking for me.' Olivia found her voice at last.

'And who would not want to search for so beautiful an example of the fair sex?' The Spaniard laughed suddenly. 'Even if she does handle a rifle like a trooper.'

'Better,' she said, making him laugh again.

He turned to Robert. 'You have taught her well, but don't you think a gun in the hands of a woman is a fatal combination?'

'It is only fatal if I want it to be,' she snapped quickly. 'And I can out-shoot any man here. Give me a weapon and I will prove it.'

Don Santandos roared with laughter, and though his men had not understood the conversation they knew something had tickled the fancy of their chief and followed suit. 'You are a trier, I give you that,' he said, wiping his eyes with his sleeve. 'But I am not such a fool as to fall for that one.'

'It was worth a try,' she said, smiling.

'I think,' said Robert, as a bowl of soup was set before him, 'I think I have a better proposition than that.'

'Oh, let us hear it. It will amuse us while we wait.'

'Wait for what?' Olivia demanded.

No one answered her. Robert stood up and beckoned to Don Santandos. 'A word in your ear, *señor*.'

Two or three of the partisans pushed back the bench on which they sat, making it overturn with a clatter, and rushed to seize Robert's arms. He stood without struggling, still looking towards their leader. 'Come,

Don Santandos, I am weak and helpless and I give you my parole.'

'No!' Olivia shrieked, knowing that his parole would bind him to refrain from trying to escape. 'You fool!'

'It seems your wife has more spunk than you do, Englishman. No wonder she preferred the company of the Frenchman.'

'I did not! Why will you not believe me?'

'Because, Mrs Lynmount, we had been watching you for some time before we took you prisoner and we saw what we saw. Would you like me to tell your husband that you were not behaving like a prisoner? Shall we tell him what we saw?'

'There is no need for that.'

'Are you afraid he would beat you?'

'He should understand that when a woman has a choice between. . .' She shrugged, allowing them to guess her meaning.

'You mean your courage deserted you and you did not fight for your honour? Oh, Mrs Lynmount, you disappoint me.'

'It was be his prisoner or be left to the mercy of his men.' She deliberately turned from him and began to eat. 'I will speak no more on the subject. If my husband is satisfied, then so should you be.'

'Are you satisfied?' Don Santandos asked Robert.

'If I am not, it is between me and my wife,' Robert said. 'I will deal with her later; there are more important things to consider now. I have something to say to you.'

'Then do so.'

'In private.'

Don Santandos stood up and signalled to his men to release Robert's arms. 'Come, my friend, we will go for a stroll in the cloisters.'

Olivia watched the two men leave the room, aware that without them she was at the mercy of the partisans, who would not be as careful of her as their leader.

They spoke only in Spanish, which was conducted rapidly and noisily with a great deal of laughter and ribald comment which was too complicated for her to follow. One or two eyed her appreciatively, but she pretended not to notice and tucked into her meal. One thing she had learned while following the drum was that if food was set before you, you ate while you had the chance, because you never knew where your next meal would be coming from. Loss of appetite because you were worried, in love or bereaved was a foolish indulgence.

After half an hour or so, Robert and Don Santandos returned with their arms on each other's shoulders, as if they had been the best of friends all their lives. Whatever Robert had had to say, it had certainly changed the guerrilla's attitude towards him. Don Santandos filled two glasses with wine and handed one to the Englishman. 'To Ciudad Rodrigo and the confusion of the enemy,' he said, clinking his glass against Robert's.

'Ciudad Rodrigo?' Olivia queried in alarm. 'Did I hear aright?'

Robert smiled at her. 'You did, my love. I leave at first light.'

'What about me?' It was almost a plea.

'You will stay here until your husband returns,' Don Santandos said.

'A hostage!' she shouted at Robert. 'You mean to leave me here as a hostage? You came all this way to find me and now you are going to abandon me to these. . .these. . .' His warning look cut off what she was going to say and she gaped at him with her mouth open.

'You will be well treated as befits the wife of an English officer,' Don Santandos said. You have my word on that.'

'I will not stay.'

'You will obey me.' If Robert hoped his quiet
manner would make her mind him, he was wrong.

'No!' she shouted. 'Never! You have no right. . .'

'On the contrary, my sweet, I have the right of a
husband. . .'

'To abandon me? I shall. . .I shall. . .' The men,
sensing a marital tiff, were laughing and waiting to
see what the English officer would do to assert his
authority, and Olivia realised she was in a very precarious position. If they discovered she was not married to
Robert, her value as a hostage would be nothing and
they would do what they wanted with her — rape her,
kill her or both, and there would be little Robert could
do to save her, even if he wanted to. Anything could
happen. She needed the protection of Robert's name,
however little it afforded, and as he and the guerrilla
leader now seemed to be on excellent terms it behoved
her to be less outspoken. She softened her tone. 'I am
sorry, Don Santandos, but Robert has had this ridicu-
lous plan ever since we were reunited yesterday. I
thought he simply wanted revenge because of what the
Frenchman had done to me. The man is dead and I can
see no point in courting trouble.'

'You flatter yourself, ma'am,' Robert said coldly. 'It
has nothing to do with you and what you did or did not
do. I will deal with that when I have more time to
consider a suitable punishment. We have a war to win.
The French must be driven from the whole Peninsula,
and, if I can help my Spanish friends to achieve that,
then that is what I will do.' He smiled at Don
Santandos. 'My wife has a French uniform coat which
will do me very well, but I need a pair of breeches.'

Don Santandos laughed, clicked his fingers and gave
an order. One of his men ran from the room and
returned with an armful of French uniforms which he
dropped on the floor. 'Take your pick,' he said. 'Their
former owners have no use for them now.'

Olivia knew the uniforms had been taken from the

solidiers guarding the baggage train. A year before she would have been horrified at the idea of someone wearing dead men's clothes, but is happened so often she had even become used to it. She watched as Robert crossed the room to select a pair of breeches, but she had not given up the fight yet. She turned to Don Santandos. 'You know, *señor*,' she said calmly, 'if Robert walks into the French lines alone he has no hope at all of succeeding in what he is planning to do.'

'He is willing to try, and if he would rather face death at the hands of the French than one of dishonour as a nobody, then I, for one, salute him. You, Mrs Lynmount, should be able to understand that.'

'Oh, I do, but is it necessary to hold me as a hostage? I am no use to you here.'

'I did not demand it; it was the captain's idea.'

'Was it, now?' She was thoughtful. Robert had wanted her to help him, so why had he changed his mind, if the partisans had not forced him to leave her behind? Was it because he was concerned for her safety or simply that he did not trust her? Either way she had to proceed carefully. 'Do you wish him to succeed?' she asked.

'Doing what?'

'Whatever it is you have cooked up between you.'

'It would help.' He shrugged. 'But if he does not it is all the same to me.'

'I could help him. With me, his chance of surviving and returning to you would be doubled. I have been in the town. I know where Ph —— ' she corrected herself quickly ' — where the Frenchman lodged. His papers and belongings are there. With them, Robert could pass himself off as a French officer. I could tell every-one how we were captured by *guerrilleros* and escaped after you left him for dead. It would be more convinc-ing, don't you think?' He appeared to be considering what she was saying and she pressed home her point.

'I also speak perfect French and he does not; he would have to remain silent.'

'As a once hanged man that would be acceptable.'

'Yes, but if he needs to ask or answer questions — what then?'

'How do we know you would not immediately make your escape or inform the French of our whereabouts?'

'Don Santandos, we do not know your whereabouts. Take us down to the main road blindfold.'

'Then how could Captain Lynmount return with his intelligence?'

'Arrange a meeting place.'

Robert returned with a pair of breeches over his arm. 'Come, my love, let us go to bed; I must be up betimes.' He paused and looked from one to the other. 'What have you been scheming now, Olivia?'

'I have been telling Don Santandos that I know my way about Ciudad Rodrigo and I speak perfect French. He is considering allowing me to accompany you.'

'No.'

'Why not?'

'Don Santandos needs a hostage.'

'No, he does not.' She turned to the Spaniard. 'You don't, do you? You will take our word?'

Don Santandos laughed, as if amused by her persistence. 'I will think about it.'

Robert made no attempt to hide his annoyance. He grabbed her arm and dragged her back to their cell. 'What are you playing at?' he demanded as soon as they were alone. 'Yesterday you would not even consider coming with me. What is going on in that perverse head of yours?'

She laughed. 'What did you say about the lesser of two evils? I do not want to be left behind with these men. Don Santandos may promise to keep me safe, but he cannot watch all his men all the time, and if I am not allowed a gun how can I defend myself? I would rather take my chances on the road between here and Ciudad Rodrigo.'

He stood and looked at her in astonishment. 'You mean you would pretend to be coming with me and then run away? Have you no honour?'

'I don't need to give my parole; only you need do that. And let me remind you of your own words yet again: "My honour is my own affair".'

He laughed. 'Do you think Don Santandos will not think of that?'

'He might not. You are supposed to be my husband and responsible for me; your word covers me too.'

'And if I refuse to take you on the grounds I cannot trust you to keep *my* word?'

'You will not refuse because it was what you have wanted all along. Now, as you are apparently fully recovered, I shall take the bed. You may sleep on the floor.' With that she sat on the edge of the bed, which was certainly not big enough for two in any case, pulled off her boots, threw him one of the two blankets, rolled herself in the other and lay down to sleep. She could hear him chuckling as he made himself as comfortable as possible, using the French uniform as a pillow.

She had become accustomed to sleeping lightly, and his efforts to creep from the room just before dawn woke her. She sat up immediately, pulled on her boots, and followed him. 'Did you think you could leave me behind?' she queried. 'It was not very *galant* of you.'

'Don Santandos will not let you go,' he said, striding along the dark corridors as if he had the eyes of a cat. 'I mean to travel fast.'

'I can out-ride you any day.'

He laughed. 'Boasting again, Olivia? Do you know, in ancient Rome, boasting which could not be substantiated was considered a crime?'

'Don't change the subject. Yesterday, before we came here, you wanted me to go with you; you almost begged me to help you.'

'Begged, Olivia? I never beg.'

'Asked me, then. What has changed your mind?'

They came out of the corridor into the huge room where they had dined the evening before. No one had cleared the table; it was still covered with half-eaten food, half-filled wine glasses, chicken bones, empty bottles. Don Santandos was already there. He had swept aside the debris at the end of the table in order to spread out a map. He folded it up when he saw them and beckoned them over.

'Good morning, Captain.' Then to Olivia, 'Good morning, Mrs Lynmount. Have you come to bid your husband a fond farewell?'

'No, I go too.'

He turned to Robert. 'What do you say, my friend? Will she be an asset or a liability?'

Robert laughed. 'The question is, will she be more of a hindrance to you? Her presence might very well cause dissension among the men, especially as you have no women in your party at all.'

'You think I cannot control my own followers?' he demanded. 'Why should I even try?'

'You gave your word, Don Santandos, as I have given mine.'

'So I did.' He laughed. 'What she needs is a duenna.'

'Certainly not!' Olivia snapped, painting a mental picture of a huge Spanish woman set to guard her against the men and watch her every move. She would never have a moment to herself, nor be able to escape.

'I fear she would be a handful even then,' Robert said mildly. 'Let her come; I will take responsibility for her.'

'I wish you would not talk about me as if I were baggage,' Olivia put in angrily. 'I have something to say in what happens to me; I am not an inanimate object.'

They both turned to look at her and then simul-

taneously burst into laughter. 'Oh, my darling,' Robert
said. 'I love you even more when you are angry.'

His declaration silenced her. It had slipped so easily
from his tongue. Was that because he was practised at
lulling women with words of love, or because it was
true? She stopped her errant thoughts instantly. They
were both acting out a charade and the reality was very
different. At this particular moment, they were useful
to each other, and hers was the greater need.

'I do not envy you, Captain,' Don Santandos said. 'I
think I would rather face a regiment of Boney's crack
troops than be married to such a one. Take her. Take
her and I wish you joy of her.' He smiled and turned
to Olivia. 'We fetched the mule. You will find your
bundle in the doorway over there and water to wash in
your room. Go and make your preparations.'

Olivia was reluctant to obey in case Robert still tried
to leave without her, but, as usual, he seemed able to
read her thoughts; he reached out and touched her
arm. 'I will wait here for you, my dear. Make haste.'

As she left, Don Santandos opened the map again.
When she returned, refreshed and, once again, dressed
in her own skirt and blouse, they were still deep in
discussion. Seeing her, Don Santandos smiled and
folded up the map and the two men went out to the
courtyard with Olivia silently following, every nerve
tense in case they should, even now, try to leave her
behind. A small escort party was assembled in the
courtyard where Robert's horse stood ready saddled
and beside it a grey which was almost as big. It was a
beautiful mount, better than any Philippe had had.

'I am afraid we have no side-saddle, Mrs Lynmount,'
Don Santandos said.

Robert laughed. 'My wife is accustomed to riding
astride. She has been doing it ever since she was old
enough to sit a pony.'

Olivia opened her mouth to ask him how he knew
that, but bit her tongue instead and went over to the

horse's head to make its acquaintance, stroking its nose and fondling its ears. 'You are a beauty,' she said, then to Don Santandos, 'What is he called?'

'Pegasus.'

She laughed and, in one swift movement, leapt into the saddle. 'The winged horse. I like it.' The animal was restive, but she controlled it easily. 'How are we going to explain the horses when we arrive in Ciudad Rodrigo?'

'You will not have them then. Remember you have escaped a hanging. You will arrive footsore and bedraggled.'

'Oh.' She was crestfallen, but she could see the sense of that. 'Shall we make a start?'

She did not notice one of the escort ride up alongside her until he threw a bag over her head and held it down as she struggled. 'Be still, Mrs Lynmount,' Don Santandos said mildly. 'It is only until you are down the mountain.'

'But I cannot see where I am going.'

'Your husband will lead you.'

She assumed from this that Robert was not to be blindfolded and it made her wonder once again what he had said to the partisan leader to make such a change in their relationship. Either they now trusted each other or each was playing a game of deception, a kind of double bluff. And she was in the middle of it.

The reins were taken from her hands and the horse moved forward. It was uncomfortable and unnerving not to be able to see, but Pegasus seemed sure-footed enough; all she had to do was keep her seat. At first she was aware that they were on a reasonably smooth road and then that they had branched off and were moving very sharply downhill. She could hear the river not far away and the scuffing of hoofs on the uneven ground. She tried counting the sounds as they moved over a particular piece of stony ground, one horse, then another, then another. There was a rider ahead of

Robert, who was leading Pegasus, and there were several more, perhaps as many as four, following her. And the path must be narrow for them to be riding single file. There seemed to be no hope of galloping off alone and escaping—not yet. At some point, the *guerrilleros* would have to leave her and Robert to finish the journey alone; then she would try her luck.

She tried to gauge their direction by the feel of the sun on her back and the sound of the river, and guessed they were making their way down the mountain on the opposite side of the gorge from the one she and Robert had taken two days before. If that was so, before long they would arrive at the village where the bridge had been blown. And not too far from that was the main road into Portugal. She would be patient.

Her guess had been right. When the sun was at its highest, they reached the valley floor, and here they sweltered, particularly Olivia, muffled as she was by the bag over her head. She cried out to be released.

'Let her out,' she heard Robert say to someone. 'If you do not, she will faint and fall off.'

She heard Don Santandos laugh and say, 'I had forgotten her.' The bag came off her head and she drew in great gulps of air before looking about her.

They were riding down the main street of the village she had seen from the other side of the river. There were women at the doors of their homes and children playing in the street, but few men. Husbands, sons and fathers, she guessed, were with the partisans in the hills. They stopped at the door of a house next to the church and a thin, agile-looking priest came hurrying out of the house and shook the guerrilla leader by the hand. 'Welcome, Miguel, my old friend.' He eyed Robert and Olivia as he spoke, unsure whether they were friend or foe, especially as Robert was wearing the French uniform. 'Prisoners?' he queried.

'Yes and no, Father Peredo. They have a role to play and I need you to make sure they play it well.

This is Captain Robert Lynmount and his lady wife.
Their story is an interesting one.'

The priest, who could have been no more than forty,
smiled and held out his hand to help Olivia dismount.
'Señora, you are welcome to Villa de Fuentes. Come
inside and take some refreshment. We have been all
but cleaned out again by the bluecoats, but they do not
know all our hiding places.' He chuckled and led the
way into his house. It was sparsely furnished but
gloriously cool. 'Sit down, please.'

'Where are the French?' Robert asked him as they
obeyed.

'In Ciudad Rodrigo, but likely to move out at any
time.' He laughed again and clicked his fingers at a
servant girl and ordered food and wine to be brought,
before continuing. 'They have been held up, as usual,
for lack of supplies. It seems the countryside is much
poorer than they had been led to believe. And they are
maddened by the blowing of the bridge.'

'Good,' Don Santandos said, making himself at
home in the priest's most comfortable chair. 'We have
plans for delaying them further, but they depend on
the Englishman here.'

'He has been wounded?'

'He has been hanged. He is a thief. He is also a
deserter.'

'And you trust him?' The little priest sounded
astonished.

'There are deserters from both sides hiding in the
hills,' Don Santandos said mildly. 'Buzzing gnats, who
are no more than a nuisance, but if one of them has a
compelling reason for wanting to help us, why should
we turn him down? But you must watch him.'

'I, play nursemaid?'

'You are allowed to come and go freely among the
French soldiers but, you must admit, they do not
altogether trust you. We need another string to
our bow.'

The priest laughed. 'It is as well they cannot see all I do. But what is the Englishman going to do?'

'The *señora* came out of Ciudad Rodrigo with a French officer; she will return with one.' He laughed. 'Slightly the worse for wear.'

'I see.'

'I want you to make sure they stay with the French until they find out when the army is marching and in which direction.'

'Supposing we cannot find that out?' Olivia asked. 'Supposing someone discovers we are impostors?'

'You had better pray that does not happen,' Miguel Santandos said, as the servant arrived with the food. It was simple but substantial and they were all silent while they ate, each busy with his or her own thoughts. Olivia was beginning to wonder what she had allowed herself to be drawn into; every word Don Santandos uttered seemed to be loaded with menace and the opportunity to escape was looking less and less possible.

Half an hour later, Don Santandos rose to go. 'I will bid you goodbye, Captain,' he said to Robert. 'Leave the horses here — the *padre* knows where to hide them. If you return alive with the information we seek, then you are welcome to keep them as a recompense for your services.' He smiled ruefully, as if reluctant to admit a weakness. 'The black is useless to us in any case — he would not let anyone else near him; one of my men has a lump the size of a hen's egg on his shin.'

Robert grinned at Olivia with a look that said clearly, Did I not tell you so?

Don Santandos turned from them and knelt at the feet of the priest. 'Bless me, Father, before I go.'

'Do you not go to see your wife?' the priest asked, making the sign of the cross over the supplicant's bent head.

'No. Each time I do, it is worse. When the enemy is defeated, then I will go home.' He rose and shook Robert by the hand. 'Good luck, my friend. We shall

be on the look-out for you.' He turned to Olivia and
grinned. 'Goodbye, my valiant *señora*.' Then he left
the room, followed by the rest of his men, leaving
Robert and Olivia facing the priest.

'I will show you the road,' he said.

They followed him from the house and he stood in
the road with the wind blowing his skirts about his legs
and pointed towards the east. 'A mile or so along the
road you will find a shrine, behind which is a narrow
path. It will take you across country and bring you out
on the road again two miles short of the town. But be
careful, the bluecoats are everywhere. Do not speak
English. You, Captain, would do well not to speak at
all. Are you armed?'

'No. The *guerrilleros* would not have been so careless
as to leave weapons where we could take them.'

The priest's face creased in a smile and he took
Olivia's hand. 'God bless you, child. May the good
Virgin reward your courage with a long life and fine
sons.' He turned to Robert. 'Look after her, Captain,
and may the Lord shine on your endeavours and bring
us victory.'

They bade him goodbye and set off down the road
on foot, striding side by side, until they were out of
sight.

'Now what?' she demanded when they had been
walking in silence for half an hour.

'What do you mean?'

'Are you still going to Ciudad Rodrigo? Are you
determined to put your head in another noose?
Because if you are, let me tell you I shall not be there
to shoot you down a second time.'

'If you could do it again.'

'Of course I could. If I had a gun. . .'

He laughed. 'Do you know, I am rather glad you do
not? I should feel decidedly unsafe.'

'If I had wanted to shoot you, I would have done so
when I had the chance.'

'Instead you saved me,' he said softly. 'Why did you do that?'

'I was angry, I told you. They had hanged one husband; I. . .' She stopped suddenly. Whatever was she saying? 'It seemed the only thing to do. And you had stolen the mule for me.'

'You did not know that at the time.'

'No.'

He turned to look at her. There was a purpose and lightness in her stride which suggested she could keep walking all day—not a bit like Juana, who was so delicate he was almost afraid to touch her, lest she shatter. Juana would have demanded a carriage and a trunk full of clothes before she went anywhere at all. He smiled suddenly. Juana would never have allowed herself to get into this kind of situation in the first place. Olivia looked just as delicate with her finely chiselled features and slim frame, but her appearance was obviously deceptive. Had she always been so sturdily independent, he wondered, or had she learned it in the hard school of an army marriage?

'Who taught you to shoot?' he asked. 'Was it your first husband?'

She smiled. 'No, Tom never felt comfortable with a gun, even though his father worked for my father. Papa manufactures arms, you see. When I was quite small I used to go out with Papa testing new weapons, and that's when I learned to shoot.'

'What did your mother say to that? Surely she did not approve?'

'I never knew my mother. Papa is all I had.' Her light laugh was a little unnatural. 'I think he was disappointed I was not a boy.'

'I am sorry,' he said softly, resisting the impulse to take her arm.

She shrugged. 'Don't be. I had a wonderful childhood.'

'But growing up was painful, eh?'

She looked up at him sharply. Did he really understand or was he just making polite conversation? 'It was precarious to say the least, but done with now. All I want is to go back home and be with my father again.'

'Instead you are tramping towards an enemy-held town with a man you do not trust, in a cause you do not support. . .'

'Who said I did not support it?' she demanded. 'Just because I think you are mad, it does not mean I do not want us to win this war. But it is for armies to win battles, not lone men and women.'

'Armies are made up of lone men, each doing his duty as he sees it.'

'But you have no duty; you have been discharged. Why were you turned out, by the way?'

'You heard Don Santandos. I am a thief.'

He watched her carefully for signs of shock or outrage, but there was nothing to see but clear green eyes in a countenance which smiled more often than it frowned. Why was she always so damned cheerful? She had nothing to be cheerful about.

They turned off at the shrine as they had been directed and walked along a narrow path which ran through a cherry orchard, although most of its trees had been stripped of their fruit, probably by a hungry soldiery. There were bee skips among the trees which reminded him forcefully of the aftermath of the summer battles the year before; honey was a favourite with the troops and they risked being stung to loot it. He shook himself; he did not want to be reminded of looting in any shape or form. He forced himself to think ahead, to plan what he would do once he was in Ciudad Rodrigo. It would not be easy, but with Olivia. . .

'Robert!' She had walked ahead of him and was standing at the edge of the orchard, pointing. 'Look!'

He hurried to join her. 'Don't you know better than to stand so openly? Has the army taught you nothing?'

'Look,' she said, ignoring his criticism. 'There are English soldiers down there. What are they doing so far from their lines?'

'Reconnaissance,' he said. 'Making maps, by the look of it.'

'Shall we go down and meet them?'

'No!' He spoke sharply. 'I am Captain Philippe Santerre, don't forget. You may go if you wish.'

She looked at him in surprise. 'You mean you would not try to stop me?'

'I am not a man to hold a woman against her will.'

'Very well. If I am no longer needed, I will go.'

He did not answer and she set off slowly, half expecting him to call her back, but when he did not she began to run. The soldiers were moving cautiously between the trees, watching the road which led into the town, but they did not seem to be concerned with watching their backs and had not yet seen her. I'd have them flogged for carelessness if they were my men, he thought, and then smiled wryly, thinking of the court-martial which had ended his right to command anyone and put him in a situation where he was so dependent on a woman.

In less than a minute, if they did not turn and see her, she would be able to hail them and then all his carefully laid plans would be thrown to the winds. But he did not care; he had no right to force her into going with him. If she died as a result of his foolhardiness, he would never forgive himself. Let her go back to her gun-making papa. Let her try to recapture her child-hood. Let her be happy. He wanted her to be happy.

Suddenly she stopped her mad dash and stepped behind a tree. Puzzled, he watched as the column carried on, moving from the trees to the cover of rocks and then on until they were out of sight over the hill behind them; Olivia had not moved. The air seemed very still and Robert realised he had been holding his breath. He let it out slowly and walked to join her.

They stood for a long moment facing each other, hazel eyes looking down into defiant green ones. The silence seemed to extend itself to the air around them as they sized each other up, each trying to guess the other's thoughts and decide how to deal with this new turn in their relationship.

'Isn't that just like a woman?' he said at last, trying to keep his voice light. 'Can't keep to the same mind for more than two minutes together. Now what are you proposing to do?'

She laughed. 'I think I shall just go on tormenting you.' She was a fool, she told herself. She had thrown away a golden opportunity, but she could not leave him to do what he had set out to do without her help. England would have to wait until his business was finished and he was free to keep his word to take her home. 'I think we ought to speak French from now on,' she said. 'And you had better begin looking as though you were in pain and lean on me a little.'

He didn't like the idea of having to lean on anyone, much less a woman, but he recognised the wisdom of what she said. He put an arm on her shoulder, trying not to lean too heavily, and together they hobbled towards the town whose walls were now clearly visible. For the first time in months, he began to feel that all was not lost; in fact, he was feeling decidedly optimistic.

CHAPTER FOUR

THEY were stopped at the town gate by a blue-coated sergeant, whose white shoulder-straps gleamed with newly applied pipe-clay. He levelled a musket at them as they hobbled towards him, feigning exhaustion. 'Identify yourself,' he commanded Robert.

'Lieutenant Philippe Santerre and Madame Santerre,' Olivia said. 'I speak for him.'

'Oh, and what has taken his tongue?' He stepped up to Robert, pushing the muzzle of the musket into the buttons of Philippe's old coat and peering into his face. 'My orders are to let no one in without the password.'

Olivia noticed Robert's fists clenching and his jaw tighten and was afraid he would try and speak. 'He cannot talk; he has been hanged and left for dead,' she said quickly. 'By the *guerrilleros*.'

Robert grinned lop-sidedly and ran his finger along the inside of the bandage round his throat, giving the soldier a glimpse of the rope marks.

'The guerrillas?' he queried. 'And where did this happen?'

'In the hills. I do not know exactly.' Although he had spoken to Robert, it was Olivia who answered.

The sergeant turned to eye her, from her French army boots, up over her skirt and dust-covered white blouse to defiant green eyes. 'And what were you doing in the hills?'

'Hunting.'

'And did you have permission to leave the town?'

Robert nodded and then stopped and put his hand to his throat, pretending pain. Olivia touched his arm. 'Don't try and talk, my dear, the sergeant understands.' She turned to the soldier. 'You do, don't you? We

81

were hungry and went looking for food. You know what these pigs of Spanish are like; they give nothing. The lieutenant is lucky to be alive at all. He needs rest. Let us go to our quarters, for pity's sake. He can report to his regiment later.'

He looked from her to Robert, who opened his mouth to speak and then shut it again, then back to Olivia. 'How did he survive?'

'I cut him down. Please let us through. We will go to Colonel Clavier in the morning.'

'Very well, but mind you do, for I shall report seeing you, so do not think you have got away with flouting the regulations and wandering about a hostile country-side on your own. This is no picnic, you know.'

'We know,' she said, as he waved them on.

They made themselves stumble agonisingly slowly past him until they were in a jumble of streets and lost among the townspeople and the thousands of soldiers who were quartered there and seemed bent on having a good time, for many of them were drunk.

'Who does he think he is?' Robert grumbled in a whisper as they quickened their pace. 'In our army a mere sergeant would not be allowed to speak to an officer like that.'

'He was only doing his duty.'

'And not very well either,' he said.

'Perhaps not,' she said. 'But you would certainly not have been allowed through without me.'

'Modesty is not one of your virtues, is it?' He turned to grin down at her as they turned up a narrow thoroughfare where houses with iron-railinged balcon-ies trailing geraniums crowded together, where women gossiped at the doors and children played on the cobbles. 'I never met such a forward woman.'

'You had better be quiet,' she said sharply. 'You can't speak, remember?'

They walked side by side without exchanging another word until they came to a bakery, though there was little evidence of any baking being done, and here she led the way up a stone staircase which went up to an outside balcony with two doors along it. She pushed open the first and went inside. He followed.

The room was dim and cool. It contained a large bed, a chest of drawers, a cupboard and a few chairs. There was a rug on the floor and a thin curtain at the window; a poor enough lodging for an aristocrat like Philippe but better than many of his compatriots enjoyed. It was just as they had left it; a pair of boots stood by the hearth from which ashes spilled, a shirt hung over a chair and Philippe's sword was propped against the wall. Robert strode over and picked the weapon up, balancing it in his hand appreciatively. The action seemed a kind of sacrilege to Olivia, a violation of Philippe's privacy; it made her feel as if she had betrayed him. She hated the Englishman for making her feel so guilty, not only about the sword but about that kiss in the monk's cell. It meant nothing, of course; it had simply been an expedient thing to do at the time, but she could not forget her own shameful reaction to it.

'Put that down!' she snapped.

He looked up from contemplating its beautifully fashioned hilt and stared at her in surprise, then slowly replaced the weapon against the wall. 'His papers and belongings, isn't that what you said? So that I can impersonate him.'

'Yes, but not that, not his sword.'

'Why not? I am an officer, I need a sword and he has no use for it now.' He smiled suddenly. 'Unless you claim to be as good a swordsman as you are a rifleman and want it for yourself. Is that it?'

'No, I have never learned the art.'

'Oh, blessed relief! I thought there was nothing I could do that you could not do better.' He went to the window, which looked out on to a narrow alley between the rough-plastered houses. 'Is it because you cannot bear to see your husband's belongings in the hands of someone else?' he asked, with his back to her. She did not answer and he turned to look into her face. 'That's it, isn't it? You loved him — you loved the Frenchman, your country's enemy.'

'But not *my* enemy. You don't understand. I can't explain and you have no right to accuse me; you have too much to hide yourself. And just because I agreed to help you, it does not mean you can march in here and make free with Philippe's belongings. You should not take for granted that you will have everything of his.'

'No,' he agreed, smiling at her vehemence; she appeared not to have understood him at all. 'Now, if you would be so good as to hand over Lieutenant Santerre's papers and his spare uniform and overalls, that would suffice.' His tone was clipped. 'I can always acquire another sword.'

She bent to pull a chest out from under the bed. 'Then what?' she asked. She had given no thought to what would happen after this moment. Had he supposed that taking her husband's name entitled him to other rights? The idea of sharing the room with this too handsome, too confident, oh, too everything man made her tremble. She could not look at him in case her eyes betrayed her thoughts. 'Now we are here, what are we going to do?'

'*We*, my dear Olivia? *You* do not need to do a thing. I asked you to get me past the guard and into the town; your job is done, you need stay no longer.'

She was so taken aback, she could not speak. How wrong she had been! He had not even considered her feelings at all and was quite prepared to turn her out. 'You ungrateful wretch!' she exploded.

'I did not say I wasn't grateful, did I? I simply give you a choice, to stay or to go.'

'Which is no choice at all. Do you expect me to turn right round and go out of the town again? What do you suppose our friend at the gate would say if he saw me leaving again so soon? And alone.'

'I've no doubt you could find a ready tale; you seem to be able to do that at the drop of a hat.'

'Then that is what I shall do. Goodbye, Captain Lynmount.' She picked up a small bag of coins from the chest and put them in her pocket. Philippe's clothes she flung at him, so that he was smothered and by the time he had extricated himself she had gone.

He cursed roundly and sank on to the bed with shirts, overalls, underdrawers and hose in his lap. Of all the inept fools! He had bungled what he had wanted to say and it was no wonder she had stormed out. The truth was that he did need her; only she could substantiate his story and make it convincing. She knew the ways of the French army and could prevent him from doing things he should not do, or failing to do things that he should do, which might give him away as an impostor. And he had to find out the number and disposition of the French forces. How many guns, how many wagons, how much ammunition, when they were going to march and where. Her help would have been invaluable for that; it had nothing to do with his personal feelings at all. He would not admit to having any.

But he had meant what he said about choice, even if he had not said it very well. It was unfair of him to expect the same degree of patriotism from her as he felt and he did not want her to think she had to stay with him if she did not want to. It would be dangerous and he had no right to insist that she share it with him. He smiled, remembering her courage. Danger would not put her off; she seemed not to acknowledge its existence. But that was dangerous in itself; over-confidence brought its own perils. Perhaps he was better off without her; at any rate he was not going to chase after her. He had run after a woman before and regretted it. If she came back on her own, then he might consider offering an explanation, but if she did not. . .

Of course she would return; where else would she go? She had pointed out herself how suspicious it would be if she left the town again so soon. She would do nothing to jeopardise his mission, would she? He stood up, threw the clothes behind him on the bed and paced the room. Could she, would she, inform on him? Just because she had been born English, that did not make her a patriot. And she had married a Frenchman. A woman did not marry unless she believed in the same things her husband did. Was she a danger to him? Should he go looking for her or should he forget about her help, leave now and find a safer hiding place? Or should he go to sleep, confident that when he woke she would have returned and he could trust her?

He fell back on the bed again and stared up at the cracked ceiling. She was an extraordinary woman, not exactly beautiful but with fine bones and expressive eyes and the figure of a goddess. She was down-to-earth, apparently fearless and always cheerful in spite of the blows that fate had dealt her. If she did not return, it was going to be hellishly difficult without her. . .

Olivia's temper had cooled almost as soon as she reached the street. Perhaps she had been unreasonable, for how was Robert to know how she felt about Philippe? Not love exactly, but a kind of fondness which came of his kindness and her gratitude. You could not easily throw that aside. Seeing that room again and his belongings, so familiar to her, had made her realise what none of the past three days had done — that he had truly died, and not in battle, which was something she knew she could accept, but in a particularly cruel and unnecessary way. Whether she had been in love with Philippe or not was none of Robert's business. His business was to spy, and the sooner he accomplished that, the sooner she could hold him to his end of the bargain — to take her safely home. And home was where she most wanted to go.

She walked past the castle with its crenellated keep and ivy-clad walls, patrolled by uniformed guards of Napoleon's northern army, to a market-place where those few traders who still had goods to sell had set out their stalls. Quarrel or no quarrel, they needed to eat; she began bargaining with a stallholder over the king's ransom he demanded for a cabbage. Three nights before she had taken one from a garden for nothing and feasted well on cabbage soup and stewed hare. Was that only three nights before? It seemed like a lifetime.

'Twenty pesetas,' the man demanded. 'And cheap, considering it had to be brought in from the country and the hills are swarming with *guerrilleros*.'

'They are your own countrymen.'

'To be sure, but they do not hold with co-operating with the French — *Afrancesado*, they call me, but I have a wife and five little children. . .'

'I understand. But twenty pesetas! That is altogether too much.'

If Philippe had been with her, he would have paid for the cabbage without a murmur, because wealth meant nothing to him, except its power to obtain the unobtainable. It was there for the spending and when his allowance ran out he simply wrote home for more. He could not have been more different from Tom, whose life had revolved around money, or, rather, the lack of it. Tom had begrudged a shilling for food when it meant he had less to gamble. He had always been convinced of being able to recoup his last losses on his next card game and make a fortune as well; it had always been the same. It was funny how she had reacted to Tom's penny-pinching by being extravagant herself, and to Philippe's generosity by being careful of his money. It was his money she was spending now and

she felt badly about that, especially when one of the
beneficiaries would be an Englishman, the enemy of all
good Frenchmen.

'Come, *señora*; if you don't have it, others will, so
make up your mind,' the rough voice broke in on her
thoughts. 'I've cherries too, and honey, but they are
for special customers.'

Special customers, Olivia realised, were those prepared to pay the exorbitant prices, but what choice did
she have? She paid for cabbage and cherries and moved
on, pushing her way through the crowds.

'Next week, I heard the colonel tell the major.' The
man's voice caught her attention. She turned to see a
corporal and the sergeant who had stopped them at the
gate, sitting on a shell-shattered wall, smoking filthy
clay pipes and sharing a flask of wine, drinking it
straight from the bottle. 'The advance guard is to go
and clear the way.'

Olivia walked past them and then turned in at a
break in the wall and made her way along the other
side of it, so that she could eavesdrop without being
noticed. If she could return to Robert with some of the
information he needed, then perhaps he would not
dismiss her so lightly.

She was so busy planning Robert's come-uppance
that she failed to notice how close she had come to
where they sat and that they had stopped speaking.
One of them, alerted by her shadow falling across
them, turned and startled her.

'An eavesdropper, by heaven. Or were you thinking
of something a little more diverting, my pretty?'

'No, no.' She backed away. 'I was dreaming. . .
wasn't looking where I was going.'

'Dreaming, eh?' the sergeant said. 'You are the one
who came with the man with no voice, the man who
was hanged.' He turned back to his companion.
'Hanged by the guerrillas, so she said. He had the rope

marks on his neck so I suppose it is true; you couldn't fake those.'

'I must go back to him,' she said.

He caught her arm. 'No so fast. Where is this heroic fellow of yours?'

'At home, resting.'

'And where is home?'

'Over Señor Antondan's bakery.'

'Has the lieutenant seen a doctor?'

'Not yet.'

'Nor reported to the colonel, I'll wager.'

'No.'

'It had better be one or the other. Either the doctor gives him a note or he reports for duty; he should know that.'

'He does. He'll go when he has rested.'

'Then I think you should see the colonel in his stead. A man left to hang and a woman with wit enough to wait until the hangmen have left and then cut him down and bandage him up is a story which will interest him. He will want to know where and when this happened.'

'We will see him tomorrow.'

He jumped down from the wall and took her arm. 'I think you should see him today. Now.'

'I do not want to go now. I must go back. Ro. . . Philippe will be anxious about me.' If he is still there, she thought, remembering their quarrel. 'I came out to buy food. . .'

'Food! I doubt he's ready for food; you are wasting your time and pesetas. No, *madame*, you come with us.' By this time the other soldier had stationed himself on her other side and there was no escape.

'Very well,' she said. 'But let us make haste; I have much to do.'

They escorted her to a house close to the castle where Colonel Clavier had made himself comfortable in one of the wealthier citizens' homes. As they entered, they passed a man coming out whose round,

rather flabby face was vaguely familiar to Olivia, and
she spent the next few moments wondering where and
when she had seen him before. He was in civilian
clothes and, because she had become so accustomed to
the dark blue jackets of the soldiers, his brown wool
coat and yellow silk cravat confused her memory. Was
he a private citizen or a soldier out of uniform, a
comrade of Philippe's? Could he denounce Robert?
Were the Englishman's plans to be thwarted before he
had even begun?

She stood to one side to allow the man to pass — a
courtesy he took for granted, except that he smiled in
a patronising way. He did not show any sign of having
recognised her and she supposed she had been mistaken. She forgot him as a dig in her ribs reminded her
that her escort was becoming impatient.

'Come, *madame*, I thought you were in a hurry,' the
sergeant said, then to the guard who stepped forward
to bar their way, 'I've brought the colonel a tasty
morsel for his dinner and she has a story to tell will set
your hair a-curl.'

'Is that what I am to tell Colonel Clavier?' the guard
demanded. 'Jacques Mortand, you should come with a
better tale than that if you want to disturb the colonel.'

'This woman, wife of Lieutenant Santerre, has been
up in the hills with the guerrillas; surely that's a tale
worth listening to.'

The guard conceded this and disappeared down a
long hallway, then knocked on a door at the far end.
A voice bade him enter and he disappeared, to
reappear a minute later and beckon Olivia. 'Madame
Santerre, the colonel will see you.'

She moved forward slowly and entered the room,
followed by the sergeant, who had no intention of
missing the story if he could help it.

Colonel Clavier was a corpulent man whose uniform
coat was stretched almost to bursting-point across his
middle, held there, it seemed, by a quantity of gold

braid. He was standing by the empty fireplace with a
brandy glass in one hand and his other resting on the
mantelpiece, where his plump fingers drummed a
tattoo in the dust. He watched her for a moment, then
left the hearth to sit at a desk which stood in the middle
of the room. Olivia, facing him, hoped she was hiding
the nervousness she felt.

'Your name?' he demanded.

'Olivia Santerre, wife of Lieutenant Philippe
Santerre.'

'You are not French,' he said, catching the traces of
an accent.

'No, Colonel. I came from England.'

'English!' His surprise was obvious. 'What are you
doing in Spain?'

'When men go to war, their wives have little choice,
and it matters not whose side they are on.' She hoped
her evasive answer would satisfy him. 'I was English
and now I am French.'

'Is that so?' He appeared to be amused.

'So my husband told me when we were married.'

'And you are loyal to France?'

She faced him defiantly. 'Of course.'

'You have been in the guerrillas' camp?'

'Yes.'

'You know, of course, that the guerrillas are a source
of some annoyance, like fleas, jumping and biting?
They must be squashed, don't you agree?'

'Yes, Colonel, most decidedly. They tried to kill my
husband. . .'

He waved her to a chair, while the sergeant stood by
the door, apparently forgotten. 'I think you had better
begin at the beginning.'

She sat down on the edge of the chair, poised for
flight, though she could not have escaped with the
sergeant blocking the doorway. She told him about
going hunting and being captured and Philippe being
hanged, all of which had the ring of truth, and she did

not have to pretend to be upset; the memory was still painful. 'They left him for dead,' she said.

'Why did they not hang you too?'

'I told them I was English.'

'And they believed you?'

'Yes, enough to have doubts about killing me. They just rode away, laughing. I suppose they thought I could not find my way down the mountain. After they had gone, I cut Philippe down.'

'How? Did they leave you with a knife?'

She paused, wondering why she had not thought of that. She could hardly change her mind now and say she had shot him down. They would not believe that anyway; even those who had actually seen the frayed noose which had been about Robert's neck had hardly credited it. 'I found a discarded bayonet.'

'And then?'

'My husband was still alive, so I nursed him a day and a night until he was strong enough to move and then we found our way back.'

'Where is this guerilla camp?'

'In the mountains to the north-east, I think,' she said evasively. 'I do not know exactly. They blindfolded us.'

'But you found your way home, it seems.'

'We were lucky,' she said. 'I could not locate the path again and I think my husband was in too much pain to take note of where we were going.'

'That is a great pity,' he said, and she thought she detected a threat in his tone. 'Because I want you to show us the way to this mountain hide-out.'

'I cannot. All mountain tracks look the same to me.'

'Then your husband will take us. . .'

'He is weak, Colonel, and he cannot talk. His neck is lacerated and his voice has gone. . .'

'He can write, can he not? And ride? He is an officer, not an ignorant peasant.' He turned to the sergeant. 'Fetch him.'

The sergeant obeyed with alacrity and Olivia dared
not protest. Her only hope was that Robert would
maintain his silence and do nothing to arouse suspicion.
She realised with a growing awareness that now her
tale had been told and she had claimed Robert as her
husband she was in the subterfuge so deeply there
could be no extricating herself. She had to play the role
to its end. She had thought herself in a scrape when
Philippe died, when she was fleeing from the guerrillas
and trying to find her way back to the British lines;
now she was in a worse one, and still it was her own
fault.

Why did she let such things happen to her? No
sensible, well brought-up young lady, English, French
or Spanish, would allow it; they would be branded as
unacceptable to society if they did. She would never be
able to hold up her head in a London drawing-room
again. Not that she set much store by that; here, in
Spain, was the real world, here was life in the round,
the living and the dying. But she did not fancy the idea
of dying just yet.

'Tell me all about yourself.' The colonel pulled up a
chair close to where she sat and smiled at her in a way
which left her in no doubt what he was thinking. 'You
have courage and beauty too, worthy of something
more than a mere lieutenant. How did you meet him?'

'In Oporto,' she said, remembering what Robert had
said about the English colony there. 'My father was a
wine merchant. Philippe used to come to our house
when he was quartered in the town. My father liked
him.'

'Even though he was French?' He reached out to
touch her arm. She pretended not to notice, wishing
she felt a little cleaner and tidier; it was difficult to
behave with any hauteur in the circumstances.

'Why not? Philippe was. . .is. . .a good man, and
my father was anxious I should marry. He wanted to
see me settled; he was dying, you see.' She buried her

hands in the folds of her skirt and crossed her fingers
to ward off the retribution for all the lies. She was
amazed at how easily they tripped off her tongue. She
prayed Robert would say and do nothing to contradict
her.

'Did you not want to return to England?'

'No. I had left it as a child; what was there to go
back to?'

'But a mere lieutenant! Surely you could have had
your pick of half the officers in the French army.'

She smiled at his flattery. 'Colonel, Philippe Santerre
comes from a very distinguished and noble family. The
fact that he is a lieutenant is only a matter of short
duration. He would have been promoted before now if
he had not been wounded at Talavera and his regiment
all but wiped out.'

He threw back his head and laughed. 'Well said,
madame, well and loyally said. We shall have to see
what we can do about this lieutenant of yours. A post
at headquarters, I think, eh?'

'Colonel. . .'

'No need to thank me now,' he said, smiling and
putting up a chubby hand to touch her cheek; it felt
cold and moist on her skin. 'Once he is on my staff,
you will be able to show your gratitude in the proper
manner. We can ensure that he is kept busy and you
are, shall we say, entertained.'

Olivia took a deep breath. 'Colonel, you flatter me.
I am sure I would be a great disappointment to you;
my English upbringing. . .'

'Englishwomen are cold, you mean?' He laughed
again and reached out to grasp her thigh. 'What is it
they say? "Still waters run deep. . ."'

She shot from her seat and backed away from him.
'I am not still waters, Colonel, I have a vicious temper.
I throw things. . .'

'Better and better.' He laughed and sat back in his
chair to look up at her, appraising her bright cheeks

and angry eyes, letting his glance rove down to her trim waist and over her dusty skirt to her boot-clad feet. 'You are hardly in a position to act the innocent, are you? Don't you want a decent pair of shoes and a gown that does more for you than that rag you are wearing?'

'They are practical.'

'They are enough to put a man off his dinner. . .'

'Good!' she retorted.

He rose and took a step towards her. She backed away, looking round for a way of escape, but there was none. 'No,' he said, laughing again. 'You are certainly not still waters; you are a turbulent ocean with heaven knows how many hidden currents. Navigating them will be a source of great enjoyment.'

Mercifully they were interrupted by the arrival of the sergeant with Robert, who wandered in behind him as if he were being made to attend a rather boring tea party, except that his eyes were alert and took in the scene at a glance — the colonel with his hands on Olivia's shoulders and, judging by her high colour, they had not been exchanging the time of day. He was surprised how angry it made him feel.

The colonel turned and looked him up and down. 'Is it true?' he demanded. 'Is it fact that your wife has a fiery temper?'

Robert looked from Olivia, who was trying to convey a message with her eyes for him to agree without actually nodding her head, then to the colonel. Robert smiled and opened his mouth to speak, but all that came from his throat was a hoarse whisper. The colonel turned to Olivia. 'What did he say?'

'He said, "Truly remarkable,"' she translated for him. 'I told you he could not speak. I must do the talking for us both.'

Colonel Clavier drew paper, pen and ink from his desk drawer and signalled to Robert to sit at a small table by the window. 'You will draw a map of where the guerrillas are hiding,' he said.

'We did not know where we were being taken,' Olivia put in, as Robert took up the pen and dipped it in the ink. 'I told you they blindfolded us.' She watched in horror as Robert began sketching.

'It seems your husband remembers more than you do,' the colonel said.

'He is making it up, to stop you interrogating him,' she said. 'He had enough of that from the guerrillas. He was much too ill after I had cut him down to mark the route we took coming back down the mountain.'

The colonel straightened up from looking over Robert's shoulder and scrutinised her face. She felt herself going very red. 'Why are you being so difficult, *madame*? One would almost think you wanted to prevent us from finding these bandits. I hope that is not so?'

'Of course not. I want them found,' she said quickly. 'I was only thinking of my husband's weakened condition. . .'

'He does not look weak to me, *madame*. In truth, I think he is quite capable of reporting for duty.' He turned to Robert. 'That is so, is it not, Lieutenant?'

Robert, who had laid aside the pen and was waving the paper like a fan to dry the ink, nodded agreement.

'Then I will arrange for you to be attached to my staff,' the colonel went on, taking the rough map from Robert. 'I can use you as a guide.'

Robert stood up, clicked his heels and bowed his head in obedience, then turned to take Olivia's arm and escort her from the room.

'*Au revoir, madame*,' the colonel called after them. 'You had better be on hand when your husband reports for duty—until he can talk again, that is.'

Olivia and Robert walked in silence along the tiled hallway, past the guard and out of the front door. The heat of the July sunshine reflected off the cobbles and rose to meet them, but both had become used to it and hardly noticed it. They were more concerned with hurrying away from any watching eyes in the house they had just left. As soon as they were well away and in one of the many narrow alleys which criss-crossed the town, Olivia let out her breath in a huge sigh of relief. 'Now what are we going to do?' she demanded. 'We will be under the eye of that lecherous monster all day, every day.'

'He is evidently very taken with you. What did you do to him?'

'What did *I* do?' she squeaked. 'You think I like being mauled by that fat pig?'

'You didn't seem to be trying very hard to stop him.'

'How could I? If he had any idea who you really are. . .'

'You mean you endured it for my sake? I find that hard to believe.'

'Believe what you like,' she snapped. 'It will not make a jot of difference in the long run; we'll be found out, and I'd rather leave before that happens.'

'What? With our mission unaccomplished?'

'*Our* mission! Not two hours ago, you were telling me I did not need to stay.'

'That was two hours ago.'

'What is different now?'

'My appointment to the colonel's staff and his evident attraction to you.'

'All the more reason to go. We'll never keep up the deception.'

'We will. We have to. And you can deal with him, I'll lay odds.'

'Even if I can, you will never carry it off. I do not know what madness made me agree to help you. Let's leave now and go back to our own lines. . .'

'Our own lines, my dear Olivia? Where might they be?'

'Wherever General Craufurd is.'

'And where is that?'

'How on earth should I know? Perhaps Don Santandos will tell us.'

'Not he. He does not trust you any more than I do.'

She stopped walking to turn angrily on him. 'Just what are you implying, Captain Lynmount? If I am not to be trusted, why did you encourage me to bring you here, right into the lion's den? I could hand you over right now. The sergeant of the guard is over there. The one we met at the gate.' She nodded her head towards a group of soldiers standing round a lone guitarist who sat on the edge of a broken limber singing a sad lament about a soldier leaving his love to go to war. 'I could call him over.'

'Do so, if you wish,' he said laconically. 'It will be interesting to hear how you explain away your previous story and why you did not denounce me when we were in the colonel's office. Good as you are at telling a tale, I doubt you would be very convincing.' He smiled but there was no humour in his hazel eyes. 'And, of course, I could explain that you have never really thrown off your English loyalties, in spite of my generosity and kindness to you. I am Lieutenant Santerre, a loyal subject of Napoleon, remember?'

'And how do you think you will manage to say all that when you are supposed to be unable to speak? I am your voice, or had you forgotten that little detail?'

'*Touché, madame.*' He laughed suddenly. 'It seems we are inextricably bound together. It is worse than being married.'

'And what do you know of marriage?'

'Nothing, thank heaven.'

'Then do not speak of things you know nothing about.'

'And I suppose two husbands, both dead, makes you an expert on the subject?'

'That was a cruel thing to say.'

He suddenly became contrite. 'I am sorry, Olivia,'

he said softly, taking her arm. 'That was unforgivable of me. I humbly ask pardon.'

'Why is it,' she mused, more to herself than him, 'that whenever I decide to break free of you something happens to bind us even more surely? It is certainly not your charming manner.'

He roared with laughter and Olivia became aware that the group of soldiers had turned to look at them. 'It's not funny,' she hissed. 'You are making us conspicuous.'

His laughter turned to a lop-sided grin as they resumed walking. 'Our being bound together, as you put it, is not of my choosing, Madame Santerre.'

'Nor mine.'

He smiled down at her. 'Then let us say it was an unkind fate, then we need not blame ourselves or each other. Let us accept the inevitable and make the best of it. The sooner I have done what I came to do, the sooner you can be released from an association you find so abhorrent.'

'What have you come to do?'

'Better you do not know the details.'

'Why not?' she demanded, then added, 'Oh, I see, because I am not to be trusted.'

'I trust you with my life; is that not enough?'

'What did you draw on that map?' she asked, changing the subject abruptly.

'The way to the monastery.'

She was appalled. Telling the whole French army where they could find Don Santandos was tantamount to his murder. 'How could you?' She rounded on him. 'They will all be killed.'

'Why this sudden concern for a bunch of *guerrilleros*?' he countered. 'They killed your husband and they tried to kill me.'

'That was before they knew who you were. They trust you now, at least enough to let you go. And they will have no mercy if you betray them. And Father Peredo has been set to watch us.'

He smiled wearily; trying to appease Olivia without putting her in any more danger than she was in already was an exhausting business and he wished he did not have to do it. 'In war it is often necessary to do things which are distasteful,' he said. 'Sacrifices have to be made. It is vital that the French trust me. . .'

'And so you sacrifice your allies. I hate it! I hate you! And even more I hate myself for betraying Philippe.'

'He would understand,' he said softly. 'Believe me, Olivia, he would understand.'

She was silent. There seemed nothing that they could say to each other which did not rub them raw and, like it or not, they had to stay together, at least for the time being. They needed each other. England had never seemed more desirable than it did at this moment; she was surprised how emotional she felt about it. Angry with herself for her weakness, she turned from him so that he should not see her tears, and noticed the sergeant and his companions eyeing them with curiosity. She smiled weakly at them and grabbed Robert's arm to alert him to the danger. He looked towards the men and grinned, just as they ambled over, drawn by curiosity.

'This is the man the guerrillas cannot kill,' the sergeant said to his companions. 'He was hanged and yet he lives. Show my friends the mark of the rope, Lieutenant.'

Robert obliged them, pulling aside his bandage. The weals on his neck seemed as livid as ever and Olivia strongly suspected he had done something to make them seem worse than they really were.

'My!' one of them said.

'How does it feel?' asked another.

'He cannot speak. His voice has been permanently damaged,' Olivia said.

'Is that so? How will he do his work?'

'I am his voice,' she said. 'Where he goes, I go too.'

One of them laughed. 'A man who needs a nurse-maid is hardly a man for a battle.'

Robert grunted, grabbed him by the front of his uniform coat and lifted him clear of the ground.

'Don't!' Olivia cried, fearing that Robert's wrath would betray them both. 'Let him be. He didn't mean anything. . .'

'No, no, I meant no disrespect,' the man squealed helplessly. 'Let me down, Lieutenant.'

Robert released him so suddenly that he fell to the ground, then glared round at the others, trying to convey his fury and a threat without speaking. Olivia marvelled at his control. Angry as he was, he had not uttered a word, either in English or French.

'Best be off,' she said to the soldiers. 'The lieutenant may have lost his voice but he still has the power to punish you, if you cause trouble.'

They drifted away, but she was worried. Robert had gained a reputation he could well have done without. Instead of melting into the background of a busy garrison town — difficult enough with his great height — he had become notorious as the man who had escaped a hanging, the man who had to rely on his wife to communicate. She pulled on his arm, trying to make him leave the scene, where everyone seemed to be staring at them and, to her mind, could see right through their subterfuge.

'You should have ignored them,' she said, when they were safely away and walking down a quiet side-street towards the bakery. 'All you did was draw attention to us and that is the last thing we want.'

'Why? I do not intend to skulk in dark corners. That is not the way to gain intelligence, and Lieutenant Santerre has nothing to hide.'

'But Captain Robert Lynmount has.'

'Who is Captain Robert Lynmount?' he queried,

drawing her arm through his and smiling down at her.
The changes in his mood were like quicksilver. 'I know
nothing of a Captain Robert Lynmount.'

'Neither do I,' she said tartly. 'He is a stranger to me.

It was true. She knew nothing of him at all, nothing
of his background, his family, his likes and dislikes, his
loves and his hates. He had been in love, he had told
her so, but he had never married. Had he been
disappointed by a lady? Did that account for his less
than chivalrous manner towards her?

Honesty made her smile to herself; she had hardly
invited chivalry. How could a man feel protective of a
woman who could shoot as well as he could, who rode
a horse as well as he could and, worst of all, refused to
admit to any feminine feelings like helplessness and
fear? How could a man feel protective of a woman who
wore a soldier's boots? She looked down at her feet;
how long was it since she had worn shoes? It had been
at Toulon, when she and the wounded Philippe had
gone home. His parents had been horrified by her
appearance, and rightly so, and Madame Santerre had
insisted on buying her a whole new wardrobe. But it
had all been so ridiculously extravagant and she had
known how useless the garments would be in Spain.
She had left them behind when they returned. But it
would be pleasant to be softly feminine now and again,
especially now.

She stopped her thoughts abruptly. She was not out
to impress this enigmatic man beside her and it would
be folly to try. He looked on her as a comrade in arms,
another soldier, a spy perhaps, but never a woman.
That being so, she had best play her part well and then
he would keep his promise to tak her home, and the
sooner the better.

'What are you thinking?' His voice, still a little
hoarse, broke in on her thoughts. 'You have not
spoken for at least five minutes and that is not in the
least like you.'

'How do you know what is like me? You know no more about me than I know about you.'

'We ought to remedy that,' he said, then spoiled it by adding, 'For the sake of our story. You must tell me all about Lieutenant Santerre—his background and family and your life with him. I must do nothing that is out of character.'

'You are enjoying this, aren't you?' she demanded, pulling her arm from his to face him squarely. 'It's like play-acting to you. You forget these are real people here, in this town, that Philippe was real and I am real. I think you want a new identity because you do not like your old one. Perhaps the disgrace of Captain Robert Lynmount is more than you can stomach. . .'

She knew she had gone too far when she saw the smile leave his face and his hazel eyes harden until they flashed an anger which made her tremble. She waited for the tirade, perhaps a denial, but nothing happened for fully a minute, while they glared at each other in animosity. Then he took her arm again and spoke so softly that she was taken aback.

'One day you will regret saying that, Madame Santerre, but in the meantime let us go home and you can tell me all about Philippe and the ways of the French army. Your chances of surviving to go home to England are dependent on my success and, reluctant as I am to say this, I need you in order to achieve it.'

She turned her head away because there were tears streaming down her cheeks and the last thing she wanted was for him to see them. She did not know why she was crying; he had said nothing she did not know already, he had broken no promises to her and it was not his fault she was in the mess she was in.

She lifted her hand and surreptitiously brushed away the evidence of her misery. 'You are right, of course,' she said, her voice brittle with the effort of sounding practical. 'I will do what I can. The sooner it is all over, the better.'

CHAPTER FIVE

EVERYWHERE the French were preparing to continue their advance. Guns and limbers and caissons of ammunition were being drawn up along the roads on the western outskirts of the town, wagons of food and carts full of forage were being trundled in from the countryside. Soldiers from the commissary's staff were going from house to house, from farm to farm, from vineyard to vineyard and orchard to orchard, taking what little food and wine was still to be found in a country almost stripped bare by earlier foraging. The people grumbled, but they dared not refuse. They put their faith in the *guerrilleros* in the mountains to set them free. 'The English have abandoned us,' they said. 'And soon they will abandon the Portuguese too. So much for their promises. Bonaparte was right — the wretched Leopard has no stomach for a fight; he knows nothing but retreat and still more retreat. We must rely on Don Santandos and our own men in the hills to set us free.'

'And you have betrayed them,' Olivia said to Robert when she heard this. 'No wonder the Spaniards do not trust the English.'

'They do not understand conventional warfare,' he said. He had been promoted to captain and given a post on the colonel's staff, which was as good a place as any to gather the intelligence he needed, but it also meant he had to watch the colonel flirting openly with Olivia. She was adept at holding the fellow off without antagonising him, but he was glad the army was on the move at last; he would not have been able to hold himself in check much longer. He wanted nothing so much as the satisfaction of punching the flabby regimental commander on his soft and bulbous nose, and

104

before long he would have done it. Now, in the middle week of July, they had been given orders to prepare to march and Robert had returned to their quarters to collect his gear.

It was small wonder he looked so tired, she thought; he had been sleeping curled up in a chair every night since they arrived, in order to leave the bed for her. He had not even hinted that they should share it, which was just as well because if he kissed her again she knew she would be every bit as weak as she had been before. He had curtly refused her offer to change places when she'd suggested he needed a good night's sleep. That and the strain of being in the company of the colonel's staff all day without being able to utter a word was beginning to tell on him. He could not keep it up much longer and she dreaded to think what would happen to them both when they were found out. Death would be the least of it.

'You cannot fight a battle without planning it first,' he said, waving the razor he was using to shave himself. 'That is the trouble with the Spaniards — they either rush in without a thought about how they will extricate themselves if things go wrong, or they turn tail and run at the slightest resistance. Look what happened at Talavera.'

'They are not cowards.' She put a bowl of thin soup on the table, with a loaf of hard bread which had cost her dear, then fetched a spoon from a cupboard drawer. 'They are just disorganised. It would be better if you helped to organise and lead them instead of making things worse by telling the French where to find them.'

'There was a reason for that,' he said mildly. He cleaned the soap from the razor and threw the contents of the bowl out of the window. There was a shout of annoyance from someone in the alley. Robert looked out and waved cheerfully to a Spaniard who had taken off his soaked hat and was shaking it up at him, then

turned back to pick up his new coat. She had paid the
tailor with Philippe's money, realising that the old one
was really too short for him and Philippe, aristocrat
that he was, would never have worn anything so ill-
fitting. It was important to keep up appearances. 'The
advance guard marches out today,' he went on.

'And you with it?'

'Yes.' He picked up a haversack from the corner and
began stuffing his buttonless red jacket into it.

'Why don't you get rid of that coat? If someone
should see it. . .'

'I took it off a dead British soldier, a certain Captain
Robert Lynmount. . .'

'He is not dead.'

'To all intents and purposes he is.'

'You are a fool. It isn't as if it were a new one. It is
a rag which won't even do up properly.'

He put the rest of his kit on top of the red jacket and
closed the mouth of the bag. 'You never know, one
day Robert Lynmount might need it again.'

'I can't make up my mind about you,' she said,
turning her head on one side to look at him as if doing
so made her able to judge him the better. 'I cannot
decide if you are driven by pride or a determination for
revenge, and, if it is revenge, who is going to be on the
receiving end—the English, the French, or Don
Santandos and his men?'

'Does it matter?'

'Was it a woman?' she asked suddenly.

'A woman?'

'The reason you are here and not fighting beside
your own countrymen.'

'It is not a matter that need concern you.' He paused
to look closely at her, wondering if he would ever be
able to talk about that day, months ago now, when he
had stood rigidly to attention while the buttons and
braid were torn from his coat. It was forever in his
mind—the humiliation and the shame, the injustice

and the helpless rage he had felt. And she dared to question him about it!

'I have bought an old landau for you to travel in at the rear with the other women,' he went on, carefully controlling his voice. 'The driver will be waiting outside when you leave.'

Finding a coach, and horses to pull it, was a miracle in itself but she chose to ignore that. 'Oh, so you don't need me any more? How will you go on if you want to speak?'

'There will be little opportunity for conversation when we come up with the British advance guard. I shall just have to make do with signs. I am not having you riding up at the front; it's no place for a lady.'

She laughed suddenly. 'I didn't realise you thought of me as a lady at all. I am simply your voice.'

'And a damned sharp one at that.' He sat down at the table and picked up his spoon. 'Where's yours?'

'I'll have mine later.' He would not eat it if he knew there would be none left for her and he needed it more than she did. 'If I am not to leave when you do, there is plenty of time.'

'Do you know the route?' she asked, sitting opposite him and putting her elbows on the table in order to rest her chin on her hands. 'Which way do you go?'

'To Villa de Fuentes first and then. . .'

'Do they know the bridge has been blown?'

He smiled as he wiped a piece of bread round his plate to mop up every last drop of soup. 'If they don't, they will when they arrive.'

'Then what? Will they go south to the plains or take the road to the monastery?'

'Whichever it is, I do not want you anywhere near, do you hear? You stay with the baggage train until we reach Villa de Fuentes and then go to Father Peredo until I can arrange for you to be transferred to the allied lines. General Craufurd will pass you back and see you get home.'

So that was it. She felt suddenly deflated, as if she had been drinking champagne and the light-headedness had worn off, leaving her heavy as lead and miserable as a wet Sunday in England. She shook herself. What had she expected? That he would fall on his knees and ask her to stay with him forever, to marry him? The mental picture of him doing anything so uncharacteristic brought a smile to her lips. It would not occur to him to think of her reputation back in England and she certainly did not want him to sacrifice himself for that. Being married to a martyr was not her idea of a good life. And besides, had she not sworn never to marry again? Had she not said she was done with all men? Was theirs not a perfectly practical arrangement, which had to come to an end some day? Had she not hoped and prayed it would end soon?

'Very well,' she said meekly.

Her unexpected obedience took him by surprise. 'You have understood me?' he queried, looking up into her face, which betrayed nothing of what she was thinking. 'I want no hot-headed, ill-considered actions, nothing done to put either of us in danger, do you hear me?'

'I hear you, but what are you going to do? Are you not going back to the British lines yourself?'

'No. I gave my parole to Don Santandos.'

'And then betrayed him!'

He stood up, towering over her, his face white and drawn with fatigue. It took more than a few sleepless nights to bring him to his knees, though she seemed to have the knack of wearing him down with accusations he could not refute. He stared down at her oval face with its halo of red-gold curls for a long time without speaking, and then, tempted beyond endurance, he grabbed her shoulders in both hands and brought his mouth down to hers, crushing her lips in a kiss which was at once savage and demanding. Taken by surprise, she did nothing until he released her and then she put all her frustration and insecurity into a sharp slap across his cheek. 'That was never part of our bargain.'

'I beg your pardon,' he said bitterly, rubbing the pink mark she had made on his face. 'Above all, we must keep to our bargain.' Then he turned from her to put a pistol in his belt, strapped on his sword, picked up his shako and haversack and left the room, clattering down the stone steps to the street.

Trembling uncontrollably, Olivia sank on to the bed and put her head in her hands. If she was so sure he was a traitor, why had she helped him? Did that make her a traitor too? Had she been one before she ever met him? Marrying a Frenchman was hardly the act of a patriot, so why did she condemn him for something she had done herself?

She had had her reasons and so, presumably, had he. He was such a confusing mixture of bitterness and cheerfulness, hate and anger, brute strength and gentleness. He could, against all reason and without apparently intending it, stir her latent passions to full flood, and it took all her self-control to keep her from throwing herself into his arms whenever she watched him moving about the tiny room in his shirt-sleeves and figure-hugging breeches. If he inadvertently brushed against her, shock-waves ran with tingling intensity through her body. He could be cruel too, but no more than she was. With her it was a defence, a way of keeping him at a distance where she could deal with him; his reasons she could not even guess at.

She rubbed her hand across her mouth as if to erase the memory of that brutal kiss and then jumped to her feet to go to the window. He had mounted the miserable excuse for a horse he had bought from the commissary and was riding down the street, followed by half a dozen urchins, who called after him for alms. He threw them a few coins and then trotted to the square where the advance guard was mustering for the march. He did not look back.

She sighed heavily, ate the last of the bread, then picked up her own bundle and went out to the street.

A young Spanish boy came out of the shadows and touched his forelock. He was about thirteen, she guessed, though he was so undernourished he might have been older. He wore nothing but a ragged shirt and trousers held up with what looked like part of a soldier's crossbelt. 'I am Pedro,' he said. 'The *capitán* said I must look after the *señora*. Come.'

The huge column had just been given the command to move. Ahead rode the senior officers, surrounded by cavalry, their colourful plumes bobbing and harness jingling, then cuirassiers, with their breastplates reflecting the glare of the sun, then infantry in ranks, headed by their regimental colours and guarded on their flanks by sharp-shooting voltigeurs, and behind them the limbers, pulled by heavy horses, the ammunition caissons and finally the baggage wagons.

The vehicle the boy conducted her to was so dilapidated, it was almost falling apart; the springs had gone and the stuffing had come out of the torn upholstery, but Olivia was the envy of all the other women who were obliged to walk in the rear of the column or ride atop the baggage in the wagons. She was strong and healthy and there were many who were not; to the consternation of Pedro, who expected to be punished by Robert for dereliction of duty, she surrendered it to the sick and expectant mothers and took her place with the walkers.

Thus it was she was far behind the front of the column when it arrived in the narrow village street of Villa de Fuentes, and Robert, going back to look for her, found the coach overflowing with squabbling women and very young children, but no sign of her. Pedro, shaking in anticipation of a beating, told him that the *señora* would not ride in the coach and that if many more crowded on to it, it would collapse. The women would not listen to him and he would be glad if

the *capitán* would turn them off. Robert smiled and
drew the boy out of earshot. 'Let them have it, Pedro,'
he whispered in Spanish. 'You go back for Señora
Santerre and take her to father Pedro. Tell her to stay
there until I come.'

'*Sí, señor.*'

'And not a word to anyone, you understand?'

The boy grinned. '*Sí, señor.* I tell no one you have a
fine voice, that you are a friend to Spain.'

Robert smiled as he watched the boy dodge back
through the laden wagons, tired horses and half-starved
mules to where the last of the column struggled along
on foot, then he returned to Colonel Clavier, who was
surveying the remains of the bridge.

'Damned guerrillas,' he muttered. 'They must be
taught a lesson they will not forget in a hurry.' Then,
seeing Robert, he demanded, 'Did you know the bridge
had gone?'

Robert shook his head.

'We'll deal with this pestilence before we go any
further. You'll lead us to them, Santerre, you'll lead us
to them, even if we have to climb over that damned
mountain to find them.' He pointed to a peak which,
even in summer, was capped with snow. 'If they can
survive up there, so can we.' He opened the bag on the
pommel of his saddle and pulled out the map Robert
had drawn. 'We'll take two companies and the six-
pounder; anything heavier will be too cumbersome.'

He looked up at Robert who mouthed the word
'*Quand*?' When?

'Tonight. We'll go under cover of darkness. If they
don't see us coming, they won't know what has hit
them until it is too late.'

Robert, nodding in agreement, wondered how a man
as stupid as Clavier had ever managed to become a
colonel. If he thought two companies of soldiers and a
gun, which meant horses too, could move against the
guerrillas, either in darkness or daylight, without being

seen and heard long before the guerrillas were seen
and heard, he was a fool.

'How long will it take to reach them?' the colonel
broke in on his thoughts.

Robert held up four fingers.

'Four hours. As long as that?'

Robert made signs to indicate the steepness and
roughness of the terrain.

'Then go and eat, Captain,' the colonel went on.
'Make love to that lovely wife of yours and report back
in two hours, ready to lead the way.'

Robert came to attention and bowed his head to
acknowledge the order, though there was no question
of obeying it. He smiled wryly. Even a kiss had
provoked a resounding slap and put an end to any
thoughts he might have had that she would welcome
his advances.

'It were as well you said nothing to Madame Santerre
of your destination,' the colonel added as he turned
away. 'I still think she has a sneaking regard for that
bandit.' He gave a barking laugh. 'I do not altogether
understand why women idolise the most uncouth of
men. They seem to delight in savouring the uncivilised.'

Robert hid his smile as he moved away; the colonel
himself, for all his gold braid and plumes, was far more
uncouth than Don Santandos with his ragged goatskin
coat and matted beard, but that was something the
Frenchman would never understand. He would be glad
when he could get Olivia away from it all.

He found her at the home of Father Peredo, along
with a dozen small children of camp followers whom
she had taken there to be given food and somewhere
to sleep. The good priest's servants were busy trying to
look after them, muttering under their breath about
having to look after French urchins when the Spanish
children in the village were just as hungry and whose
fathers were also required to fight. 'Children are children the world over,' Father Peredo said. 'Fetch the

village youngsters to share the food; let the little ones learn to love their enemies, even if their parents cannot.'

Olivia, seeing Robert, put down the two-year-old she was nursing and went to him. 'You look tired. Come and sit down.'

'Why did you give the coach away?' He sank into a chair and looked up at her. Her simple skirt and blouse were dusty from travel, her hair had been blown by the wind into a tangle and her face had caught the sun, but her eyes were still full of life and a smile played about her lips; he marvelled that she was as cheerful as ever.

'I did not need it, others did. What is happening?' She nodded towards the outside, where the sounds of an army could easily be heard—the shouts of command, the jingle of harness, the creaking of wheels on the sun-hardened road, horses, singing, women calling out as they caught up with their menfolk. 'Has the colonel seen that the bridge is gone? What did he say?'

'He is going into the hills to look for Don Santandos.'

'When?'

'Tonight at dusk.'

'And you are going to show him the way.' He did not answer and she pressed her point. 'You are, aren't you?'

'Yes.'

'Why?'

He did not want to argue with her; he would rather have snatched a few minutes' sleep. 'I have been ordered to.'

'By a fat, ignorant French pig of a colonel! I am not going to stand by and let you do it.'

He smiled wearily. 'And how do you propose to stop me?'

She stood looking down at him, green eyes flashing anger, and then turned abruptly and called to Father Peredo, who was marshalling the children into the dining-room. 'Robert is going to lead the French army

into the hills to find Don Santandos,' she told the priest
when he joined them. 'He has betrayed his friends. . .'

If she had thought her disclosure would shock Father
Peredo or shame Robert she was mistaken. The priest
looked from one to the other and smiled. 'Captain
Lynmount must do as his conscience dictates. . .'

'Conscience!' she squealed. 'He has no conscience. I
do not know what his game is, but he must not be
allowed to sacrifice the guerrillas for it.'

'They know the odds,' Father Peredo said calmly.
'And so does Captain Lynmount. You, my child, must
not interfere.' He turned to Robert. 'You know what
you are doing?'

'Yes, and so does Miguel Santandos.'

'You will need a decent horse,' the priest said.
'Yours is in an old hut in the hills behind the church,
safe and well-fed, but ready for some exercise.'

Olivia stared at them both, unable to believe her
ears. Had she been mistaken in Father Peredo too?
She opened her mouth to protest and then shut it
again, but that did not mean she accepted either
Robert's decision or Father Peredo's judgement on it,
nor had she any particular feeling for the men who had
killed Philippe, but they were supposed to be allies in
this monumental struggle against Napoleon and it was
not fair that they should be sacrificed. She listened
carefully to Father Peredo's instructions on how to find
Thor and watched Robert leave. As soon as the
children had been returned to their mothers and the
priest had gone to say mass in the neighbouring church,
she changed into a pair of Philippe's old overalls,
crammed a beret over her curls and crept out of the
house to find Pegasus.

The hut was hidden in a fold of the hills which rose
up behind the village and had probably been used as a
shelter by the goatherds who looked after the village
flocks. It was only a one-roomed building, half-stone,
half-wood, but big enough to conceal two horses. If the

French had known the animals were there, they would have been confiscated and the villagers severely punished.

She approached carefully but there was no one about and Pegasus gave her a snicker of greeting as she opened the door and slipped inside. She found his bridle and saddle lying in a corner and five minutes later was riding him out and down the hill, keeping in the twilight shadows.

She had been going only a few minutes when she remembered seeing the guard at the monastery looking over the bridge at a path which led up from the gorge bottom. Was that an alternative way up from the village? If so, where did it begin? She could only think of one place and that was at the foot of the other bridge, the one in the village. She turned her horse towards it, wondering how she could pass the French troops camped around it; they would be thickest at that point and on their guard. Boldness, she decided, was the answer; in the darkness she could pass for a French soldier. She turned back and rode down the middle of the village, whistling to herself, apparently off-duty and at ease, though inside she was tense as a coiled spring and praying no one would stop her.

Camp fires glowed among the trees of the orchard which bordered the road as the women went about their tasks of cooking the evening meal and the men eased off their boots and sat in stockinged feet to clean their weapons ready for the morrow. Many of them carried wine in their canteens, a flogging offence in the British army but common practice among the soldiers of Napoleon, and there was already a great deal of drunkenness, ribaldry and lovemaking. Not that Olivia blamed them for that; they needed something to lighten a miserable existence. She had thought Tom was badly off, but his life had been luxury to what the common French conscript had to endure.

She slumped in the saddle and dropped her head on

her chest, as if tipsy herself, apparently letting the horse have its head, and arrived at the bridge without being challenged. Now she had to find the beginning of the path and must be careful not to arouse suspicion.

'If you keep going you will ride straight into the river,' someone called after her. 'Don't you know there is no bridge?'

She roused herself and raised a hand to acknowledge she had heard, but did not turn towards the man; the twilight had given way to a bright moonlit night and she dared not show her face. She dismounted awkwardly, as a drunken man would, and led her horse into the trees beside the road, muttering something about the damned Spanish wine giving her a belly-ache. The soldier laughed and turned away.

She tethered the horse to a tree and began exploring along the top of the gorge through which the river had cut its path, making her way from the bridge northwards. At first it seemed so sheer that there was no way down, but half a kilometre on she found a track and went back for Pegasus. The path was so steep, she had to lead the horse and before long she was beginning to doubt the wisdom of bringing the animal, but, having begun the descent, she was determined to keep going, glad that the roar of the water covered the sound of the horse's hoofs and the clatter of loose stones, which she kept dislodging and which cascaded down to the river, glinting far below her in the moonlight.

She dared not look down but kept close to the horse's head, murmuring encouragement, more to help herself than Pegasus, desperately hoping that she had been right, and that when they reached the bottom there would be a level path, and she would not be faced with having to climb back the way she had come. If that happened she had lost all hope of overtaking the column marching to the monastery.

At last the path levelled out and she found herself on a well-worn track which followed the line of the river very close to the bank. In spring, when the river was swollen by melting snow, it would be underwater, but now, in July, it was almost dry and was an easy ride. She mounted again and set off at a walk, not daring to go faster, for down in the valley bottom there was no moon. Her main task now was to locate the path leading up to the monastery and she was gambling that it was no worse than the one by which she had descended.

An hour later, she poked her head over the top of the cliff close by the bridge, and looked about her. The monastery building was in darkness and she could see no guard patrolling the road. For the first time she began to have doubts. Had the guerrillas left the monastery to the advancing French, or, worse, had the French already arrived and taken it? Was the way to northern Portugal open to the invader? She led Pegasus forward into an olive grove on the lower slope, where she tethered him to a tree, stroking his nose and bidding him stay quiet, before creeping forward to find the answer to her questions. The moon had gone behind a cloud and she was glad of the darkness as she darted silently from tree to tree, peering up at the grey stone walls, looking for a light in a window, the reflection of a weapon, anything to tell her that Miguel Santandos and his men were still there, still watchful.

The next moment she was flung off her feet and all but throttled by an arm coming out of the darkness and encircling her throat. She landed heavily on her back as her assailant flung her to the ground and sat astride her. The moon came out from behind a cloud and for a brief second she could see his head outlined against the night sky and the knife gleaming in his upraised hand.

'Robert!'

'My God, Olivia!' The knife clattered to the ground and he rolled off her and sat back on his heels to stare into her pale face. Her eyes were brilliant with fear and he found himself shaking at the thought of what he had been about to do. 'What in hell's name did you think you were doing?' he demanded, taking refuge in anger. 'I was going to kill you.' He looked down at the French overalls she wore and then back up at her face. 'How did you get here?'

'On Pegasus.' She sat up and shook the dry dust from her hair. 'I came to warn Don Santandos you had betrayed him and were leading the French to attack him.'

'You fool!' He scrambled to his feet and held out his hand to help her up. 'Why can't you behave like a woman and leave the fighting to men who know what they are about? You could have ruined everything.'

'That was my intention.' She ignored his hand and stood up beside him. 'Forewarned is forearmed. At least I would have given Don Santandos a fighting chance.'

He smiled ruefully. 'And I, all unknowing, was to lead the French into an ambush?'

'I suppose so.'

'And was I to be given a fighting chance?' He was both exasperated and admiring, and he wished he dared release her, but she was so unpredictable, he could not trust her to stay at his side. 'Where did you leave the horse?'

'Tethered to a tree near the bridge.'

'Then let us fetch him.' He took her arm and began propelling her towards the bridge. She struggled but he hung on to her. 'I am a fool,' he said, between gritted teeth. 'Fool to think that you thought well enough of me to trust me and do as I asked. Now you must take the consequences.'

He did not slow his pace as she stumbled along beside him. 'What are you going to do?'

He did not answer but tightened his grip on her arm until she had to bite her lip to stop herself crying out. 'Robert, please, you are hurting me.'

'If you insist on denying your womanhood to dress and behave like a man, you cannot afterwards complain if you are treated like one. From now on, you will take orders like a soldier or the consequences will be what every soldier can expect if he neglects his duty.'

Behind them she could hear the French patrol— boots scuffling on the hard road, the rumble of the gun's limber, the sound of harness and hoofs. They would be alert and watchful, she knew, but until they were within a few hundred yards of the building they would not know how narrow the road was, nor how little cover there was around the bridge. She looked up at Robert, wondering whether to attempt to make him change his mind and join the guerrillas, but he did not look like a man open to persuasion; his jaw was set and he was looking straight ahead.

'Come,' he said as they reached the horse and he untethered it. 'Mount up.'

She obeyed silently. He took the reins and led her out on to the road and towards the approaching patrol, turning his back on the monastery. If Don Santandos was there and looked out now and saw them, she would hardly blame him if he put a bullet into their backs. 'Robert,' she said, in desperation, 'let's go to the monastery, please.'

He turned to look up at her. She was not sure but she thought he was smiling. It was just like him to laugh when there was nothing to laugh at. 'Are you suggesting that Captain Philippe Santerre should desert?'

'No, he never would. I am asking Robert Lynmount to come to his senses and make up his mind whose side he is on.'

'He knows which side he is on.' He stopped walking and the horse nuzzled into his shoulder. Absent-mindedly, he stroked its nose as he looked up at her. 'You may join Don Santandos if you wish. I will not stop you.'

'But you will not come with me?'

'No.'

She was silent. If she went, what then? Where did she want to go? Home? Was that still her goal? Whatever he had done, could she turn her back on him and ride away? Oh, what was happening to her? It was the second chance she had been given and the second time she had hesitated. All she had to do was turn Pegasus towards the convent. Why couldn't she do it?

'Come, Olivia, you are not usually so indecisive and I have no time to waste.'

Her answer was to click her tongue at Pegasus and set him off to where Colonel Clavier, determined to lead the assault himself, was deploying his troops. He had sent one group up the hillside to try and approach the monastery from the bare mountain above it, while others were dispatched into the trees on the lower slope and ordered to approach as near the front of the building as possible. The signal to begin the assault would be the firing of the six-pounder, which had been drawn up on the road itself.

He was puffing and blowing, riding from one section to the other. 'There you are, Santerre,' he said irritably. 'Where the hell have you been?' Then, remembering the captain could not speak, added, 'Get back to your post by the gun.' He turned away, ignoring Olivia. Thankfully she realised he had not recognised her in the overalls, though the disguise would not stand up in daylight.

'Go to the rear and stay there,' Robert said, as soon as the commander was out of earshot. 'That is an order, and heaven help you if you disobey.'

'Yes, sir!' She gave a mock-salute and pulled on the reins to turn Pegasus. Robert turned from her with a chuckle. She was irrepressible, but he would not have her any other way and now he could not imagine life without her. Later, when all this was over. . . But he would not let himself think of the future; he had no future.

Olivia had hardly gone a hundred yards when she heard a fusillade of shots coming from the monastery. So Miguel Santandos was there and he had seen the danger and fired first. She turned in the saddle to see two men fall, but the French were trained soldiers and were soon returning the fire. She heard the six-pounder boom once and then an ear-splitting explosion. Pegasus reared in terror. She calmed him and turned back along the road, her only thought that Robert might be hit and she had to go to him. The little cannon was nothing more than a heap of twisted metal and its crew lay sprawled in death around it.

She spurred the horse forward. 'Robert! Oh, let him not be dead! Let him be alive.' She was torn apart by guilt as she jumped from the horse and ran to the bodies. Why had he been so stubborn? Why hadn't he gone to the monastery? Why, oh, why?

'Here!' Robert's voice came from behind her. She turned in relief. He was standing a little way off, his eyes gleaming in a blackened face, but apparently uninjured. She ran to him. 'I ordered you to the rear.' It was the sharp voice of command and held no forgiveness. She paused, unsure of herself. 'You want to be a soldier,' he said, holding out a rifle and a bandolier he had taken from one of the casualties. 'Then be one. Take this to the rear and watch our backs. Fire a warning if you see anything.'

She took the weapon and turned from him. He was hard and unyielding and she wondered why she had ever thought him anything else but a ruthless soldier, and a mercenary at that. And she had almost fallen in love with him! How thankful she was she had discovered the truth before she made a fool of herself.

The battle continued with concentrated small arms fire until she began to wonder who would run out of ammunition first, but after two hours the shooting

became more desultory, and then Colonel Clavier
ordered the drummer to beat the retreat. He had lost
too many men and the monastery seemed impregnable.

In the confusion, as the men gathered to return to
the village, Olivia went in search of Robert. She found
Thor, tethered near by, but no sign of him. He was not
among the tired, defeated group who lined up in the
road, nor among the wounded being transported back
in the ammunition wagon, nor, she discovered as she
searched the hillside, among the dead. Leaving Pegasus
with Robert's horse, she made her way slowly back up
the road, looking from right to left, stopping to listen
every now and again, alert for the sound of footsteps
or the groans of someone wounded. She found him at
last, standing alone by the parapet of the bridge,
apparently deep in thought. He looked up as she
approached. Was he still angry with her? His
expression gave nothing away.

'Are you satisfied with your night's work, Captain?'
she asked, taking the offensive, which was her usual
way of dealing with his anger. 'I wonder how many
loyal Spaniards have gone needlessly to their deaths
tonight?'

'None at my hands.'

'How can you be sure? And now that the colonel has
been sent back to Villa de Fuentes with his tail between
his legs, what next? I cannot imagine that is the end of
the matter. He is hardly likely to give up fighting and
go back to France to keep chickens, is he?'

A fleeting smile crossed his face. 'Don Santandos
has only to hold the monastery until General Craufurd
arrives in a day or two, then he will be able to recapture
his village.'

'How do you know the general will come?'

'I do not, but Miguel Santandos seems confident of
it.'

'You have spoken to him?' She was astonished.

'Before the attack. I was coming from a meeting with him when I found you, skulking in the trees.'

'Then you led the French into a trap? It was planned all along?'

He smiled. 'Of course.'

'You might have told me. I should not have. . .' She paused. 'Oh, I see, you did not trust me.'

He sighed, and put his finger under her chin to lift her face to the moon, which had come out from behind a scudding cloud. Her beret had fallen from her head and her soft curls framed her face. In spite of the soldier's overalls, she looked very feminine and very vulnerable. 'What you do not know, my lovely Olivia, you cannot tell. It is safer that way.' He lowered his face and kissed her gently on the lips; it was a kiss of forgiveness and this time it provoked no retaliation.

'Are you going to join Don Santandos now?' There was a slight tremor in her voice.

'No, I go back to the village. There will be reprisals and I must do what I can.'

Olivia was horrified. 'You can't do that! If the colonel finds out you led him into a trap. . .'

Robert smiled. 'Why should he?'

The whole idea of returning was so senseless that she could not believe he meant it, but, looking into his eyes, she saw nothing to make her think he was jesting. 'But they were already mustering when I left; they will be halfway down the hill by now. How will you explain your absence?'

'I will think of something. I could have been wounded. Or taken prisoner and escaped.'

'Just as you were hanged and escaped! The same trick will never work again. And how will you speak? Has your voice been miraculously restored to you?' She laughed, a high-pitched, unnatural sound that seemed loud in her ears and made her realise how near to hysteria she was. 'And with an English accent too!'

'I will manage.'

'Robert, you have done what you were asked. Don Santandos expects no more. We can go back to our own lines from here.'

'No!' Robert shouted. 'Damn you, woman, you still don't understand, do you? I *cannot* go back.'

'Then we had better set off at once; the longer we delay, the worse it will be to convince the colonel.'

'Oh, no. You, my lady, you will stay with the guerrillas. I hesitate to burden Don Santandos with you, but he owes me that and he will hand you safely over to General Craufurd when he comes.'

'You will have trouble enough explaining your absence,' she said amiably. 'But explaining the loss of a wife as well. . .' She took his arm as if they were out for a moonlit stroll. 'Do not make it more difficult for yourself.'

Robert knew she was right and, in spite of her wilfulness or perhaps because of it, did not want to be parted from her; he allowed himself to be persuaded but not without a great deal of grumbling, which had no effect on her at all.

They went back to the horses and set off in the wake of the returning patrol, down the mountain path, back to the village, riding in silence. They had said all there was to be said and talking only seemed to make matters worse between them. On the way they passed the broken six-pounder and the bodies of several French soldiers, and although the colonel had been sensible enough, or coward enough, to realise how high the odds were against him and had withdrawn before too many casualties had been inflicted, he would not let it rest there, they both knew that. There would be other trials to come.

The sun was just coming up behind the distant mountains as they neared the village. Down by the river a working party was already busy trying to build a temporary bridge strong enough to take the troops, with their horses, wagons and heavy guns, across the river. Colonel Clavier had decided not to risk the monastery road again, nor did he want to detour south where the British rearguard was most active. The rest of the regiment, dispersed among the orchards and olive groves, were stirring for another day and the clatter of pots and the sudden flaring of a fire announced that breakfast was on the way.

In the village street a few inhabitants were making their way towards the church, whose bell tolled for early mass. Olivia found it difficult to believe that a few hours before she had been in a battle, that men had died, and before long the whole process would be repeated. Wherever Napoleon's army went, there went death and destruction. How could anyone condone that? It made her blood boil. And Robert? What game was he playing? But it was no game; he was deadly serious.

'We had better establish what happened,' she said as they rode down into the village. 'If I am to speak for you, then I must know what to say.'

'I was there beside the six-pounder when it blew up. The explosion knocked me out. I was out for a long time. When I came to, the men had withdrawn, leaving me for dead. As usual you had disobeyed orders and come looking for me. That will have to do, but you must make it sound convincing.'

'How did the six-pounder come to blow up? The guerrillas only had small arms; they could not have disabled it.'

'It jammed; they do sometimes, you know. The charge went off inside it.' His chuckle told her that he had caused the explosion; he had been telling the truth when he said no Spaniard had died at his hands. She felt immeasurably relieved.

The story seemed to satisfy Colonel Clavier and Olivia came to the conclusion that he was a very stupid man. He was also very angry. He was convinced that some-

one in the village had warned the guerrillas to expect
the patrol so that instead of encountering them on the
open mountain he had found them in an unassailable
position in the monastery. He questioned Robert long
and hard but Robert, through Olivia, denied knowledge of the existence of the monastery. His map had
shown the way to the camp where Philippe had died.
The colonel might have been more sceptical if anyone
but Olivia had been trying to convince him, but he was
without his usual mistress, who had declared the heat
and the flies and the constant sniping of the guerrillas
insupportable and had fled back over the Pyrenees,
leaving him looking for a replacement; Olivia had
intrigued and fascinated him ever since she had been
brought to him in Ciudad Rodrigo; he believed her
because he wanted her and instead turned his attention
to the villagers, threatening to massacre the whole
village if the culprit was not delivered up to him in
twenty-four hours.

'What are we going to do?' Olivia asked Robert later
that morning, when she heard about this. 'Do you
think he really will carry out his threat?'

'I expect so.' He had come back from supervising
the building work to have a meal and was sitting near
the open door of their lodgings looking out on the
square, where all the equipment, guns and wagons had
been drawn up, waiting to proceed. Small children
swarmed around them, poking and prying and being
driven off by the few men left to guard them.

'But there are only old men, women and children in
the village; all the fighting men are in the hills.'

'Then he will take women and children.'

'Robert, we cannot allow that to happen.'

'No, I must tell him the truth, give myself up.'

'No!' Her cry was one of anguish. 'You can't! You
must not!'

He turned to smile at her. She was wearing the
brown dress she had taken from the empty villa and

had a multicoloured shawl draped across her shoulders. It had been given to her by one of the women whose children she had helped the day the French had arrived. Her feet were encased in slim black dancing slippers with silver buckles which he guessed had come from Philippe's pack; the Frenchman had obviously been something of a dandy as well as a soldier. 'Olivia, I have no choice.'

'Yes, you have,' she said. 'We will evacuate the women and children, take them to their men in the hills. They will be safe there.'

'All of them?'

'Why not? We could go after dark, in small groups. The colonel cannot punish them if he cannot find them.' She paused, her eyes alight with mischief. 'Father Peredo will help organise it. I am going to see him now.' She tied a knot in the shawl and turned to leave. 'Go back to your duty, soldier, this is woman's work and the less you know about it the better.'

He threw back his head and laughed. It was the first time she had heard him laugh since the attack on the monastery and somehow it made all the difference. She would enjoy taking the children to safety under the noses of the garrison.

It took all day to arrange with Father Peredo and the enthusiastic Pedro to help her. They went stealthily from house to house, giving careful instructions, emphasising the need for silence, swearing everyone to secrecy, and by the time dusk fell again everyone was ready. The soldiers who were busy trying to rebuild the bridge and those few who were off-duty and gathered at the inn or on the streets failed to notice that there were fewer villagers than usual seeing to their wants. The women and children left their homes in family groups at set intervals and made their way into the olive groves, where their appointed leaders took them down the steep cliff to the path by the river and to safety.

It was dawn again when Olivia returned to her lodgings, thoroughly satisfied with her night's work. When reveille sounded in less than an hour's time, the colonel would find a village without inhabitants and no one on whom he could take out his ire but his own men. Robert was not at home and she supposed he had found somewhere more comfortable to sleep. She smiled as she flung herself on the bed; poor Robert, she really did cause him a few problems but he would be proud of her tonight. She wondered why it was important that he should be proud of her. He was nursing a grievance that filled his mind; to him she was nothing but a necessary encumbrance and one he wished himself rid of. That being so, why had she refused to take the opportunities she had been offered to leave? Why stay with him?

The answer, she admitted, as she drifted off to sleep, was that she needed him as much as he needed her. Just how much or why, she would not allow herself to speculate; it was far too disturbing.

Relax with **FOUR FREE** Temptations

PLUS A FREE CUDDLY TEDDY AND SPECIAL MYSTERY GIFT.

plus two FREE gifts!

Temptations offer you all the age-old passion and tenderness of romance, now experienced through very contemporary relationships. And to introduce to you this powerful and highly charged series, we'll send you **four Temptations plus two FREE gifts** when you complete and return this card. We'll also reserve you a subscription to Reader Service which means you could enjoy:

■ **FOUR BRAND NEW NOVELS** sent direct to you each month.

■ **FREE POSTAGE AND PACKING** we pay all the extras.

■ **FREE MONTHLY NEWSLETTER** packed with special offers, competitions, author news and much more.

■ **HELPFUL FRIENDLY SERVICE** telephone our Customer Care team on 081-684 2141

Turn over to claim your
FREE Temptations and FREE gifts.

NO STAMP NEEDED

Mills & Boon
Reader Service
FREEPOST
P.O. Box 236
Croydon
CR9 9EL

FREE books and gifts claim

Yes! Please send me four Temptations and two FREE gifts without obligation. Please also reserve me a subscription to Reader Service; which means that I can look forward to four brand new Temptations for just £7.40 each month (subject to VAT). Postage and packing is FREE. If I decide not to subscribe I will write to you within 10 days. Any free books and gifts will remain mine to keep. I understand that I may cancel or suspend my subscription at any time. I am over 18 years of age.

7A3T

Ms/Mrs/Miss/Mr _____

Address _____

_____

_____ Postcode _____

Signature _____

Offer closes 31st March 1994. The right is reserved to refuse an application and change the terms of this offer. One application per household. Overseas readers please write for details. Southern Africa write to Book Services International Ltd., Box 41654, Craighall, Transvaal 2024. You may be mailed with offers from other reputable companies as a result of this application. Please tick box if you would prefer not to receive such offers. ☐

MPS
MAILING PREFERENCE SERVICE

CHAPTER SIX

OLIVIA slept until the midday sun made the room like an oven and woke her. For a moment she could not decide what was different about the day; it was as hot as ever, the room looked just as it had been when she fell asleep, but there was something not quite right. She rose and opened the door; the sun beat down on the dusty square, a dog lay panting in the shade of a solitary eucalyptus, a cat stalked a wall, but there were no wagons, no guns, no soldiers that she could see. She went back into the room. Robert's kit, his uniform, his boots and shako, his sword and pistol, his ammunition pouch, everything had gone; there was nothing to show that he had ever been there. She washed and dressed hurriedly and went to see Father Peredo. In spite of being up all night, just as she had been, he had been working at his desk for some hours, and was expecting her.

'Colonel Clavier has received orders to abandon the mountain route and go south to join the remainder of the army advancing on Almeida,' he told her. 'They marched out while we were taking the women and children to Don Santandos.' He smiled suddenly. 'A detachment has been left behind to hold the village and keep the French supply lines open, but the rest have gone. With God's help Miguel will soon re-take the village and the people will be able to return.'

'And Robert?' she queried.

'He went too.' He watched the expressions chase each other across her face — perplexity, then hurt and finally anger. 'He left instructions that I was to see that you go to Don Santandos and from there to General

Craufurd.' He opened a drawer of his desk and withdrew a folded sheet of paper. 'He left you a letter.'

She took it from him, broke the seal and scanned it hurriedly. But it told her no more than the priest had done. Robert had decided to stay with the French troops.

> You have done all that was asked of you and more. You deserve your reward. Go home to England and enjoy your life. Know that there is one here who wishes you the greatest happiness. Think of me sometimes, in the comfort of your own home, as a man you might have come to know a little better if circumstances had been different. *Adieu*, little leopardess.

She was surprised, as she stood with the letter in her hand, to find her vision blurred by tears. She brushed them away, angry with herself for her foolishness. What else could she have expected? Their meeting had been a chance encounter in the middle of a war and, for a time, they had been useful to each other, but that was all.

All! By heaven, it was not all! He had been hurt and dishonoured and he bore the internal scars of that; it did not mean he was beyond redemption, that she could stand by and let him ruin himself still further with his foolhardiness. She screwed the letter up into a tight ball and threw it into the empty hearth, smiling rebelliously at the priest. 'If he thinks he can throw me off like an old glove, then he is in for a surprise,' she said and, turning on her heel, left the house with Father Peredo's laughter ringing in her ears.

She did not hesitate, but packed all her belongings into a tight roll and took it out to the hut where Pegasus was hidden. She saddled him up, fitted her bundle to the pommel and set off in a south-westerly direction. With the craggy mountains at her back, she passed through pine and eucalyptus woods, then rolling hills covered

with vineyards, small farms and orchards, heavy with
the scent of flowers and buzzing with honey bees. Alone
on the road, far behind the marching army, she felt at
peace; the war seemed a million miles away.

But that was an illusion; it was round every corner,
behind every craggy rock. Hidden eyes watched the
roads, ready to strike wherever a smaller than usual
force, a baggage cart left too far behind, stragglers
from the main march, made an easy target. Nothing
was safe from the *guerrilleros* who stretched taut
French nerves to breaking-point and caused their
already elongated supply lines to snap under the strain.
It had taken weeks to re-supply the army after the
taking of Ciudad Rodrigo, but now they were on the
move again, still under orders to drive the leopards
back into the sea.

But taking the Portuguese border stronghold of
Almeida would be a very different proposition from
taking Ciudad Rodrigo. The only way to enter the
town was by crossing bridges and going through tun-
nels, and its huge star-shaped fortifications were in
much better repair than those of the Spanish town had
been. Robert had spoken of it as almost impregnable,
which was why Colonel Clavier had been so anxious to
make a name for himself and find a way into Portugal
which avoided it. His hopes for promotion and an easy
life among the generals and marshals of the Napoleonic
campaign who seemed not to share the hardships of
their men, but to travel with all the accoutrements of
luxury, including their mistresses, had been balked by
Don Santandos and his handful of partisans and he was
a very angry man. He did not fancy Almeida, whose
Portuguese garrison was headed by a British brigadier
who would not easily surrender. The colonel took his
time marching his men across the plains to rejoin the
rest of Masséna's army. It was then, in the half-light
just before dawn on the twenty-fourth of July, he found

himself face to face with General Craufurd's
skirmishers.

Olivia, who had been riding Pegasus for twenty-four
hours with only occasional snatched minutes of rest,
heard the sounds of battle some way off and dug her
heels into the horse's side to make him gallop. Her
place was with the women of the regiment, waiting as
always, with the supply wagons in the rear, waiting,
hoping and praying for the safety of their men and for
the moment when the firing ceased and they could go
forward to find them, alive and well, wounded or dead.
It had been the same when she had been with Tom,
the same with Philippe, and she could do no less for
Robert, in spite of his rejection of her. What she could
not understand was his willingness to take part in an
action against his own compatriots; he must be made
to see that he would never regain his claws that way.

She came upon the baggage train grouped in a field,
several miles short of the scene of the battle, and
stopped to ask what was happening.

'They've joined up with Marshal Ney's corps,' she
was told by a burly pipe-smoking woman driving a
wagon from which she sold drink and other personal
items to the troops. 'Seems they've caught Craufurd
with his pants down.' She laughed. 'His backside is
exposed and our cavalry are cutting him to pieces.'

Olivia hid her dismay at this news. 'And the
infantry?'

The woman shrugged her shoulders in the direction
of the noise of guns. 'Who knows? We can only wait
and hope.'

That was the worst of it, the waiting, but it had to be
endured. Olivia dismounted and sat with the women in
the shade of a copse of pine trees, all of them tense
and listening, trying to judge from the changing sounds
how the battle was going. At times it seemed
uncomfortably close and they began to wonder if it
would overwhelm them, then the noise receded, as the

English struggled to return across the bridge to the far bank of the Coa and safety. It was much cooler now and heavy clouds were sweeping down from the distant mountains; fighting in the rain when it was difficult to keep guns and ammunition dry was even worse than fighting in the searing heat when the midsummer sun took its own toll of casualties.

The baggage train eased its way forward in the wake of the battle, ready to provide fresh ammunition when needed and, later, treatment for the wounded and comfort to the weary. Olivia, riding Pegasus in a deluge of rain, a little ahead of the other women, found herself shivering, but it was not so much the downpour, coming after so much heat, which caused it, as the uncertainty of what she would find round the next bend.

She remembered discovering Tom in the aftermath of the battle of Oporto, the horror of a battlefield when the fighting was done, the cries of the wounded, the shrieks of dying horses, the tattered shreds of colourful uniforms, the smoke and the stench of death. And Tom, dying in the middle of it all.

She had to find Robert. She knew, as she searched the soaking ground around the approaches to the bridge where body was heaped upon body, that finding him alive and unharmed was the most important thing in her life at that moment. She would come to terms with what that meant to her later, when she had time to spare for such self-indulgence.

Craufurd's snipers, safe now behind the rocks on the west bank, took pot-shots at anyone moving on the approaches to the bridge, but the battle was over and, as far as the British were concerned, disaster had been averted. Olivia joined other women who moved about the battlefield in a kind of trance, searching for their men, crying with relief when they found them injured but alive, or moaning in despair when they found them

dead or, not finding them at all, looking further afield
in case they had been carried off or had deserted.

Olivia, leading Pegasus, found no sign of Robert and
was hopeful that he had somehow escaped having to
do battle with his own countrymen. He had been
attached to Colonel Clavier's staff, so if she could find
the colonel she might find the man who filled her
thoughts and had filled them ever since the last time it
had rained — the day they met. She made her way to a
tiny hamlet she had passed on the road and here she
found the regimental command post set up in the inn.
The colonel, she was told, had been ordered to Marshal
Ney's headquarters to account for his actions.

'And Captain Santerre?' she asked the soldier who
guarded the door.

'Not here. Haven't seen him since. . .' The soldier
racked his brain. 'Since we joined up with the rest of
the corps.' He pointed across the street. 'Try the cellar
of that house; there are injured being looked after
there.'

She thanked him and hurried to cross the street, her
thoughts so far in advance of her feet that she did not
look where she was going and ran straight into the
arms of a tall, heavily built man wearing a brown frock-
coat and a top hat. He held her to steady her.

'Sorry,' she said and did not realise until she heard
his gasp of surprise that, in her agitation, she had
spoken English. She looked up and found herself
meeting the blue-eyed gaze of the man she had seen
coming out of Colonel Clavier's house in Ciudad
Rodrigo, the one she had half recognised.

It came to her, like a clap of thunder, where she had
seen him before, and she could hardly believe her
memory. She had known him as Mr Rufus Whitely
when he had visited her father in the early days of the
war. Her father had treated him cordially and shown
him round the manufactory and talked to him about
the armaments being made there. Their visitor had

shown particular interest in the new rockets being developed and tested on a secret site on their estate. The tests had not been successful — the rockets had been decidedly erratic in their trajectory and unstable to say the least; they were as likely to wipe out one's own people as the enemy. Her father had been undaunted and was still working on the missiles when she left home. What was Rufus Whitely doing in Spain, and among the French at that?

'Mr Whitely,' she said, ready to brazen out her own indiscretion. 'What are you doing here?'

If he was surprised at her use of his name, he hid it well. '*Madame*?' he queried in French.

'Don't you remember me?' she persisted. 'Olivia Pledger, I was then. You visited us in England. As I remember it, you were particularly interested in Papa's rockets.'

She watched as he concealed his surprise behind narrowed eyes; he was cool, she would give him that. 'You are mistaken, *madame*.'

'I think not. What are you doing here, with the French?'

His glance flicked over her dress and back to her face. 'I could ask you the same thing,' he said, apparently deciding not to continue with his denial. 'Is your father here?'

'Certainly not! He would never. . .' She stopped. 'I am here because I am married to a French soldier.'

He looked round at the busy street, where troops and stretcher-bearers hurried back and forth and horses clattered up and down, harness jingling, then back at her. 'I think we should talk,' he said in English. 'In private.' He took her arm and led her to the inn where the guard stood aside to let them in without even questioning them. He led her through the house on to a cool, vine-covered terrace where tables and chairs were set out for the inn's customers, now driven away by the arrival of the French soldiers. 'Sit down.'

'Why should I? Who do you think you are, dragging me away like that? I have other things to do. My husband. . .'

'Your husband?' He took her arm and pushed her into a chair and sat beside her. 'You had better tell me about this husband of yours.'

'Not until you tell me what you are doing here. You are English, or that is what you were pretending to be when you visited my father. From the Secretary for War, you said. Was that true?'

'Of course it was true.' He paused. 'Madam, I must ask you not to divulge a word of what I am about to tell you to a living soul. I may assume you are a loyal subject of King George, in spite of appearances?'

'Appearances can be deceptive,' she said.

'Quite so. My appearance is not what it would seem either.' He smiled and reached out to touch her arm with a hand that was warm and sweaty. 'I am an agent of the British, here at the express command of Viscount Wellington himself. I have an important task to do, do you understand?' She nodded and he went on, 'I must insist on your oath of secrecy.'

'Of course.'

'You must speak of this meeting to no one. If I find you have breathed so much as a hint that I am not the friend of Colonel Clavier I seem to be, then. . .' he sat forward and drew a finger slowly across her throat, roused to a perverted desire by the fear in her expressive green eyes '. . .I shall denounce you to the French as an English spy and you will die horribly. You understand?'

'Yes.' She looked him straight in the eye, so that he found himself drawing back from her. 'You have nothing to fear from me. As it happens, the man who is passing himself off as my husband is also English, masquerading as a French soldier.'

He looked startled, his eyes widened and she noticed

his hands tighten on the arms of his chair, but he quickly regained his composure. 'A deserter.'

'No,' she said, without thinking. 'Not a deserter. Someone like you, working behind the lines.'

'Tell me about him. What is his name?'

'Captain Philippe Santerre is the name he is known by, but it is really Robert Lynmount.'

'Lynmount!' He sat bolt upright, then laughed. It was a harsh sound which frightened her. 'So this is where he has got to. I suggest, ma'am, that you stick to Philippe Santerre; Lynmount is not a name to be proud of.'

'What wrong has he done?'

'You do not know? He is scum, my dear, scum.' He stood up so that he overshadowed her. 'Forget you ever knew him.' He put a hand on her shoulder. 'More than ever, I must insist on your promise not to betray me. The successful outcome of the war could depend on you keeping your word. Say nothing; particularly say nothing to that miserable cur of a man who calls himself your husband. Husband!' He laughed suddenly. 'You would be very unwise to put your faith in him.'

She rose beside him, her fists clenched at her sides. 'You have no right to say that, none at all. What do you know of him?'

He smiled, as if at some secret jest, as he took her arm to escort her back through the inn to the street. 'A great deal, but do not distress yourself, my dear, your loyalty does you credit. Only remember, your allegiance to your country comes above all else and in the absence of any higher authority that means me. Put yourself in my hands, be patient and you shall be amply repaid.'

'I want no payment for being a good patriot,' she snapped. 'All I want is to go home.'

'Then you shall, but let me advise you against attempting to leave on your own; it could be danger-

ous, fatal even.' Was he threatening her? His voice was
silky smooth, but it held a menace that terrified her
more than the idea of physical violence. 'I will make
the arrangements myself. Wait for my instructions.' He
smiled. 'You may be able to do me a small service at
the same time.'

At the door of the inn he doffed his top hat to her
and left her with a smile and a final warning to
remember what was at stake if she failed him.

Olivia stood staring after him for a long time after
he had gone, her thoughts in a turmoil. Had he been
telling the truth about himself? He had been very
plausible and his story had sounded almost too fantastic
to be a lie. What was, in some ways, more important
to her—had he also been correct about Robert? His
words echoed in her brain—'not a name to be proud
of'. 'Scum'. 'Cur'. Were they the measured words of
cool judgement or was there more to it than that? She
could not ask Robert, even if she could find him,
because she had given her word.

Robert. Where was he? She crossed the street
towards the house with the cellar full of wounded men,
trying desperately to compose herself.

She had gained the opposite side when a hand
touched her arm and, keyed up as she was, she turned
like a startled hare, ready to bolt. But it was Robert.
He had a bandage round his head and his uniform was
filthy with mud and dried blood.

'You are wounded.' Her relief at seeing him alive
mixed with the doubts that Rufus Whitely had planted
in her mind made her confused and ill at ease; she
could hardly look him in the eye.

'A mere scratch. What in Hades' name are you doing
here? I thought you would be on the other side of the
river by now, on your way to Lisbon. Did you not read
my letter? Father Peredo. . .'

'Father Peredo is not my keeper,' she snapped. 'And
neither are you.'

'No, by heaven, or I would muzzle you like a dog.'
He moved to take her arm and she involuntarily
flinched away from him. Puzzled by her reaction, he
let his hand fall to his side. 'Oh, I see, he has been
filling your head with scandal. I am surprised at you,
Olivia, believing his lies.'

'Whose lies?' she queried. 'I don't know what you
mean.'

'Don't you?'

'No, and it is more than careless of you to be talking
at all in public, let alone in English. Or don't you care?
Have you already made your deal with the colonel? Is
that why you tried to leave me behind?'

He grabbed her hand and dragged her across the
road to the stables beside the inn and pulled her inside.
It was dark and cool and quiet but for the snort of a
horse and the loud purring of the inn's cat, which lay
curled up on a bale of straw. 'Having you with me is
worse than being shot at,' he said savagely. 'At least in
battle I can shoot back.' He pulled her into his arms,
holding her tightly against him and crushing her mouth
with his, filling her traitorous body with an unbearable
yearning. She felt herself melting into him, wanting
more.

She tore herself away at last, and stood facing him,
nostrils flaring and hands shaking. 'I suppose that is
your idea of shooting back,' she said, close to tears. 'I
can tell you now, I will not endure it.'

'No?' His smile was crooked. 'Then why are you still
here? Why do you continue to haunt me?'

'I. . .' She stopped. She could not tell him that ever
since the battle she had been filled with a terrible fear
of losing him, that wherever he went, whatever he did,
she wanted to be at his side. She had never felt like
that about Tom or Philippe; this was new and both
terrifying and exhilarating. If it had not been for
meeting Rufus Whitely, she could have been happy,

but now her mind and emotions were at loggerheads and she was thoroughly confused.

'What are you up to, Olivia?'

'Up to?'

'Yes. What were you talking about?'

'When?'

'Just now. You and that. . .' he paused to moderate his voice '. . .that dandy in the frock-coat and top hat.' He took her shoulders in his hands as if he would like to shake her, but instead he held her away from him to look into her eyes, confusing her more than ever. 'What did he say about me?'

'Why should he say anything about you? Do you know him?'

'I know him.' He laughed grimly. 'Whatever he said his name was, I can tell you it is Rufus Whitely, Captain Rufus Whitely, a British officer. I suppose he has been captured, caught out enjoying himself and not on the field of battle, by the looks of it.' She realised he was referring to Mr Whitely's civilian dress. 'Of all the ill-luck.'

'Yes,' she said, seizing on the explanation he had inadvertently given her. 'It is unfortunate to be captured, but better than being killed and,' she added with heavy emphasis, 'especially being wounded by your own people.'

'I was thrown when Thor was startled.' He laughed. 'My wound, such as it is, was caused by falling against a tree. And I was referring to my own bad luck in running into that blackguard, not his.'

'Why should his being captured be bad for you?' she asked warily, surprised that he should admit to being thrown. 'He won't betray you.'

'No?' His cynical smiled spoiled his normally handsome features. 'I fully expect him to do just that.'

'Don't be silly. What has he to gain?'

'The temptation to offer a juicy bit of intelligence to the other side in exchange for freedom must be more than tempting to a normally patriotic soldier; to Whitely it would be irresistible.'

'I think you are being unjust.'

'What has he been telling you?'

'Nothing.'

'Nothing, Olivia?' He scanned her face. 'I watched you go into the inn; you were alone together for at least half an hour, long enough to tell each other your life histories. Does he know you are English?'

'Yes. We had met before, in England.' She paused. 'We spoke of that.'

'Oh.' This piece of information quietened him for a moment, though she could not tell what he was thinking.

'You do not like him, do you?' she persisted.

'I do not.'

'Why not?'

'I have my reasons.' He paused, wanting to allay his own doubts but reluctant to question her more closely for fear of stirring up her curiosity and finding himself on the receiving end of a grilling. He would not lie to her and he did not want to tell her the truth, not yet. 'Has he given his parole?'

'He did not say.'

'He must have done to be allowed to move about so freely. Keep away from him, do you hear? I forbid you to speak to him again. He is trouble.'

He was so vehement that she was left more bothered than ever. If Rufus Whitely was truly a British intelligence agent, then why was Robert so afraid of him, unless he had something to hide? Were her doubts about Robert well founded after all? Was he the traitor? Was that why he had refused to return to the British lines — because he dared not? She did not want to believe it; her whole being cried out against the idea.

Her dilemma was made worse when they heard the following day that Don Santandos and his guerrillas

had been taken by surprise on open ground, where
they were most vulnerable, and suffered a mauling by
a company of skirmishers from Philippe's regiment.
The prisoners were brought into the French camp in
heavy chains to be questioned. Olivia, anxious to know
what had happened, decided to risk paying the colonel
a visit during his interrogation of the men. He had
returned from headquarters with orders to continue
the march, but his personal feud with Don Santandos
and the humiliation he had received at the guerrilla
leader's hands still rankled. He was adept at finding
excuses for not obeying orders, and a broken axle on a
supply wagon and a shortage of horses had furnished
the latest one.

The prisoners were stubborn and insisted on being
treated as prisoners of war, but the colonel ridiculed
that idea. 'You are not troops,' he said, leaning back
in his chair and surveying the ill-assorted men who
stood facing him, manacled together. 'You are rabble;
you have no idea how to fight. The mighty armies of
the Emperor have occupied your country; it is at peace
with France. You are spies, in the pay of the hideous
Leopard, nothing more, and for that you will die.'

Olivia tried to argue on the prisoners' behalf. 'They
are too ignorant to be spies,' she said, smiling sweetly
at the colonel and reaching out to touch his arm. It was
a provocative thing to do and she hoped she could fend
him off when the time came. 'They are only trying to
defend their homeland.'

'Barren mountains and sour vines,' he said. 'For that
they are willing to die. Then I give them their wish.'
He turned to the guards. 'Take them away and shoot
them.' He returned his attention to Olivia. 'For your
sake, I give them a quick death. Now, my dear, what
shall we do to while away the time? A carriage ride, a
little picnic?' He was stroking the back of her hand
with his thumb as he spoke, making her scalp tingle.
She needed all her wits about her now.

'But won't that be dangerous?' she queried. 'The guerrillas might be looking to avenge their comrades.'

'Then they will die too. We will take an escort.'

'But it would surely spoil our picnic. All that noise and commotion.'

'True,' he said meditatively. 'Then let us have supper here. Afterwards. . .' He did not finish what he was about to say because he was interrupted by Robert, who marched in and saluted.

'What is it, man?' the colonel asked irritably.

Robert, giving Olivia a look that was almost an accusation, pointed outside to where the sounds of mustering troops could be heard—a drum roll, shouts of command, marching feet.

Olivia went to the window from which she could see the village square, with its few stunted cork oaks and slim poplars. It widened out at the end where the church stood and it was here that the troops had been assembled to watch the execution. The prisoners, their hands bound, stood with their backs to the church, facing a dozen voltigeurs who kneeled in the dust, their muskets primed. An officer and the regimental doctor stood to one side and, to her surprise, Rufus Whitely was with them. Angry because of her helplessness, she turned away.

'The firing squad is ready for your inspection,' Olivia said, blessing Robert's intervention but more concerned about the guerrillas than her own peril. 'Will you not spare them?'

The colonel smiled. 'No, my dear, not even for you. If I did that, there would be anarchy and every tinpot peasant would rise up, thinking we had gone soft. They know the risks they are running when they defy me.'

'Then will you excuse me?' She dared not continue the argument; he would not hesitate to mete the same punishment out to her if she crossed him, but neither could she stand by and appear to condone it.

'Naturally I will,' the colonel said, pushing his bulk

out of his chair. 'There is no need for you to witness such things. They are the inevitable consequence of war, but not for you to worry your pretty head over. I will see you later.' He put his arm round her and pulled her close against his side, drawing a hissing breath of annoyance from Robert. 'About eight, shall we say?' He picked up his white-plumed cocked hat and settled it on his head, before straightening his uniform jacket. 'Lead on, Santerre.'

It was a reprieve for her, but only a short one. Olivia watched them march out side by side, the tall upright Robert whose uniform fitted his slim figure to perfection and the fat, waddling Clavier; she could not suppress a smile at the enormous conceit of the colonel even to think she would prefer him. Somehow or other she had to avoid that assignation. Her reverie was interrupted by a shouted command and a volley of shots which made her wince. Her thoughts went to the families of the men who had died; had they been with their men on the battlefield or were they safely at the monastery? What could be done to help them?

'Why were they out in the open at all?' she asked Robert when he joined her that evening at her bivouac fire among the pine trees by the roadside. 'They should have stayed at the monastery.'

He sat on the ground and held his hands out to the warmth, for the rain had made the air cooler. 'They went to meet General Craufurd, but you know what happened. The general found himself in action and had to beat a hasty retreat.'

'And left the guerrillas to their fate.'

'He may not have known they were so close, and in any case there was nothing he could do. If I know the Peer, Craufurd is already in hot water for venturing over the river at all and risking his men and guns.'

'And Don Santandos?'

'He has taken the survivors back to the hills.'

'Where are their families?'

'I do not know. I hope they had sense enough to stay where they were and not follow their men.'

'It's my fault,' she said miserably. 'I took them from their homes and there was no need for that.'

'You did not know that at the time, so do not blame yourself.' He spoke softly. 'We must think about you.'

'Me?' she queried in surprise. 'What about me?'

'General Craufurd has put himself out of reach; I cannot see how I can hand you over to him now.'

'What makes you think you can hand me over to anyone?' she demanded. 'I am not a piece of baggage. When we go, we go together. It is more important to return to Villa de Fuentes and do what we can to help the villagers. Without their men, they will be in sorry straits.'

'No. There is work to do here.'

'French work! Enemy work! I begin to wonder about you, Robert Lynmount.'

'Only begin?'

He was smiling at her through the blue smoke of the fire; it gave an ethereal quality to his features, a kind of misty glow which made him seem not quite real, a ghost conjured up from her imagination. But for what purpose? To help her escape? But she had refused all the opportunities she had been offered to do that. To give her love? No, he did not love her and, she told herself firmly, she did not want a third marriage; she had had enough trouble with the other two. To prove she was as good a soldier, as effective a spy as any man? That was more like it! The difficulty was deciding who was the spy and who the traitor, who to trust and who not.

Miguel Santandos was a patriot—there was no doubt about that; perhaps he could advise her. But Don Santandos was many miles away and her problem was here on the border between Spain and Portugal, with a lustful French colonel, a British agent and a disgraced Captain of Hussars.

   Which of them posed the greater danger, not only to
her, but to the whole British campaign? She refused to
believe there was anything more to her dilemma than
that. Love did not come into it; she would fight that
idea to the very end, even though it made her
miserable.

   'Tell me the truth,' she said slowly, stirring the fire
with a stick, making the flames leap around the kettle
of mutton stew she was cooking for his evening meal.
'Just what are you about? What is this work that has to
be done?'

   'Why is it so important that you should know?'

   'So that I can help and not hinder.'

   He threw back his head and laughed. 'You would do
better to find a way out of the scrape you are in. You
should have known that making sheep's eyes at the
colonel was a chancey thing to do and would achieve
nothing. I advise you to make yourself scarce from now
on, unless, of course, you really are enamoured of the
man.'

   'Enamoured?' she squeaked. 'Of that. . .that. . .
Robert, how could you think such a thing? I only went
to see him so that I could learn more about what had
happened and try to persuade him not to kill the
guerrilleros. You know that.'

   'I know nothing. I can only guess what goes on in
that beautiful head of yours.'

   He was infuriating, she decided, to pay her a compliment in that offhand way, as if he were not even aware
of what he said, just as he had once said he loved her
when she was angry. 'I could say the same,' she said. 'I
can only guess what is going on inside your head, and
it seems to me that it is decidedly muddled. Why won't
you tell me?'

   'Curiosity killed the cat.'

   'And satisfaction resurrected it,' she snapped.

   'I am not joking,' he said, pulling a stick from the
fire and holding it up to watch it burn in his hand. 'You

are playing with fire. If the colonel realises you are no longer the wife of one of his officers, then nothing can save you.'

'I know that.'

'Of course, he may already know.'

'How?'

'Whitely may have told him.' He pushed the flaming brand back under the pot.

'If he had, I would have been arrested by now and you too. Besides, whatever you think of him, Captain Whitely is an Englishman, just as you are. Why don't you work together?'

'That would be trying to mix oil and water, my dear. It cannot be done.'

'Why do you hate him so?'

'I do not hate him, I despise him. An officer who gives his parole and then is too afraid to wear his uniform. . .'

'There may be a good reason for that,' she said slowly. 'You are not wearing yours.'

'That is different. As soon as I have done what I have to do, I will wear it again.'

'Even without its buttons?' She knew, as soon as she spoke, that she had touched a raw spot, and if he had been going to tell her anything he would not do so now.

He stood up suddenly, towering over her. 'I have to inspect the piquet lines. I suggest you find a way of avoiding the colonel tonight and tomorrow we will devise a plan to send you home. Goodnight, Madame Santerre.'

She watched him striding through the trees towards the road, cursing her foolish tongue. They had nearly, very nearly, come to an understanding. He had been on the point of taking her into his confidence, and she had had to taunt him about that uniform. 'What about your supper?' she called after him, taking the blackened kettle from the fire, but he did not turn back.

She could not sleep that night. She was used to sleeping out of doors and often, in good weather, preferred it, but tonight the ground seemed extra-hard and the wet trees dripped water on to the thin blanket she had used to cover herself. Robert did not return and she tossed and turned, wondering where he was. Had he, in his anger, betrayed himself? Had he met Rufus Whitely? What would they have to say to each other, or would they dispense with words and come to blows?

Something hit her shoulder. She sprang up, seizing the pistol she always had under her hand, but there was no one near but a voltigeur and his wife, curled together under the canvas from a cart, both snoring loudly. She turned to look about her and stood on a pine cone with her bare foot. She collapsed on to her blanket giggling; to be startled almost to death by a falling cone was certainly not the behaviour of a soldier and a spy.

All hope of sleep gone, she put on her old boots, rolled up her bedding and, tucking it under her arm, went to take Pegasus from the horse lines. She was glad she still had him and knew that it was only because she was a favourite of the colonel's that she had been allowed to keep him. The colonel. Was it too much to hope that he had forgotten their assignation?

She decided it was and she would have some fast talking to do in the morning if she stayed in camp. She could leave, of course, but that would mean leaving Robert, and that was something she was not prepared to do. When she was with him they were constantly at loggerheads, as if the breath of their co-existence lay in argument, that without it both would expire. When they were apart she remembered the good things about him — his chivalry, his concern for her comfort, how he had stolen for her and found a carriage for her even though she had rejected it, how gentle his big hands were even when he was angry—and there were times when she tried him sorely.

She would find him and apologise, persuade him to return to the camp fire for his supper, try to ease his hurt. Love, she told herself for the hundredth time with less and less conviction, had nothing to do with it.

The horse lines were patrolled by guards, but she knew she would have no trouble persuading them to let her have Pegasus; they were quite accustomed to her comings and goings. 'The colonel was looking for you, I hear,' one of them said, as she untied her horse. 'He sent the drummer to find you.'

'Did he? I had better go and find out what he wants.'

They laughed. 'Don't you know?'

She joined in their laughter as she found her saddle among the heap on the ground. 'Have you seen Captain Santerre?'

'Oh, you are safe there, sweetheart. The captain rode out half an hour ago on that great black horse of his.'

'Rode out?' She was instantly alerted. 'Where? Who with?'

'He was alone,' the second man said. 'He went that way.' He pointed. 'Gone to do a bit of reconnoitring, I should think. You will be safe until dawn.'

She ignored his innuendo as she mounted and set off in the direction he had pointed out, her good intentions forgotten as she galloped to catch up with Robert. Whatever he was up to, she would be a part of it.

It was full day before Robert came near enough to the guerrilla hide-out to be challenged from a rocky promontory by two guards armed with carbines.

'Is Miguel Santandos with you?' he shouted up to them. 'I must speak to him.'

They scrambled down the rocks to the path. 'Come with us,' one of them said, pulling him from his horse while the other put a bag over his head. Then they took his arms and propelled him forwards on foot.

Unable to see where he was going, he stumbled several times, but the hands gripping his arms kept him upright. No one spoke, not even Robert, who knew protests at his treatment would be in vain. They trusted no one and he could not blame them for that.

His blindfold was removed when they entered a huge cave. Here were the remnants of the guerrilla force, sitting round a camp fire. They looked tired, defeated men, their clothes were ragged and many of them were wounded, but their eyes still had the fire of battle in them and they watched Robert warily as he moved forward, peering in the gloom from one to the other.

'Where is Don Santandos?'

'Not here.'

'He survived?'

'Oh, he survived,' said the huge black-bearded man with a chest like a barrel and hands which looked capable of strangling a bear. Robert knew him as José Gonzales, Don Santandos's second-in-command. 'Which is more than his wife did.'

'His wife?' queried Robert.

'Yes. They caught us on the plains, a whole battalion of them, wiped us out but for the handful you see here. She ran after him, flung herself into the worst of the fighting, screaming his name. A shell landed. . . nothing left to bury.'

'I am sorry, *señor*.' The sympathy seemed inadequate. 'But what were you doing out in the open? You must have known it would be suicidal. You fight best in the hills; no one better.'

'We were going to meet Craufurd, to ask him to look after our families, but you know that already. . .'

'No. I understood you had sent a message to him, no more than that. He could not break off an engagement to come to you and he had his orders.'

'We would have met the general without trouble if

someone had not pointed that misbegotten French colonel in our direction and caused a battle which need never have happened.'

'That is nonsense. The colonel. . .'

'The colonel!' The man snorted with derision. 'What do you feed him to keep his hungry hands off your wife, Captain?' He ducked as Robert's clenched fist shot out, then laughed. 'English! Bah! And English women are worse than the men. You told the fat French pig where to find us; you betrayed us and for that you will undoubtedly die.'

'I did nothing of the kind.' He was calmer now, realising anger would do no good. 'Nor did Olivia, I swear to it. I want to help you. I can help you. I know the disposition of the French forces, and the route and timing of their march. It is something the English commander-in-chief would very much like to know.'

'How will that help us?'

'One day Spain will be free, but you will not do it by yourselves. You need the help of Wellington's army.'

'Bah!' The big man spat. 'That is always retreating. There are no leopards left in Spain and soon there will be none in Portugal, but you know that. It is why you and your gun-crazy wife have thrown in your lot with the French. We let you go and you betrayed us.'

'No. Find Don Santandos; he will speak for me. He knows the truth.'

'Naturally we will send for him; he will want to witness your death-throes. What a pity you did not bring the *señora* with you. We could have had a double execution. But we will get her later, never fear.'

Robert thanked providence that Olivia was many miles away in the comparative safety of the French camp. He had returned to their bivouac very soon after leaving it, to find her curled up under a blanket and his supper cooling on the embers. There were others near by; she would be safe until dawn when he planned to return. He had given some thought to bringing her and trying, once again, to persuade her to stay with the guerrillas in the expectation of Wellington making a push and returning to Spain, but had decided against it until he could talk to Miguel.

His only regret was that she would never know how he had met his end and would go through life thinking he had deserted her. He wondered idly, as the partisans trussed him up like a Christmas goose, how she would fight off the colonel. That she could do so he did not for a moment doubt. Now, when it was too late to do anything about it, he knew that his disgrace had been for a whim, a passing fancy, a spoiled child. That was all Juana was or ever could be. Olivia was different. Olivia was everything that Juana was not. Olivia was. . . He smiled wryly as his bonds cut into his wrists; Olivia was simply Olivia and there was no one else quite like her.

CHAPTER SEVEN

OLIVIA flung herself from her lathered horse outside Father Peredo's house and hammered on the door. 'Come on! Come on!' she murmured impatiently, then pushed past the startled Pedro almost before the door was properly opened.

'My dear child!' Father Peredo met her in the hall. He had a sheaf of papers in his hand, as if she had interrupted his work on them. 'What has happened?'

'The *guerrilleros*, the village men, are going to kill Robert. They say he betrayed them. You must stop them.'

'Where are they?'

'In the hills. Oh, please come. It may already be too late; they are only waiting for Don Santandos to return and then. . .'

'Where is Miguel Santandos?' He went back into his living-room and put the sheaf of papers in a desk drawer. She hovered in the doorway.

'I do not know.' His deliberate slowness was irritating her. 'Come, please. Only you can save him.'

He smiled. 'You think I should?'

'Of course. You know he would not betray his friends.'

'Do I?' He looked up from locking the drawer to smile at her. 'Do you?'

'Of course I do, and so do you.' She surprised herself with the swiftness of her response; she had not hesitated at all.

'Good. We will go now and you can tell me what happened as we ride.' He called to Pedro and sent him scurrying for a horse, then he left her, telling her he would join her outside.

She returned to Pegasus, who really ought to have been rubbed down and allowed to rest, but she needed to ask yet more of him before that could happen. He nuzzled up to her as she patted his nose; it was almost as if he understood. 'Good, brave fellow,' she said, as she mounted again. 'Don't let me down now.'

Pedro led a horse up the village street from wherever he had been hidden, just as Father Peredo came from the house. The priest had changed from his frock to breeches and shirt and she was surprised how much younger and stronger he looked without the enveloping skirts. 'Come,' he said, throwing himself lightly into the saddle. 'Lead the way.'

She wanted to gallop but he would have none of it. 'Do you want to kill that horse?' he queried.

'Better than having Robert killed.'

'That young man is special to you, is he?'

'You know he is. He is my husband.'

'Is he?' he enquired mildly as they rode side by side over the new wooden bridge.

She looked across at him and felt the colour flood to her cheeks. He knew the truth! 'It makes no odds,' she said defiantly. 'We had to say that.'

'Of course, I understand, but it is something you should remedy before too long. It is not good to live with a man as you are doing.'

'We are not. . . We do not. . .'

He smiled. 'That is good, but it cannot be easy; better to marry and have your union blessed in the sight of God.' He paused, having obviously said all he was going to say on the subject. 'Now, tell me what happened.'

'Robert rode out from the camp in the middle of the night. I followed.'

'Why?'

'Why?' she repeated. 'Does it matter why? I wanted to talk to him, and heaven knows that is difficult enough in the French camp, where he is supposed to be dumb.'

'He is still keeping that up, is he?'

'He has to.'

'Yes, of course. So you followed him and then what?'

'It took some time to pick up his trail, but I came within sight of him at last and he was heading into the hills. I could have hailed him. . .'

'But you did not.'

'No.'

'You wanted to see where he was going. You were suspicious of him. . .'

'No,' she said quickly, then laughed. 'Well, perhaps a little curious. I saw him being stopped by two men at the entrance to a pass. They did not seem too friendly, so I kept well back and followed.'

'You were not seen?'

'I do not think so. I left Pegasus behind and crept forward on foot. The men took Robert into a cave. I heard them say they were going to execute him.' She smiled wryly. 'And me too, if they could catch me. I left in a hurry.'

It sounded so easy, the way she told it, but it had meant crawling in the heather and broom for what seemed hours and freezing at every sound. She had toyed with the idea of rushing into the hide-out and demanding Robert's release at the point of her pistol, but she knew that would never work and instead had returned to her horse and ridden for Villa de Fuentes as if the hounds of hell were at her heels.

'Do you think we could go a little faster? Don Santandos may have returned,' she said.

'Do you have no faith in that man of yours being able to talk his way out of trouble?'

'I am not at all sure he wants to. In some strange way I think he imagines he would welcome death as an end to his problems. He seems not to mind risking his life.'

'It is a soldier's lot.'

'Not the way he is doing it. Something has happened in the past, something which has left him embittered, and he will not talk of it.'

'One day, when he has learned to trust again, he will.'

'If he lives that long,' she said, digging her heels into her horse's flanks and leaving him to follow.

His horse, though an inferior one, was fresh while hers was not; he was easily able to keep up with her and it was he who was in front when they were hailed by the new look-outs at the approach to the hide-out. The midday sun was high in a clear sky, but up here in the mountains where the wind soughed through the passes the air was chill. She shivered as she dismounted and waited, with growing impatience, while the priest spoke to the men. Then they were waved on and led their horses through the narrow pass. At the far end, the mountain broadened out into a plateau where goats grazed on the sparse grass and broom, and here they were met by José Gonzales who conducted them into the cave.

It was so dark in there after the bright sunlight outside, Olivia saw nothing but dark shapes and the whites of a dozen pairs of eyes. She heard her name being called and turned towards the sound. Robert was sitting with his back against the wall, his hands tied behind him and his legs tucked up almost to his chin and bound there. She ran to kneel beside him, reaching out to touch him. 'Thank God you are safe.'

He grinned, his teeth showing white in the darkness. 'Can you never stick to your own affairs, my dear? Must you be forever trying to embroil yourself in mine?'

'They are one and the same,' she said. 'Has Don Santandos returned?'

'He is expected any time. I see the good priest has

come to give me the last rites; I am sorry I am not a Catholic, but perhaps he will overlook that little point.'

'Last rites be damned!' she said.

'Tut, tut, my dear,' he said, smiling. 'That is hardly the language of a lady; it would cause no end of raised eyebrows in an English drawing-room.'

'We are not in an English drawing-room, nor will we ever be again if we cannot extricate ourselves from this scrape.' She included herself in that prediction without even thinking about it. 'And Father Peredo has not come to administer last rites, he has come to try and free you, but if you will do nothing to help yourself. . .'

'How can I help myself, trussed up like a chicken and surrounded by fools who do not know the truth when they hear it?'

She was glad they were speaking in English; the guerrillas would take exception to being called fools. 'Let us hope Don Santandos is more ready to listen.'

'I gather he has been driven crazy by the death of his wife; he is not behaving like a rational man. I am told he is even now stalking the French columns, determined on single-handed revenge.'

'On you?'

'One must suppose so; it is what these people believe.'

She wondered if she dared begin trying to undo his bonds. She looked around her. The priest and José were talking earnestly together, both facing towards the prisoner. 'Did you tell the colonel where to find them?'

'How could I? Until yesterday I thought they were safely in the monastery.' He was not even angry, as he might once have been at such a question. 'You saw them more recently than I did when you took the women and children to them. Did they speak of moving out then?'

'Not that I can recall.' His wrists were raw where the rope had bitten into them. She began picking at the knots, trying not to hurt him and uncaring that she was being watched. 'If you did not do it and I did not do it, then someone else betrayed them.' She turned from him towards the partisans. 'Will someone lend me a knife?'

They laughed at her temerity, but no one gave her one. Father Peredo came over and knelt on the other side of Robert. 'Why did you come here?' he asked him. 'They told me you rode into the pass as if you had nothing to fear.'

'I did not know I had. I had given my parole to Don Santandos and, as far as I knew, I was trusted. I had dispatches to send to the British and I came to ask for someone to act as a courier. And to escort the *señora* to safety.'

'It does not matter about me,' she said, though no one appeared to hear her.

'Why not go yourself?' the priest asked.

'No, I am more useful where I am.' He tried to lift his bound hands. 'Or at least where I was before this happened. The longer I am away, the more difficult it will be for me to explain my absence.'

'If, as you say, you knew nothing of Miguel's plans, how did you know where to find our men last night?'

'One of the *guerrilleros* told me before. . .before he was executed. Garcia, I think his name was.'

'We tried to save them, truly we did,' Olivia put in. 'They were not tortured.'

Father Peredo turned and looked up at José Gonzales. 'You are in control now. What do you say? Would Garcia have told our friend of this hide-out if he thought he was the traitor?'

The big man looked perplexed. He was unused to command because Don Santandos had always been their leader and Miguel had never delegated a decision in his life. 'Where are these dispatches?' he asked.

'They were in my saddle-bag,' Robert said. 'But I

am sure you have emptied that already, so I have no idea where they are.'

The guerrillas had found the papers but they had been written in English and, apart from the absent Miguel, there was no one who could read them. José raised his hand and clicked his fingers. 'Give the papers to the Father,' he said. 'He will tell us if we should believe the Englishman.'

Olivia held her breath as Father Peredo read the documents, but if she had hoped he might read aloud she was disappointed. He folded them carefully and smiled at Robert. 'You need a courier?'

'Yes. Whether I live or die at the hands of your compatriots, that intelligence must be sent. Do you understand?'

'I understand. And if you are allowed to live?'

'Then I go back and, with luck, there will be more dispatches to follow those.' He nodded towards the papers in the priest's hand.

'And the *señora*?'

'My wife?' He looked towards Olivia. 'Take her to safety.'

'Father Peredo knows I am not your wife,' she said, while the priest turned to translate to his compatriots. 'He knows you cannot make me do anything on the grounds that I have vowed to obey you.'

'What has that to do with anything?'

'If you go back to the French army, I go with you and it's no use you arguing.'

'I have long ago learned the futility of that,' he said. 'If I want you to stay anywhere, the only way it can be achieved is to tie you up.'

She laughed. 'You are the one who is tied up, not me.'

He held up his bound hands to José. 'Cut me loose, there's a good fellow,' he said in Spanish. 'I need to give the *señora* a beating.'

The big Spaniard laughed and produced a wicked-looking knife from his belt with which he cut through the bonds in seconds. 'Sometimes it is necessary to beat our wives or they lead us by the nose. The English have never learned this truth.'

Robert began massaging his hands and legs to return the circulation to them. 'Thank you, my friend.' He stood up and stamped his feet a few times and then pronounced himself ready to leave.

'Do one thing for me,' José said, as he escorted them from the cave and out into blinding sunlight. 'Find the devil who betrayed our people. Find him and kill him for me.'

'That I will do,' Robert said. 'You have my word.'

The partisans all came out to see them off. They shook hands with each in turn, then took their horses from the young guerrilla who had brought them forward. 'Send your families back to your village,' Robert said, as they prepared to ride away. 'Father Peredo will see they come to no harm. And leave here yourselves. Go back to the monastery — today — do not linger. There must be no more fighting on the plains. Leave that to Wellington's leopards.' He turned to Olivia. 'Come, little leopardess, we have hunting to do.'

Olivia followed obediently. Her horse had been rubbed down and given water and oats, and although he was tired he was by no means finished. They walked in order to rest him.

'Where are we going?' she asked, as they made their way down towards the distant valley.

'Back to the forward lines, back to Colonel Clavier. Where else?'

'He was looking for me last night.'

'I hope he did not find you.' It was said laconically, but somehow his words cheered her.

'No, but when we get back he will want to know the reason why.'

Robert was thoughtful for a moment. 'We quar-

relled. I am a jealous and violent man. You were afraid
to go to him for what I would do if I found out.'

She laughed, not knowing how true his description
of himself was. 'And what have I been doing all day?
And, more to the point, what have you been doing all
day?'

'You have been sulking. . .'

'I do not sulk!' she retorted quickly.

He turned to look at her, smiling. 'No, I give you
that. But nevertheless today you did.'

'And you?'

'I had been told where the survivors of the guerrillas
were hidden, I went to reconnoitre.'

'And?'

'I found their camp, but it was deserted. They have
obviously given up after their defeat at the colonel's
hands and gone home.'

'And if he wants to know where the camp is, will
you tell him?'

'Certainly. He will find no one there; Father Peredo
will see to that.'

'I take it I am to be the one to tell the colonel all
this?'

'Yes, you recovered from the sulks as soon as you
saw me coming back.'

'If I had decided not to return with you, what would
you have done?'

He laughed. 'Ah, but I knew you would.'

'You are impossibly conceited!'

'No more than you.'

She pretended to raise her whip to him, making him
duck, but instead she touched Pegasus with it, and the
horse, rested now, set off at a canter. Robert did not
trouble himself to go after her and after half a mile she
stopped to allow him to catch up. In silence they rode
down on to the metalled highway and turned westward,
taking the road they had covered in darkness the night
before, back to the French advance on Almeida.

But this time it was different. Their relationship had changed subtly; although not exactly harmonious, the razor-sharp edge had gone from it and they found they could talk together without acrimony.

The town could hold out indefinitely, he told her as they rode, certainly until Wellington advanced, which he would do as soon as he was in a position to win a decisive battle. He did not envisage having to fire in anger against the allies.

At first it seemed he was right. The French lay siege to the town on August the fifteenth and ten days later they were still there, still surrounding it and growing hungrier while they fired cannon balls at its walls and were sniped at by the defenders whenever they showed their heads.

'Why they don't invest it and carry on their advance I do not know,' Robert said on the evening of the twenty-fifth, when he returned to the derelict peasant hovel a couple of miles from the city where Olivia had set up house. 'They will lose the initiative. Wellington will be here any day now.'

'So much the better, surely?' she said, taking the pot from the fire and dishing food on to a tin plate.

She was adept at making a home in the most unpromising places and it was better than living out-doors with the men or crammed into the farmhouse with the colonel. She had cleaned its two rooms and built a fireplace in order to cook whatever food could be scavenged — she was good at that too — and she had found straw for bedding.

Robert was very often the officer of the guard or leading a patrol, or out on some secret errand of his own, and was rarely there at night, but when he was they retired to separate rooms to sleep. It was not something they had arranged formally; it just happened that way. Even so, it was a lifestyle that in England would brand her as a harlot, ruined beyond redemp-tion, but this was not England and nothing was normal and the irony of it was, she was as chaste as any respectable widow could possibly be.

She tried to convince herself that that was how it suited her, that she was immune to Robert's physical attractions, that she had not noticed his muscular torso when he bathed in the nearby river, that the touch of his hand did not make her yearn for something more. They did not quarrel so often now but neither did they share their thoughts. She knew no more about him than she had at the outset; he remained an enigma.

'Yes, of course,' he went on, unaware of her turbulent thoughts. 'But if they hang about here until the winter rains they will never drive the leopards into the sea. It is the key to the whole war. Without the British presence in the Peninsula, there would be no stopping the Emperor; the world would be his.'

'Then the longer Almeida holds out, the better. Could we not smuggle ourselves in there? I would rather be with our own people than out here. We are likely to go hungrier than they are.' She was referring to the old problem of food supplies. Everything the country had to offer had been taken or destroyed by the inhabitants to keep it from the enemy and anything sent over the hundreds of miles of supply lines stretching from France had precious little chance of arriving. The troops were being driven to eat dogs and cats, and more ammunition was being expended on shooting wild birds than on the enemy, who were safe behind their walls with full larders.

He appeared to be considering the idea and she watched him carefully. Just lately he had seemed to be softening towards the idea of returning to his own people; once or twice she had caught him saying, 'When we return. . .' as if it were a possibility. He seemed to have aged several years in as many weeks, as if the strain of living a lie, and a silent one at that, was too much for him.

'Tomorrow,' he said now. 'Tomorrow I will find a way into Almeida.'

He was afraid that if she did not soon return to a civilised life and revert to being the real lady who lurked beneath the old blue uniform jacket and peasant skirt which was more often than not hitched up to her knees she would never make the transition at all. Sometimes when he looked at her, with her face flushed from the cooking fire and her hair lying in curly tendrils about her cheeks, he would imagine her in a London drawing-room, dressed in silks and lace, with satin slippers on her feet instead of those old boots, and diamonds in her hair.

Not that she would be any more desirable then than now. He no longer tried to delude himself; he wanted her in his bed, wanted to demonstrate a love he could not find the words for. But he would not take her until she wanted it too. And if she never did, well, then, he would have to bottle up his feelings and look after her until she needed him no more.

He had to keep reminding himself that she was not with him by choice; her aim was, and always had been, to return to England. But why had she not gone when she had been given the chance? Why did she insist on his accompanying her? Was it sheer perversity? He wished he knew.

She was too thin and she worked too hard, not only looking after him, roaming the countryside persuading the people to part with a little food, but also for the other women and children who camped around the city only just out of range of its heavy guns. Sometimes her scavenging took her within sight of the snipers who lined the city walls and a musket ball would send her scuttling back to safety. She seemed to lead a charmed life, as if she had her own private guardian angel sitting on her shoulder. He was glad of that, because she ignored all his warnings and did exactly as she pleased. Her obvious wilfulness—he hesitated to call it shrewishness as others did—had had one good effect: Colonel Clavier had given up trying to seduce her.

She had told the colonel such an exaggerated tale of her husband's jealousy and what he would do to anyone who so much as looked at her that the stupid man had been frightened out of his wits and had turned his attention to the widow of one of his officers, killed during the encounter with Craufurd. Madame Falaise had no husband to exact revenge and she was in such dire straits financially, she was grateful for the colonel's protection. But how long that would last, Robert did not know; it would be better to take Olivia out of the man's reach.

'Be prepared when I come for you,' he said. 'When I come off watch.'

She was ready, but the way was made for them in quite a different manner from the one he had envisaged and it was not until afterwards that they found out how it had happened. The French were still bombarding the town in the vain hope that it might weaken the defences and demoralise the garrison, and it was sheer bad luck that one of the shells should land on a trail of gunpowder, left by a leaking barrel, which led straight to the open door of the cathedral where the ammunition was stored. Robert and Olivia were moving stealthily through a cornfield between the French lines and the city walls when they were nearly thrown off their feet by the explosion. She flung herself into his arms and stared open-mouthed as the cathedral, the castle and half Almeida were sent into the air in a huge billowing cloud of smoke and flame.

'We could have been there,' she said. She was shaking and he held her close against him, stroking her hair in an unconscious gesture of reassurance. She had washed it that morning in something that made it smell of lavender and it transported him back to his child-hood and the scent of the garden after rain and the bees buzzing in the lavender bush. It made a stark contrast to the stench of gunpowder and burning wood, the crash of masonry and windows exploding. 'If we had gone yesterday or that had happened tomorrow. . .' She shuddered. 'Oh, those poor people!'

'Your guardian angel has come up trumps again,' he said, trying to make light of it, but there was a catch in his voice which made her turn her head to look up at him.

'My guardian angel?'

He smiled and his hazel eyes softened at the sight of her, this brave and lovely girl whose endurance and cheerfulness knew no bounds. 'Yes, I always imagine a little cherub sitting on your shoulder, taking care of you.'

She laughed. 'But you take care of me.'

'Not very well, I am afraid.' He nodded his head in the direction of the burning town. 'And now we had better wait and see what the consequence of that is before we venture in.' Reluctantly he released her and they turned to go back to their old quarters.

They could hear wave after wave of cheering coming from the French besiegers who, after the initial surprise, had realised what had happened; they were jubilant. Two days later the garrison commander learned that someone had let the French know there was no ammunition left, and after that there seemed to be little point in trying to brazen it out; he surrendered.

Napoleon's men stormed over the bridges which spanned the deep moat and ran into the city, cheering, looting, raping and stealing anything and everything worth carrying. By the time Robert and Olivia arrived, they were drunk and uncontrollable. Olivia had never seen them quite so bad in all the time she had been with them.

Robert was furious — extraordinarily so, she thought, as he fought with one soldier who came out of a villa carrying a large gilt mirror and a sack full of loot. His

anger was so violent, she thought he would kill the
man. Quite apart from the fact that it was accepted
that French soldiers would plunder every town they
captured, it was certainly not the proper thing for an
officer to brawl with a private. Robert was also shouting in English, and that worried her more than anything. She tried to drag him off before they attracted a
crowd.

'Philippe!' she screamed, hauling on his shoulder and
hoping the use of his French name would bring him to
his senses. She was in danger of being struck by flying
fists, but she did not think of that.

'Philippe! Let him be!'

He became aware of her only when a blow intended
for his victim glanced off her cheek and she cried out.
He turned his back on the soldier, who scuttled away,
glad to escape from the clutches of the lunatic, and
took her in his arms.

'Olivia, what have I done?' He took her face in his
hands and surveyed it critically. There was a bright
pink spot on her cheek. He bent to kiss it. 'Oh, my
love, I would not hurt you for the world. I didn't see
you.'

'Nor heard me either,' she said, pretending not to
notice the endearment, telling herself that it was just
his way of saying sorry and meant nothing. 'I kept
shouting at you. You seemed like a madman. Have
you never seen a looter before?'

'Of course I have, but in Wellington's army it is a
crime which merits a flogging. The worst offenders are
hanged and left where everyone can see them.'

'But this is not Wellington's army, it is Napoleon's,
and you were screaming at him in English. We can
only pray he knew no language but French and thought
you were shouting in German. . .'

He took her arm, still looking grim, and together
they walked into the town centre where a great heap
of rubble was all that remained of the fine cathedral.

The castle had been damaged and the surrounding
houses had lost their roofs and windows. Olivia had
never seen such devastation. 'Don't you think we
should leave, while the situation here is so confused?'
she asked, convinced that the Portuguese would never
recover their fighting spirit after such a defeat. 'We
would not be missed immediately. If Wellington
decides to evacuate all his troops from the Peninsula,
you and I will be left high and dry. We should join him
before he embarks.'

'What makes you think he will want us?' It was a
strange question and she looked at him sharply but, as
usual, his rugged features gave nothing away. If only
he would talk to her about himself, tell her what was
eating his soul away, she might be able to help. More
than anything she wanted to understand what drove
him on.

'Why wouldn't he?' she demanded. 'We are English
and presumably he was glad of the dispatches you sent
him.' She turned to look him squarely in the eye. 'You
did tell him the truth?'

'That is not a question that deserves an answer and
if you doubt me that much, why do you stay? Go, if
you wish, go and tell him the truth yourself.' He did
not know why she continued to press him — he had
made himself perfectly clear; he would not go until he
had something worthwhile to take back, something not
even Rufus Whitely could take from him.

'How can I?' she demanded, meeting anger with
anger; it was part of her strategy, part of her fight
against falling in love with him, her defence, her
armour. But it was useless; she needed him and it was
not all to do with how she was going to get home.
Somehow that seemed to be losing its importance.
'Would you have me travel alone?'

'It was what you were doing when we met.'

'But, if you remember, we made a bargain.'

'That I would see you safely home if you took me

into Ciudad Rodrigo.' He could not suppress a smile at the memory of that encounter. 'But you have been given the opportunity many times and have always refused to go.' He laughed suddenly. 'What attraction do I have, that you cannot leave my side? I am not wealthy and my prospects are non-existent. And it cannot be my charm, for you have told me I do not have any.'

'That, at any rate, is true,' she said. 'But a bargain is a bargain.'

'Events have overtaken us, and why is it so necessary that I should go with you? Ask Captain Whitely if you want company.' He did not know why he mentioned the man's name; he would never allow Olivia to go anywhere with that snake. 'Where is the gallant captain? I have not seen him since. . .' He racked his brain. 'Where is he, Olivia?'

'I do not know.' She was equally puzzled by his reference. 'The last time I saw him, and that was only briefly, was when the *guerrilleros* were captured and shot. I saw him standing beside the officer in charge of the firing squad.' She paused, remembering what Rufus Whitely had told her. Had he completed his special assignment for Wellington and returned to his chief with his intelligence? Why did that not fill her with optimism? 'He may have escaped.'

'Broken his parole, you mean? Yes, I would not put that past him.'

'He would confirm the intelligence you sent, would he not?'

'Maybe.'

'Then you have nothing to fear by going back. You have surely vindicated yourself.'

He turned angrily from her, striding over to the edge of the ramparts to gaze out over the plain towards the west. There, between him and the sea, stood the British forces, his own regiment, his one-time comrades. What she asked was no more than he longed for himself, but he could not do it.

Olivia, watching him wrestling with himself, knew
now that she had lost the battle with herself; she could
no longer deny her love for him and would endure
anything to stay with him; home was wherever he was.
If he never knew it, no matter; it was enough to be
near him, to listen to his voice when they were alone
and he was free to talk, to share a joke and hear his
laughter, to watch him eat the food she had cooked, to
be there when he needed her, to know that he would
always look after her. Even to quarrel with him now
and again. She could envisage nothing coming between
them except the ghosts who haunted his dreams, who
reminded him of a past he seemed unable to put behind
him. She was powerless against that. But she would no
more admit defeat than the plucky Portuguese; their
faith could move mountains and so could hers.

They found a billet of two rooms in a house near one
of the bridges which was only slightly damaged, and
continued their masquerade, he as a loyal aide to
Colonel Clavier and she as his mouthpiece.

The usual problems presented themselves to the
occupying French forces: an even more resentful pop-
ulace — Portuguese now — and supply lines longer than
ever. The British forces had no such problems — they
had the sea at their backs and a navy that ruled the
world; they were as well supplied as the miserliness of
the British government would allow. Nor did they have
any trouble with the Portuguese, who looked to them
for salvation and willingly took their orders from the
British commander-in-chief. They had obeyed his command to pack up everything they could carry, destroy
everything which could not be moved and retreat with
him, leaving nothing behind for their conquerors. It
was weeks before Masséna was ready to march again
and by then he was undecided which route to take.

'The colonel told Madame Falaise that Wellington
has moved his headquarters back from Celerico to

Gouveia,' Olivia told Robert one day after meeting the colonel's mistress in the market. 'Is it true?'

He shrugged. 'If you can rely on French intelligence, yes, it is true.' He did not seem anything like as disappointed as she was at the news. Every time they moved a little nearer their own lines, the lines themselves receded.

'Will he never stand and fight?'

'In his own good time.' He was sitting on a battered old sofa which served as his bed at night and a seat during the day. On his lap he had a board on which he had spread a large sheet of paper and was drawing on it with a piece of charcoal. She put down the shopping she had just brought in and went to look over his shoulder. 'What are you drawing?'

'A map.'

'I can see that. What is it of and why are you doing it?'

'It is a map of the mountains north of the Mondego River.' He pointed to a line he had drawn. 'This is the road the French are going to take to advance into Portugal.'

'How do you know?'

'Because I shall put it into Colonel Clavier's head to advise the marshal that it is the one they should take.'

'Why should they take any notice of you?'

'Philippe Santerre fought in northern Portugal before, remember? He is supposed to know the terrain.' He turned his head to smile up at her, almost boyishly. 'They don't want to meet Nosey head-on, they want to come upon his flank. I have been asked to suggest a route and as my croaking attempts to talk annoy the colonel no end he has forbidden me to speak and demanded a map.'

'And is it accurate?' She was horrified to think that he had been attempting to talk.

'Of course it is accurate.'

She was angry with him. 'If you have to oblige them,

why can't you deceive them? It is tantamount to. . .'
She stopped speaking, unwilling to accuse him of
treachery again, but that was what it was. Having only
just decided she loved him and that his reasons for
what he did were patriotic, it was more than disap-
pointing to find all her old doubts returning. He was
impossible!

Unable to face another argument, she left him and
went for a walk in the town, trying to come to terms
with her own emotions, one minute full of certainty
that all would be well if she could only make him put
the past behind him and face up to the future, the next
tortured with doubts that he was still carrying on a
vendetta that only he knew about. If only there was
someone she could talk to about it, but there was no
one — no Father Peredo, no Don Santandos, no English
at all, except Governor Cox, and he was a prisoner of
war. Even Captain Whitely seemed to have disappeared, though whether she would have unburdened
herself to him she was not sure. There was something
about him she did not like. Perhaps it was because he
had spoken so ill of Robert. And perhaps that had
been justified; she did not want to think so.

She walked for hours, threading her way between
the ruined houses, past the rubble that marked the site
of the explosion, and along the ramparts. The weather
was hot, but a cooling breeze blew across the plain,
stirring the flattened cornfields, where a company of
soldiers were doing musket drill. She could hear the
distant shouts of command and then a volley of shots
which sent a flock of birds flapping skywards. The
approach roads were jammed with vehicles, guns and
limbers, supply wagons, loaded as far as the commissary had been able to load them, ready to move on.

Everywhere there were soldiers, some off duty,
others drilling, still more lining up for their meagre
rations. She was glad that Robert's position with the
colonel's staff meant that they had reasonable quarters

and the best of whatever food was available. There was
a high price to pay in the risks they took and she ought
not to make matters worse by quarrelling with him. If
only he would not do things which made it difficult for
her to keep silent; if only he would confide in her.

She heard a bugle call echoing round the city and,
knowing it signalled the call to resume the march, she
hurried back to their quarters. Robert had already left.
She put together their belongings, found Pegasus and
took her place at the end of the march.

The road, she soon realised, was tortuous to say the
least. Once over the plains, it wound through hills and
pine forests, over swiftly flowing streams and through
narrow passes. The long column, hampered by heavy
guns, caissons and wagons full of food and clothing,
moved painfully slowly. Stragglers were picked off by
the Ordenanza, an army of Portuguese militia called
up to defend their homeland. Every bit as determined
as the Spanish *guerrilleros*, they swooped down from
the hills, wearing loose breeches topped by short brown
cloaks and woollen caps and armed with the tools of
their trade — pruning knives and quince poles, sup-
plemented by old blunderbusses and captured muskets.
Masséna refused to recognise them as real soldiers and
had them executed if they were caught.

It was mid-September by the time the column
reached Viseu, a town surrounded by lofty pines where
a network of roads met like the spokes of a wheel, and
by that time the rear of the column, where Olivia rode
Pegasus alongside the wagons and the walking women
and children, was a whole day behind its head.

As soon as the column was halted, everyone scattered to find firewood and began cooking, and Olivia
rode on to find Robert, expecting him, as usual, to
have found them a billet. She had rarely come to a
night stop without having somewhere to sleep, even if
he himself slept outside with the men. His first action,

when freed of his duties, was always to look after her,
even when she was at her most provocative.

Viseu was a very ancient city, full of winding alleys
and little squares with narrow little houses interspersed
with the splendid mansions of its wealthy citizens.
Olivia rode through the mêlée of soldiers which filled
the place to overflowing, to where she could see a knot
of senior officers in conversation on the edge of the
main square.

Old Masséna was there, together with his mistress
dressed as a light dragoon, the red-headed Marshal
Ney, Reynier and Foy, the deranged General Junot,
Colonel Clavier and sundry aides. The colonel was red-
faced and sweating and waving his arms about, looking
as though he was about to burst out of his coat; his
seniors were obviously giving him a hard time over
something. Robert was nowhere to be seen and, not
daring to approach such illustrious company and
enquire after him, she dismounted to look about her
and it was then she saw Rufus Whitely, standing in the
background watching and listening.

Still in civilian dress, though he had changed his
brown tweed coat for a blue serge one, he looked
completely relaxed, as he smiled and put a finger to his
lips to warn her not to betray him. Where had he been
in the last few weeks? Why had he come back? Olivia
began to feel uneasy and wished Robert would put in
an appearance. Holding Pegasus by the bridle, she
scanned the mass of blue-uniformed men moving about
the square looking for the tall figure of Robert.

'The colonel has ordered his arrest.' Rufus had
moved on silent feet to stand beside her.

She spun round to face him, anxiety etched on every
line of her face. 'He has found out?'

'Not yet.' His smile annoyed her. 'But he will. Soon
now. Here they come.'

A path was being made between the ranks of the
men, and through it came Robert, flanked by two

sergeants armed with rifles. He was without his
sword — its scabbard hung empty on his thigh — and he
was wearing his best uniform; the trousers were white
enough to dazzle and the well-tailored blue coat with
its white cross belts, red tail facings and fringed epaul-
ettes emphasised his narrow waist and broad shoulders.
He looked straight ahead, head erect, back stiff, and
came to attention in front of the colonel.

Carefully, very carefully, she eased the rifle out of
its sling on the saddle of her horse and inched her way
forward, feeling in the folds of her skirt for the pistol
she always carried in her pocket. Two weapons were
all they had, two weapons, but they could do some
damage with them before they died. Masséna would
make the first target and one of the marshals would be
next. If God gave them a chance to reload, then others
would follow and they would go down fighting.

'Well?' the colonel said, stepping forward and standing only two paces from Robert, blocking him off from
her view; all she could see was the plume on his shako,
which hardly moved as he stood rigidly to attention.
'What have you to say for yourself, Captain Santerre?
Of all the Satan-made roads there are in Portugal you
had to show us the worst.'

Do not speak, Olivia begged silently. Please, Robert,
do not speak now.

'Acting dumb will not serve,' the colonel went on. 'I
know you can talk. People have heard you. Monsieur
Whitely, here, has heard you.' He jerked his thumb
over his shoulder to where Rufus stood, smiling easily.
'Is that not so, *monsieur*?'

Rufus moved forward to stand beside the colonel.
'Indeed and the language he speaks is English. He is
an English deserter.'

Olivia held her breath as Robert uttered an oath and
took a pace forward, his fists raised. Whitely backed
away as the sergeants seized Robert's arms and held
him. Olivia told herself to keep cool as she moved

round to come into his line of vision. All eyes were on
Rufus and no one noticed her.

'His name is Robert Lynmount,' Rufus went on
loudly enough for everyone in the vicinity to hear,
most of whom had been stood down and had just
finished stacking their arms and were on their way to
their billets or camp fires. 'He is the son of Viscount
Lynmount, a British politician — not that his father
wants to know him now.' He had the attention of
everyone including the knot of senior commanders who
had drawn closer. 'He has been disowned for the
disgrace he has brought to the family name, cut off
without a penny. He was drummed out of his regiment
and because he dared not go home he has taken on the
identity of a valiant French officer, an officer who died
in the service of his country. This man is not interested
in fighting for his own country or France either. His
only concern is plunder; he does not care who wins the
war as long as he comes out of it the richer.'

The colonel's bulbous eyes were almost popping out
of his head at this. It was obvious he was reluctant to
believe he had been so easily duped. He tried to move
away from his senior officers and put them out of
earshot. Whitely stood, with his legs apart, pointing at
Robert. 'Viscount Wellington has denounced him; he
has said you will be doing him a service if you execute
him.'

A low murmuring began among the watchers, like
the incoming tide, eddying back and forth, growing
louder with each surge. Their anger terrified Olivia,
the more so because she felt that, in some respects, it
was justified. What Whitely had said was true; Robert
had never denied being cashiered though she had never
been told the reason.

'All for a woman,' Whitely said, then smiled as he
added, 'a woman he wronged.'

'Where is she?' Robert asked, through gritted teeth.

'What have you done with her? If you have harmed her. . .'

'Juana?' Whitely laughed. 'She is in Salamanca. As soon as I have seen you dispatched to hell, I shall join her there.'

Olivia tugged on Pegasus's reins to pull him forward. Robert glanced across and saw her for the first time and almost winced. If anything was needed to confirm that Whitely spoke the truth, it was that look; it was almost as if he recognised her as one of his accusers. But what could she accuse him of? Treason? She had no right to level that at him. Loving someone too much? That was no crime. Pride? Vengeance? Greed? But this was no time for guessing games. She walked forward, knowing her own head was in the noose along with his, if she failed.

'*Cochon*!' she spat at him. 'To think I trusted you, let you wear my husband's uniform, cooked for you and cleaned for you. I am a loyal Frenchwoman, you knew that. You said you would help us to beat the British. Liar!'

His startled look was almost comical, but she dared not smile. She continued her tirade, moving closer, still hauling Pegasus after her. 'I hate you for what you have done to me.' She turned to survey the audience, assessing where everyone stood, how far it was to the nearest cover, who still had weapons and who was unarmed. 'He tricked me.'

She heard a single handclap and allowed herself a quick glance to where Rufus Whitely stood applauding. 'A fine performance,' he said in English. 'But I doubt it will save you.'

Her answer was to throw Robert the rifle and fling herself on her horse's back, pointing her pistol at Marshal Masséna. 'Try to stop us and he dies,' she shouted, as Robert leapt up behind her, kicking his heels into the animal's sides and driving him through the mass of French soldiers.

Taken by surprise, no one moved for several seconds
and by that time they were in the crowd and it was
impossible for anyone to fire without hitting their own
people. Pegasus forced a way through by sheer momen-
tum and they were halfway to the corner of the square
where a large building jutted out when the first bullets
spattered around them. If they could reach that corner,
then it was up to Pegasus to save them. She could not
fire for fear of hitting Robert.

He discharged the rifle and then grabbed her weapon
and fired that too. The shadow of the building loomed
up. 'Come on, old fellow!' she murmured, lying low
over the animal's neck. 'You can do it!'

She heard running feet behind her and more shots
and then a cry from Robert. A swift glance behind her
told her that he had been hit, but she could not stop.
He grabbed her waist and hung on as the flying horse
carried them onwards, through the town gate and on
into the pine forests. Only then dared she pull up. The
horse shuddered to a standstill, and Robert, losing his
grip, slid to the ground.

CHAPTER EIGHT

OLIVIA slid off the horse's back and knelt beside Robert. There was blood in his hair and on his forehead. She carefully lifted aside the curl that fell over his face and examined the wound. A bullet had grazed his temple, cutting a gash from the corner of his eye to the top of his ear. It was enough to produce a great deal of blood but it had not penetrated more than skin deep. She breathed a huge sigh of relief and pulled a handkerchief from her skirt pocket to staunch the flow, before tearing a strip from the bottom of her petticoat to bind it. She was amused to see that he was wearing his old red coat beneath the blue one and understood why; if he was going to face a firing squad, then he would be in his proper uniform.

'This is no time to faint,' she said to his unconscious form, her asperity hiding her concern. 'Wake up, Robert, wake up. We are not safe yet.'

He stirred and blinked. He had a blinding headache and his vision was blurred. He could see nothing but dark shapes and then a lighter one which resolved itself into a face, though it was not clear enough to recognise. The voice he did recognise. 'What happened?' he asked. 'I can't see you properly.'

'It's only temporary.' She prayed that was true. 'Can you stand?'

'Of course I can stand.' He sat up. 'God, I'm dizzy.' He touched his bandaged forehead gingerly. 'How bad is it?'

'Not bad at all,' she said cheerfully. 'It is only a graze. Come, let me help you up. We must go on before they come after us.'

'They?'

'We have the whole French army on our tail. Don't you remember?'

'I remember being marched across a square and thinking, This is it, this is the end, and worrying about you.'

'Me?' She was sure he was confusing her with a past love, because it was for Juana he had been concerned when Captain Whitely denounced him. Did he remember any of that? Who was Juana? It was not the time to torment her brain with such questions; that could come later. She stood up and bent to haul him to his feet. 'Come, we must move on.'

'Where are we?'

'In the woods outside Viseu. Any time now the whole place will be alive with voltigeurs searching for us. We must find somewhere to hide; we haven't a hope of outrunning them on one horse.'

She left him to fetch Pegasus, who was contentedly cropping the undergrowth a little way off. By the time she led him back, Robert had staggered to his feet. A little colour had returned to his face and his eyes were clearer. He might be a little concussed, but she could not wait to find out; she moved forward to help him mount. He brushed aside her assistance and climbed into the saddle, then reached down to pull her up behind him. She hesitated, but their pursuers were already in the wood; she could hear them crashing through the trees. She grasped his hand and hauled herself up behind him and, almost before she could settle herself with her arms around him, he had dug his heels into Pegasus to make him gallop.

There were shouts behind them and a few bullets whizzed through the pines, very wide of the mark. 'They can't hit a barn door at twenty paces with those weapons,' she laughed, leaning her head against the roughness of his coat. 'And there isn't a horse in their stables can beat Pegasus.'

He did not answer, still feeling somewhat fuddled by

his injury and bemused by his rescue. It was just the sort of foolhardy ploy she would attempt. It had been mad enough to succeed too, if only they could keep ahead of their pursuers long enough to lose them in the depths of the forest. But the ground was uneven and, with the onset of night, black as pitch; they would risk laming the horse if they continued. 'For our mount's sake, we had better walk a while,' he said, pulling the animal up and throwing his leg over the front of the saddle to dismount.

She jumped down beside him. 'If we left the trees, we might be able to see where we are going. For all we know we may have been going round in circles.'

'I think not; we have been going steadily uphill.'

'You think we can climb the mountain?'

'There might be a pass.'

'Then let us press on.'

He picked up the reins with one hand and took her hand with the other and they walked on, still going uphill. There was silence behind them, except for the sounds of the night, a scuffling in the undergrowth, an owl, the distant howling of a wolf which made her shudder; their pursuers seemed to have given up. He gripped her hand tighter to reassure her, but said nothing.

She looked towards him, but there was nothing so dark as a forest at night and all she could see was his dark outline. What was he thinking about? Had he remembered the accusations Whitely had made? Was he as puzzled as she was by them? Why should a man who purported to be a British agent denounce a fellow Englishman? Who was the patriot and who the traitor? Could they both be loyal? Could they both be traitors? If only she knew the truth! But what difference would it make? Would it make her love Robert any less or respect Captain Whitely any more?

'How do you feel?' she asked. 'Does your head still ache?'

'A little.'

'Do you remember what happened now?'

He chuckled. 'You threw me a rifle. I remember catching it and riding hell for leather.'

'Do you remember why?'

'Rufus Whitely,' he said suddenly.

'Yes, he had quite a lot to say.' Then, unable to remain silent on something which had been occupying her thoughts the whole time they had been riding, she added, 'Who is Juana?'

'Juana?' he repeated sharply. 'What do you know of her?'

'Whitely said that you had wronged her.'

'That is a lie!' He almost flung her hand from him, making her stumble. 'Do you make a habit of believing everyone but me?'

She recovered her footing and plodded on. 'You have never even mentioned her before; there was nothing for me to believe or disbelieve. Still, if you wish to have your little secrets, why should I care? It is no concern of mine.'

'You are right,' he said. 'It is no concern of yours.'

'I don't know why I took the trouble to save you,' she said, angry now. 'I should have let them shoot you.'

'It would have been simpler,' he said flatly. 'Except that you would have died along with me. It was a sorry tale you told; I have heard you tell much better.'

'And for what?' She was really into her stride now and uncaring what she said; dispensing vitriol dulled the hurt. 'I did what I did because I thought it might help us to go home. We are as far from that goal as ever.'

'Home!' he said bitterly. 'You heard what the man said. My father has disowned me. There is no going back. I knew that when I rode out of Lisbon.'

'Then why did you promise to take me back? Why make a pledge you had no intention of keeping?'

'I meant it when I made it. I thought. . .' He stopped, remembering how he had felt at the time — fury at the injustice, a determination to make everyone eat their words, desire for revenge, most, but not all of which had been dissipated by Olivia, who had shown him how to live again and how to laugh at adversity — especially how to laugh. 'Never mind what I thought.'

'You thought you could mitigate your disgrace. Regain your claws, I think was how you put it. That has not changed.'

'It was a foolish idea.' He tugged on the horse's reins and Pegasus followed obediently. 'I should have known how impossible it was. I should have known it even before Captain Rufus Whitely turned up. I said he would give us away, didn't I? He bargained our lives for his.'

'I don't understand,' she said, calmer now. What was the good of fighting when she had no idea what she was up against? If he loved someone else. . . Better not think about it, better to concentrate on getting out of the scrape they were in. It was her own fault anyway; he had not asked her to fall in love with him. 'He told me he belonged to British Intelligence,' she said. 'He said he was working for Viscount Wellington. If that was true, why did he denounce you? You would not have betrayed him, would you?'

He laughed aloud, making some small animal in the undergrowth scuttle away in alarm. 'You believed him?'

'Why not? When I met him before, he was working for the government.'

He stopped abruptly and turned to face her. She could see nothing of his features and wondered if his head was still bleeding and if he was still stupefied by his injury; it would account for his bad temper.

'Government?' he queried, putting his hand on her arm to detain her. 'Who told you that?'

'He did, and I must suppose he had some sort of

authorisation because Papa believed it. He showed him the rockets.'

'Rockets?'

'Must you echo everything I say, or has that blow to the head deafened you as well as addled your brains?'

'What rockets?' His grip on her arm was painful and she pulled herself away and stumbled over a tree root. He reached out and gathered her into his arms to save her. 'I am sorry, Olivia.' His voice had lost its hard edge and become gentle; it made it even more difficult for her to deal with him. Anger she could answer with anger, suspicion with suspicion, but tenderness was something she had no armour against. 'I am sorry I have been such a disappointment to you,' he said, holding her against his broad chest and laying his cheek on her soft hair. 'But now I must know everything.'

She sighed and allowed her head to rest on his shoulder; he was so strong, a bullet did no more than graze him, and she needed his strength because she felt weak as a kitten. 'There is not much to tell. Papa gave him a demonstration of the rockets.' She laughed suddenly, leaning back to look up at him. 'They were a dismal failure, flying everywhere but where they were meant to go, but Mr Whitely seemed impressed. He said the Horse Guards was still interested and would commission their use once the tests had proved satisfactory. Papa was still working on them when I left England.' She paused. 'That was the last time I saw Mr Whitely until Ciudad Rodrigo.'

'That was when he told you he was a British agent?'

'No, later, after the battle of the bridge.'

'Why didn't you tell me?'

'I gave my word not to.'

'Did you never doubt him?'

'I had no reason to.'

'But you doubted me.'

There was no satisfactory answer to that and they resumed walking, picking their way along a track which she supposed the locals used. If that was the case, it must lead somewhere.

'He has to be stopped,' he said, more to himself than to her. 'He is the traitor, not me. He is selling information to the French about those rockets, I'll lay odds.'

'He said he was on a special assignment for Viscount Wellington. He said the whole conduct of the war depended on his success. He said I could help him.'

He gave a grunt of wry amusement. 'Success, yes, but French success, not ours. He must have been considerably put out to find me in the French camp. He could not let me return to our own lines to let the cat out of the bag.' He paused. 'Of course, he could have killed me, made it look as though I had fallen in battle, there are opportunities enough for that, but it was better to denounce me; it gave him more credibility with his French paymasters.'

She felt uncomfortably guilty that she had told Rufus Whitely that Robert was masquerading as a French officer; it would have been much better if he had believed him to be a deserter and, therefore, not a threat to him. 'Do you think he has been sending false information back to Wellington, acting the double agent?'

'Very possibly.'

'Now, of course, you will have to return,' she said, almost triumphantly. 'You will have to report the facts.'

'Someone else can do that.'

'Who?' She paused in her stride to look at him. All she could see were the whites of his eyes and his teeth, and she knew he was smiling. 'Oh, no,' she said. 'You do not get rid of me like that. And, besides, who will believe me?'

He laughed. 'If Clavier can believe your tall tales, then Viscount Wellington will believe you when you tell the truth. I will give you letters. . .'

'No. You must come too.'

'I have other things to do.'

'What? What is more important than reporting a spy?' She stopped as she realised what he had in mind. 'Oh, I see, you are going to Salamanca.'

'Salamanca?'

'There you go again, repeating everything I say like a parrot. Isn't that where Juana is?'

He laughed suddenly. 'If I didn't know you better I would say you were jealous.'

'What have I to be jealous of?' she retorted. 'We mean nothing to each other, do we? A chance encounter, that's all it was, an opportunity taken to be useful to each other, and it seems to me I have fulfilled my side of our bargain but you have yet to fulfil yours.' For the first time that he could remember, there was no humour in her laughter. 'But pray do not let me detain you. Go to your Juana. I wish you joy. I can find my own way home. That, as you said, was what I was doing when we met, and nothing has changed. Nothing.'

She turned from him and stumbled through the trees, fighting her tears. A moment later, she returned and snatched the horse's reins. 'I'll take Pegasus; he was given to me. You can walk.' She threw herself on the horse's back and sent him cantering through the darkness.

She was not sure but she thought she heard him laughing, and that was enough to increase her fury. The situation was most assuredly not funny and he was a fool if he thought she would go back after that. Let him find his Spanish love; she did not want him. She did not want any man. Had she not decided to remain a widow, to go back to Papa and comfort him in his old age, to stay at home and try to be the gentlewoman? She would forget the man whose laughter echoed in her ears. Forget him! Forget him!

Blinded by tears, she had no idea where Pegasus was

taking her and he was in danger of stumbling if she continued. Her concern for her horse brought her to a stop. She slid from his back and stood leaning against him with her head in his sturdy neck, weeping oceans into his long mane.

Footsteps behind her made her spin round. He had come to find her; he was not the heartless knave she had thought him to be. 'Robert, I. . .'

A hand was clapped over her mouth and her arms were forced behind her, so that she could neither move without pain, nor cry out. 'I am sorry to disappoint you,' said a voice. 'But I did tell you not to trust that rogue, didn't I? Let you down, has he? Deserted you? He won't come back, you know.'

There was someone else with him because other hands were tying something tightly across her mouth, choking her. Then, in spite of her struggles, they bound her hands behind her back.

'Put her on her horse,' Rufus Whitely said.

She was lifted bodily and set astride Pegasus and the horse was led off with the men either side. Where was Robert? Had he heard the scuffle? How much distance had she covered since she left him? Why did he not rescue her? She had saved him from a greater force than two men, she had saved him from a whole regiment, so why could he not do the same for her? He would come, she told herself as she struggled to keep her seat; he would take them by surprise and she would be ready to do her bit, even if her hands were bound.

After a little while they came to a clearing where their horses were tethered. Olivia remained tense and listening as they mounted and led her back the way they had come. Robert had still not put in an appearance when dawn lightened the sky above the distant peaks and she was led into Viseu. She knew then that he was not going to rescue her. What a fool she had been to expect he would!

The army was preparing to resume its march; a bugle

was sounding the call to muster, horses were being harnessed and wagons tied down, but she did not doubt that time would be found for an execution before they moved. It would not take long to detail a firing squad. She resigned herself to the inevitable.

In the town centre, they came to a halt. Colonel Clavier was just coming out of his billet, strapping on his sword belt, and walking towards a horse being held by a groom at the roadside. An aide followed, carrying his plumed hat for him, ready to hand it up when he mounted. Behind them, Madame Falaise appeared, sumptuously dressed in pink satin and a matching turban whose sweeping peacock feather brushed her rouged cheek. At least, Olivia thought with a wry smile, I have escaped her fate.

Whitely led Pegasus forward. 'One down and one to go, Colonel,' he said.

Colonel Clavier looked her up and down and his lip curled. 'I never thought I would say it, but I would rather have the man.'

Whitely laughed. 'This one is more of a man than the other.'

Olivia, whose legs were free in order to ride, kicked out at him. He grabbed her foot and nearly unseated her. 'It was meant as a compliment, my dear.' He turned to the colonel. 'Lynmount will return. He will walk in on his own, I promise you.'

She tried to speak but the gag prevented her from doing more than mumbling. He reached across and untied it. 'Now, my dear, were you about to say he would not be such a fool as to come back?' He smiled. 'But I know the Honourable Robert Lynmount; I have known him since we were boys, when he lived in the big house and I lived at the rectory. His life is ruled by his notion of chivalry. I cannot afford that luxury.' He gave a bark of derision. 'He will be back.'

'That is not what you said when you tied me up.'

'No, but I wanted to stop you struggling or crying

out.' He turned back to the colonel. 'With your permission, sir, I will bait the hook.'

Colonel Clavier nodded without speaking, took his hat from the aide and clapped it on his head, then walked his horse to the head of his troops. Behind him a drummer boy, no more than a dozen years old, wearing a cocked hat which seemed to swamp him, began to beat out the rhythm of the march. Rufus Whitely stood watching the front ranks as they left the square, then turned his horse away, leading Pegasus and the helpless Olivia to the rear. There was to be no execution.

He took her to one of the canteens on wheels looked after by a huge pipe-smoking Frenchwoman, whose muscular ability was notorious among the camp followers; the women were all afraid of her and so were most of the men. They paid her inflated prices for wine and tobacco without a murmur. 'Jeanne!' he called. 'I have brought you a fare-paying passenger.'

The woman poked her head out between the canvas flaps at the back of the wagon and surveyed Olivia, from her tousled curls, over her trim figure to her scuffed boots and then feasted her eyes on the magnificent animal she rode. The girl was obviously as poor as a church mouse but the grey was worth a fortune to an army where good mounts were almost impossible to come by. She took the evil-smelling pipe from her mouth. 'I'll have the stallion,' she said.

'You shall have it,' he said equably. 'At the end of the march.'

'What good is that?' she demanded. 'The officers need horses now. Two days from now they might all be dead.'

'And so might you.' He dismounted, led Pegasus up to the tailboard of the wagon and hoisted Olivia out of the saddle and on to it. 'Five hundred francs now and the horse later.'

'I'd rather have gold.' She gave a cracked laugh. ''Tis a better currency.'

'Very well.' He tied Pegasus to the back of the wagon. 'He is to stay there, do you hear?'

'Are you crazy? That's just asking to be robbed; he'll have to be hidden.'

'No, he is to stay there. I want him seen. I want him seen *easily*.'

'If you think that will lure Captain Lynmount, you are very much mistaken,' Olivia said, guessing what he intended. 'Why do you think I was alone when you found me? We had parted, parted forever. He was going. . .'

'Just where did he say he was going?'

She hesitated and he yanked on her bonds, making her cry out in pain. 'It were better you told me.'

She was silent, prepared to endure the suffering if it meant her enemies expended valuable resources trying to find the Englishman, and especially if it put Rufus Whitely out of favour with his paymasters.

'No matter,' he said. Then to Jeanne, 'Tie her to the wagon and keep a close eye on her. She is artful, and resourceful, so watch her like a hawk.'

'And you?' the woman asked.

'Oh, I shall not be far away.'

He rode away chuckling to himself. Jeanne watched him go and then turned to do as he had asked. Olivia was tied securely to one of the iron hoops supporting the canvas of the wagon, and almost immediately they set off in the wake of the march.

The wagon, she discovered, was not only a mobile store for dispensing wine and tobacco, it was a cache for loot—gold and silver plate, jewellery, clocks, mirrors, even carpets. It was piled so high behind the normal stock, the vehicle was twice as heavy as it should have been and decidedly unstable. That was why it needed four mules to pull it and why they frequently found themselves losing touch with the rear of the column. On these occasions, Whitely would ride back — on Robert's horse, Olivia noted — and urge Jeanne and the half-starved mules to go faster.

Olivia did not know why he continued to hold her prisoner, to feed her and have her adding weight to the already overburdened wagon; Robert was obviously not going to attempt a rescue and it would have been easier simply to have shot her and been done with the inconvenience. Even more she could not understand why the French themselves allowed her to live. When she put the question to Whitely one day, he laughed. 'They think you are my mistress. Why do you think I keep returning to visit you?'

'But you have a mistress, or a wife, I am not sure which.' He had tied Thor to the wagon and joined her on the tailboard where they sat with their feet dangling over the side. From the outside she looked perfectly free to come and go and only from the inside could anyone see the rope around her waist which tied her to the structure. Pegasus was still roped to the back, plodding close enough to where she sat for her to be able to stretch out a hand now and again to give him a pat. When Rufus was not there, she found the companionship of the animal comforting.

'I do?' He looked surprised.

'Juana. You said she was waiting for you in Salamanca.'

He threw back his head and laughed. 'Yes. The bitch went off with a Spanish nobleman who has thrown in his lot with the new regime.'

'Then why did you say she was waiting for you?' Curiosity drove her to speak civilly to him, though she had earlier decided to maintain a cool silence. Robert would have been amused by that; he would have said keeping quiet was impossible for her and he would have been right.

'To goad Lynmount, why else?'

'Tell me what happened. Why was he cashiered?'

'He never told you?'

'No.'

'He was court-martialled for looting.'

'Looting?' She found that hard to believe. 'But Robert despises looters. Why, he nearly killed a soldier in Almeida for it.'

He smiled. 'It's understandable, my dear, when you know the facts.'

'Tell me.'

'He was caught plundering a flour mill. The flour had already been bought and paid for by the army for the troops, so it was doubly serious.'

'Why was he doing it?'

'For Juana. She was seventeen, olive-skinned, with sleek black hair and huge dark eyes. The fool was in love with her, still is. He and her brothers were caught red-handed. They had a cart outside the mill loaded with sacks. There was no defence and he did not offer one. He will never return to England. His father really has cut him off without a penny.'

It seemed incredible. Had Robert regretted what he had done; was that why he wanted to regain his claws? Or had the dreadful accusations Whitely made been true — Robert did not care who won the war? Was he still in love with the faithless Juana? Had he gone to Salamanca to find her? She ought to be furious that he had kept so much from her but all she could feel was an overwhelming pity.

'But you said Juana was waiting for you, not Robert.'

He laughed grimly. 'Juana waits for no one, especially one as impoverished as I was; she could not wait for me to make my fortune.' He glanced into the back of the wagon as he spoke and she realised that most of the loot was his. He could hardly blame Robert for taking food when he had thousands of pounds' worth of stolen luxuries. 'And, unlike our friend Lynmount, I have no prospects of a title.' He smiled, a twisted, secretive smile. 'Unless a grateful country rewards me with one.'

'You mean you really are a British agent?'

He turned and held up his hands, palms towards her. 'I swear to you, as an officer and a gentleman, that I have been sent here by Viscount Wellington.'

'Then it is true.'

'I said it was, did I not?'

'But the contents of the wagon are your plunder. How can you condemn Robert. . .?'

'I did not condemn him, a court-martial did that and, besides, taking from your enemies is very different from stealing from your allies. Even you should be able to see that. Every action that deprives the French of any of the means to wage war is a patriotic action, is it not?'

She laughed. 'You are plausible, I give you that.'

'But do you belive me?' He turned and pulled aside the canvas of the wagon to shout to Jeanne. 'You are dropping behind again, woman. Do you want those wild Portuguese to swoop down on us? Get a move on.'

'It would help if you got off,' she shouted back, whipping up the mules. 'And the girl. Walk a bit, can't you?'

He looked at Olivia. She seemed relaxed and at ease, friendly almost, and he was inclined to trust her, especially after what he had told her. 'Do you want to walk?'

'Can't I ride Pegasus?' She reached out and pulled a grey ear affectionately and was rewarded with a whinny. 'He needs exercise.'

'Then I shall exercise him later.' He laughed. 'Do you think I am a fool?'

'Very well, let us walk.'

He untied her and threw the rope into the back of the wagon before leaping down and holding out his hands to help her. She jumped down unaided but had not realised how cramped she had been; her knees buckled and he had to hold her upright.

He did not immediately release her. 'You know,' he said softly, looking down at the brown cotton dress, 'beneath that grimy garment there lurks a very beautiful woman.' He pushed aside the collar of the dress, revealing the depth of her throat and a little of the curving white flesh which promised paradise for the man who could plunder it. 'But this time I do not have to envy the Honourable Robert; I have you and he does not.'

'Let me go!'

He laughed. 'What can you do if I do not?'

'I shall scream. I shall denounce you as a British agent.'

'Would that be a patriotic thing to do, my dear?' He held her shoulders in his hands, caressing them with his thumbs, gradually moving aside the thin cloth which covered them. 'We should both die and then the Peer would not receive his intelligence.'

She stood rigidly to attention, neither submitting nor fighting him off, knowing that in a physical battle she was almost bound to lose. She could not understand how the British commander-in-chief could trust such a man; he was too smooth, too cocksure, too conceited for words. But did such things matter in war, if he was the best man for the task in hand? And he was right; betraying him would be betraying her country. She had to think of something else.

She glanced at Pegasus. Could she reach him? How far would she get before someone put a bullet in her back? Not far, she decided; the road was narrow and the ground on either side was steep and afforded little cover except rocks and gorse bushes, enough to hide someone on foot but not a galloping horse and rider.

'You said once that I could help you,' she said, then added quickly, 'With your work.'

'Are you serious?'

'Never more so.'

'I will think about it.' He looked up to see the wagon disappearing over the brow of a hill. He grabbed her hand and dragged her after it. 'Why didn't she shout?' he demanded, referring to Jeanne. 'We could have been left behind.' Being left behind was almost as good as a death sentence to the French columns; they always kept nose to tail the whole way, for fear of ambush.

They caught up with the wagon on the next incline and the big woman pulled the mules up and waited for them to climb aboard. Rufus felt confident enough of Olivia not to tie her up again, but they were still some way behind the rest of the column and he clambered forward to take the reins and hurry the beasts. Jeanne settled herself in the back on a pile of clothing and sat puffing at her pipe, regarding Olivia through the smoke.

'Decided to come round, eh?' she said. 'Thought you might. He's not so bad as long as you do as he says. He pays me well.'

'To look after his loot.'

'That, and other things. Letters and things. . .'

'Are you an agent too?' Olivia asked in surprise. She had heared about spies who disguised themselves so that even their own mothers would not know them but, as far as she knew, the woman had been with the regiment for years; it was the only home she had.

Jeanne's answer was a cackling laugh and a tap on the side of the nose with a dirty fingernail. 'That would be telling.'

The more Olivia learned, the more confused she became. It was no good trying to unravel it, she decided; there were too many people who were experts at deception. She had to escape. If she could find her way back to the British lines, she could ask Wellington himself for the truth, and maybe she could tell him a thing or two he did not know himself. Did he, for instance, know the French were coming from Viseu, the worst road in the whole kingdom, according to Colonel Clavier? Did he know they were expecting the army of the south under Marshal Soult to join up with them and that the whole might of the French army was poised for a decisive push to rid the Peninsula of him and his leopards?

If Whitely was truly a British agent, then he did know, but if Whitely was a traitor, if he was sending false information, as Robert had said he was, then she had to do something about it herself. Robert either would not or could not help and, besides, she had no idea where he was.

She listened to the quiet rumble of the cart's wheels, the clip-clop of the mules' tread on the hard road, the soft breathing of the two horses trotting side by side at the rear and wondered exactly where they were. How close behind the column were they? Where was the nearest village? Most important of all, where were the British and Portuguese forces?

The answer to her last question seemed to be 'very close at hand' because the silence was suddenly shattered by musket fire.

'Ordenanza!' Whitely shouted, whipping the mules in a frenzy. 'Hold on!'

The mules set off in a crazy gallop, dragging the loaded wagon all over the road. It careered from side to side, threatening to topple over, as he endeavoured to catch up with the rear of the column where there was safety in numbers. The two horses at the back were pulled willy-nilly this way and that and whinnied their protests. Olivia crawled to the tailboard to try and release them.

Now, she told herself, now is the time. If you are going, go now. She reached out to untie the horses but Jeanne, who had gone to the front to look over Whitely's shoulder, came back and saw what she was doing. She slapped her face and dragged her back into the wagon. 'No, you don't, my beauty. That horse is mine and I'm not about to let you take it.'

A bullet whistled through the canvas, leaving a neat little hole on each side of the wagon. Both women flung themselves to the floor. More bullets splattered round them, some hitting the woodwork and others breaking the wine bottles. The red liquid ran out and dripped between the floorboards. A mirror shattered. Jeanne's ability to curse was as legendary as her strength and she gave vent to her feelings with a string of oaths which went on, without her once repeating herself, for several minutes. The main thrust of her annoyance was not that she might be killed, though that seemed very likely, but that she was losing her valuable stock.

She scrambled up and made her way forward in the swaying vehicle to take over the reins. 'I'll drive,' she said. 'You shoot back; at least that might keep their heads down until we get in among the other wagons.'

'I am unarmed,' he said, bringing his whip crashing down on the lead mule. 'I came to court a lady, not make war.'

'Fool!' she screamed at him. 'Fool!'

A sound made her turn back. Olivia had succeeded in untying both horses. She had let Thor run loose, but she was using all her strength to hang on to the reins of Pegasus. She stood on the furthest part of the tailboard, ready to jump. With a scream of fury, Jeanne hurtled towards her, just as she managed to haul the horse alongside and launch herself into the air.

The crazed animal galloped past the wagon and on up the road, with Olivia struggling to pull herself into the saddle. The gunfire was being returned by the voltigeurs who defended the supply wagons, now halted and grouped in a defensive circle a little ahead of her. Pegasus had his head; she could neither steer him nor stop him. She could hear the attackers whooping as they ran from cover to cover, firing as they went,

but strangely the bullets seemed to pass her by. Even
while she struggled—she had one foot in a stirrup now
and was at least in the saddle—she recalled Robert's
comment about her guardian angel. Stay with me, she
commanded it; the Ordenanza could not know she was
their friend.

The horse took an enormous leap over a makeshift
barricade and she found herself inside the circle. There
was nowhere else to go; he shuddered to a halt,
breathing heavily and covered in a lather of sweat. 'Get
down!' someone shouted at her. 'Do you want to make
dead meat?'

She slid to the ground and turned to look for cover.
All around her, defenders were crouching behind the
barricades, firing at the rocky hillside where a flash or
a puff of smoke told them where their attackers were
hidden. Rufus had turned Jeanne's wagon and now it
was careering back down the hill it had toiled so hard
to climb. Was that the action of a brave Englishman?
she wondered. The Ordenanza were his allies, not his
enemies; he could surely convince them who he was.
A voltigeur thrust a musket into her hand. 'You know
how to load?'

'I think so.' She did not want to help them defeat the
Portuguese partisans; she fumbled with the powder and
dropped the shot. When he found her on her knees,
pretending to look for it, he grabbed the weapon back
from her. 'Women!' he said, making her smile. 'You
would at least expect them to learn how to load a gun.'

She looked about her. The wagons were all canteens
or food and clothing carts, none held ammunition, and
the French were suffering heavy casualties; she knew
they could not hold out much longer. The partisans,
firing from the rocky hillside which rose on either side
of the road, must have realised this too; they stormed
from their hiding places and advanced pell-mell down
the steep incline, while others behind them kept up the

fusillade to cover them. The voltigeurs, out of ammunition, threw down their arms.

More Ordenanza appeared from nowhere with blackened faces and wide grins. They herded the survivors into a tight group and waited for their leader to tell them what to do next.

One of them had decided that Robert's loose horse was a prize worth catching and was walking towards it, arm outstretched. He was exceptionally tall and well-built for a partisan, most of whom were small, undernourished men, and there was something about his bearing which was familiar to Olivia—more than familiar, loved. In a dream she moved away from the huddled circle of prisoners, waiting in terror to learn their fate, and walked slowly out on to the road to meet him. He had not gone to Salamanca. He had not gone home either. He was here.

He had succeeded in catching the horse and was leading it towards her. Except that he was dressed in the rough clothing of the Ordenanza and had a thin red scar running from his left eye to his ear, he looked no different from the man with whom she had galloped out of Viseu. She stopped and waited for him to come up to her, wondering if he had known she was with the column.

He walked slowly, uncertain what to say to her. For days he had watched her being pleasant to that snake Whitely, while the wagons rolled on behind the French army. He told himself he could have forgiven her anyone but Whitely. She must be convinced by now that the man was a traitor and not the agent he had said he was. Did she care?

He had laughed when she'd left him, laughed to cover up his hurt that she could doubt him. Go to Salamanca indeed! He would not travel half a yard to go to the Spanish whore; surely she knew that? Olivia would come back, for had she not always said he needed her? She had been right about other things too. He had to go home; it was where he belonged. He could make his father understand, especially with Olivia beside him to support him.

He had waited in the same place in the wood for several minutes, not daring to move in case she returned and missed him in the dark, but the minutes had stretched into half an hour and the silence around him had deepened. If she were hiding near at hand to punish him, he would at least have heard the horse. She had gone further than she had intended and was lost. For the first time in his life he had panicked. In the pitch-darkness of the wood he had blundered about, going round in circles, calling her name. His head had ached abominably and the trees into which he kept colliding had made his wound bleed again. He had stumbled, somehow regained his balance, taken a step and then — nothing.

When he had regained his senses, he had found himself lying on a couch in the home of the leader of the local Ordenanza in a village called São Jorge, a few miles north of Viseu. He had been surrounded by brown-clad partisans who, judging by his uniform, thought they had captured an important French leader and were debating what to do with him. Some had been advocating exchanging him for some of their own people, though they knew few were kept as prisoners, and others had been in favour of shooting him, after they had tortured him and found out all he knew. One or two had expressed doubts. They had known he was being pursued and they wanted to know why. What had he done that his own people should chase him? Had he deserted? And why was he wearing a red coat under his blue one?

His command of the Portuguese language was poor and the local schoolteacher had been fetched to translate into Spanish, their only common language. He had lost no time in explaining who he was and why he was there. His story had caused more heated debate, but in the end he had convinced them he was telling the truth, mainly because of the faded red coat and because he could describe Viscount Wellington — what the great man looked like, his big nose and cocked hat, worn fore and aft, his plain grey coat, his barking laugh, his victories. They could not get enough of his victories and, unlike the Spaniards, they believed in him.

'We will spare you,' their leader had pronounced at last. He was an olive-skinned, black-eyed man called Martin Davaco, fanatical to a degree and not a man to be trifled with. 'Join us; we need good men who can handle a gun. You can teach us as the General Wellington teaches our brothers, the Cacadores. But make no mistake, you are on trial.'

'My wife?' He had hoped to enrol them to help find Olivia. At the time he had been convinced she was lost in the forest.

'They say there was no one within a league of you when they found you,' the schoolmaster had translated. 'And they covered the ground well.'

'They are sure?'

'Yes. And they do not risk men and guns looking for a woman,' he had added. 'Women are changeable and unreliable. Women they leave at home when they go to war. It is where they belong.'

He had been allowed to return to the spot where they had found him and had searched in a wide circle, beating at the undergrowth with a stick, unwilling to admit he might be looking for a body. But in the end he had come to realise that Olivia's usual resourcefulness had probably come to her aid and she had found her own way out; she was not the kind of person to be beaten by a forest of trees.

He had gone back to the village and thrown himself wholeheartedly into their private war against the long columns that rumbled, day after day, through their countryside, crushing the wild flowers beneath their wheels, disturbing the animals that provided them with food, cutting down their trees, setting fire to the brush with their camp fires. Every ammunition wagon destroyed, every gun captured, every sack of flour spilled aided the war effort and helped to defeat the tyrant, and that was the creed by which they lived. It had pleased him to be involved, though his mind was constantly on Olivia, wondering where she was, if she was safe.

He had been with them as they watched the passing of Masséna's army from their hiding places among the rocks and scrub of the hillside. It had been far too big a target for their small force to attack, but their patience had been rewarded when a group of a dozen or so supply wagons had begun to straggle. He had been shocked to the core when he had borrowed Martin Davaco's spyglass and seen Whitely and Olivia sitting companionably side by side on the tailboard of the last wagon.

She had been laughing. That had hurt more than anything—that she could ride a French wagon with a traitor like Rufus Whitely and laugh. He had been forced to contain his impulse to rush down the hill and strangle the man there and then; it would have been a senseless thing to do and Martin Davaco would have justifiably thrown a knife into his back if he had tried it.

He had been forced to watch, with growing bitterness, as Olivia walked beside an enemy even more dangerous than the French troops who marched ahead of her. She had allowed the man to hold her in his arms, not only allowed it, but seemed to enjoy it. In that case, what else had happened between them? Shades of Juana's treachery tormented him. If Martin had not given the command to attack at that moment, he would have thrown caution to the winds and let off a shot at the traitorous Englishman.

Now he stopped within a few feet of her. She was

wearing a thin brown dress, a rag of a dress, but he did not see that; he saw her as he often liked to imagine her—fresh from a bath, dressed in a blue silk dressing-gown, with her hair newly washed and curling closely to her head. And smiling.

She was smiling now. Neither heard the nearby sounds of the Portuguese men barking commands at their prisoners, the braying of mules, the clash of metal as weapons were thrown down in a heap, nor saw anything but each other. The silence stretched out between them like an accusation, unspeakable, unbearable.

'Olivia,' he said, and managed a crooked grin. 'Another chance encounter, eh?' It was about the most senseless thing he could have said.

CHAPTER NINE

IF ROBERT had given any indication that he was pleased to see her, Olivia would have run into his arms and confessed her love for him. Instead she stood on the dusty road, her feet a little apart, and stared at him. Was he blind? Could he not see how delighted she was to see him? Had nothing changed? He had not altered in looks and was as handsome as ever; his hazel eyes looked straight into hers, but where before there had been humour, now there was mistrust, and where before his mouth had smiled, now it was set in a hard line of intransigence. His temple, close to the thin red scar on his forehead, twitched a little and she wondered if the injury gave him any pain. She laughed shakily when he spoke her name. 'So you do remember me.'

'Remember you?' He was puzzled.

'The injury to your head. You were having trouble remembering things.'

He wanted to say, How could I ever forget you? How could I forget the woman who made me want to live again, gave me the will to fight again, made me love her and want her above all things, and then left me? But the words would not come and instead he said, 'My memory is perfect.'

'Good. You look well.'

'I am. And you?'

'Very well, thank you.' She could not believe they were having this conversation; it was so trite, so inconsequential, when there were a thousand questions she wanted to ask him and a million things she wanted to tell him. Could they not even talk to each other any more? Had they lost even the comradeship of soldiers fighting for the same cause? She laughed suddenly and startled him, so deep in thought he had been. 'I must not keep you from your duties.' She could hear his comrades calling to him, though she did not take her eyes from his face. 'Am I to assume I am your prisoner?'

'Of course not!'

'What are you going to do with me, then?'

'I? Nothing. You are free to go where you wish, except. . .'

'Except?'

'Except to rejoin the French column.'

'What makes you think I should want to do that?'

'You seemed to be quite content to be with them until now.'

'Oh.' He had seen her with Rufus Whitely. 'I was a prisoner.'

'It certainly did not look like that to me. You were being more than civil to him.'

'That was only. . .'

She did not finish. Coming up behind him was the runaway wagon with a grinning Portuguese partisan sitting on the driving seat and two more standing in the vehicle behind him. 'We caught them!' he yelled, waving the whip. 'Come and see!'

'Ask Captain Whitely,' she said. 'Ask him if I was his prisoner.'

Robert forced his eyes away from hers and turned towards the wagon, striding up to it as it drew to a halt. The vehicle had been captured by three partisans who had broken off the main engagement to go after it. They had Jeanne and Rufus Whitely securely tied up with the rope which had once bound Olivia.

'It's crammed with booty,' one of the captors said. 'Come and see.' He dived into the back and returned with his hands full of jewellery. 'Look! We could buy a big gun and boxes and boxes of ammunition with these. And food for our people.'

Robert ignored the riches and pushed past him to

haul Rufus out on to the road. 'This one,' he said, his voice so calm that it terrified Olivia. 'This one dies. But before we send him off to hell I have a few questions I want answered.' He pushed the trembling man in front of him to the circle of wagons, where everyone else was gathered. 'Anyone who wants to see what we do to traitors, let them gather round,' he said in English.

The partisans looked from one to the other and the few voltigeurs who had survived to surrender trembled. They could not understand what the big man said, but they could see he was more than normally angry. He turned to Olivia. 'You speak Portuguese; translate that.'

'What are you going to do?' She had followed the two Englishmen into the circle, afraid for Rufus, but even more fearful for Robert. She was sure that he was about to do something he would regret for the rest of his life.

'Translate!' he commanded. 'Tell them everything I say.'

'Very well.' She turned to the assembled company to do as he asked.

'Tell them that anyone who betrays his country and cheats his friends should be shot. Tell them that this man is an English traitor and. . .'

'But Robert, he is not a traitor. He swore he had been sent by Wellington.'

'And you believed him? Was that why you were so willing to travel with him?'

'It is true, Lynmount,' Rufus said. 'The Peer did send me. Do you suppose I would come into this God-forsaken part of the country if I hadn't been ordered to?'

'You are a liar and a cheat. . .'

'So I am a liar and a cheat.' Rufus appeared calm, but a nerve twitched in his throat. 'That does not make me a traitor.'

Olivia began to translate for the benefit of the partisans, but Robert interrupted her. 'You do not need to tell them his feeble excuses.'

'They have a right to know both sides.'

'That is true,' Martin Davaco said. 'And this is neither the time nor the place to hold a trial. The French rearguard may come back at any moment to find out what has happened to their supply wagons and we cannot be caught in the open. Back to São Jorge, everyone. We will convene a court there and the schoolmaster will preside. He will know how to do it properly.'

'What about the other prisoners?' someone asked him.

'Shoot them.'

'But you cannot do that,' Olivia protested. 'They surrendered.'

'I shall tell you something, *senhora*,' he said, taking her arm and leading her away from where his men were lining up the prisoners, including Jeanne. 'Masséna refuses to recognise us, the Ordenanza, as fighting men. He calls us bandits and criminals. When our men are caught they are not treated as prisoners of war and he has refused to exchange a single one. They are tortured before they die.' He laughed harshly. 'As an example to the rest of us.' He jerked his thumb over his shoulder. 'If these prisoners cannot be exchanged, why should we keep them in idleness, eating our food? We have little enough of that.'

'But. . .'

'You would have us set them free to go on killing our people?'

'No. . .'

'Then what else is there to do? They must die.' As he spoke a volley of shots rang out and echoed round the hills. 'Now we must go. Their friends will find them and bury them. Come.'

Olivia dared not look back, knowing what she would

see if she did. She found Pegasus and climbed on his back, wishing she could be anywhere but where she was, with an angry Robert, a sullen Rufus and a crowd of barbarous partisans who had gathered up everything worth carrying and loaded it on to the mules they had taken from the shafts. Wagons were useless to them; they travelled over narrow mountain tracks and eschewed the roads. Robert set Rufus on one of the mules, tied his hands behind his back and put a noose about his neck. Holding the rope's end in his hand, he mounted Thor.

'Robert, you can't take him like that,' she protested. 'If the mule stumbles, he will be strangled. And besides, it is so undignified.'

'Undignified!' He slapped the beast to make it start. 'Why do you think he should be allowed his dignity?'

'He is an Englishman, and whatever your quarrel with him you should not forget that. And I believe he is loyal to his country.'

He turned to look at her and then wished he had not. In another minute he would have softened enough to do as she asked and he dared not risk it. He turned from her to look straight ahead at the cloud-capped mountain and the path that wound across its slopes, now in sun, now in shadow, to São Jorge. 'He has addled your wits with his caresses,' he said. 'You do not recognise lies when you hear them.'

'I do not recognise you any more. What happened to the man I knew, the one whose only wish was to regain his claws and vindicate himself? If you did wrong, you have paid the price. There is no need to go on punishing yourself. . .'

'I am doing no such thing. It is the traitor who has to be punished.'

'And having done that, having executed him without trial, what will you do if you discover, when we return to our own lines, that what he says is true, that he is a loyal Englishman and an important agent? Will you be able to live with yourself?'

He knew that she was right but he was not yet ready to admit it; he could see no further than his present fury.

They arrived in the village just as the setting sun touched the mountain peaks and turned them to a glorious and breathtaking gold. São Jorge consisted of a single street surrounded on one side by mountain slopes on whose sparse vegetation a few sheep and goats grazed, and on the other by pine woods and a stand of poplar. There was a handful of dwellings, built of stone and wood, with the living quarters, reached by outside stairs, above the stables and working areas. There was a town hall, a schoolhouse and a church.

The inhabitants, warned of their coming by a look-out, crowded round them, happy to see them safely returned. The booty they had captured was piled up in the schoolroom for all to admire and tales were told of the encounter which lost nothing in the telling. 'The Englishman brought us luck,' they said, crowding round Robert and patting him on the back.

Olivia slipped away to be by herself. No one noticed her going. The night was peaceful, the French were camped many miles to the south and nothing stirred, except a colony of bats in the church steeple, who swooped in and out of a hole in the eaves. She walked to the end of the street to stand looking out across the dark mountains to the north. Somewhere over those peaks was a green and pleasant land that was neither too hot nor too cold — her homeland — and she wished she were there.

She tilted her head to look up at the sky, twinkling with stars, the same stars she had watched with Tom the night he had proposed, the same which had lit the sky at Oporto and Ciudad Rodrigo and Almeida. They shone on friend and enemy alike. For more than two years she had been wandering from one battlefield to another, enduring blistering heat and icy winds, ill-fed and ill-clothed, and for what? So that she could lose a husband who was no more than a boy, another who was one of her country's enemies, and, worst of all, the man she loved.

To be so near him and yet so far, to speak to him and yet be unable to penetrate the wall he had built about himself, was purgatory. He had kissed her, sometimes in anger, sometimes with gentleness and sensitivity, but he had never been indifferent to her. There had always been a certain something between them, a thread of mutual respect, a passion even, that was there if never acknowledged, which ran through everything they did and said. But now even that had snapped under the strain; he was as much lost to her as if he had died along with Tom and Philippe.

She could hear sounds of revelry coming from the schoolhouse; they were celebrating their victory as if they had won the war. The war was not won yet. Her own private war was not won either. But, by heaven, neither was it lost. She would fight, she would not give up; there was too much at stake. She turned and walked slowly back to the centre of the village.

On the way she heard her name being called softly and turned to see Rufus Whitely chained to the church railings, like a puppy who could not be trusted to behave indoors. He smiled when he saw her; it did not make her feel any better about anything. 'Well, my dear, what now?' he asked.

'They are going to try you tomorrow.'

'I have already been tried and found guilty. Only the execution is to come.'

'No. They are not barbarians.'

'Oh, but they are. Did they give those poor fellows on the road a chance?'

'There was a reason for that.'

'Oh, I know the reasons.' He laughed. 'And I do not

blame them for killing Frenchmen, but I am an Englishman, one of their allies.'

She smiled crookedly. 'That is what the trial will be about—to discover the truth.'

'What do you think?'

'I do not know what to think. Robert. . .'

'Robert Lynmount is an embittered and jealous man; there is no hope that he will be impartial. And his new friends are so enamoured of him, they will lap up everything he says.'

'Why do you hate him so?'

'My feelings do not come into it, but his certainly do. Olivia, you are the only person who can help me. I must get back to my regiment. I have important intelligence. . .'

'I cannot help you.'

'Yes, you can. Untie me, for a start.'

'You will not cover a hundred yards before they shoot you down. There is a guard.'

'Not now, later, when they are all asleep. I doubt they will leave me here all night. Come and find me.'

'They will come after you. Why not put your faith in these people and Robert's good sense? I will talk to him again.'

'He is past listening to anyone.'

'I must try.'

'And if you fail? And if the battle is lost, even the war itself, because intelligence did not reach the commander in time, what then?'

'I will not fail.'

It was an awesome responsibility and one she did not relish, especially considering she still had lingering doubts, but there was only one way forward and that was for all three to go back to the British lines, to stand side by side before Viscount Wellington and let him be the judge.

'If you fail,' he said as she began to walk away, 'then you must set me free, whatever the cost.' He paused and gave a short bark of a laugh. 'And because you will never be forgiven for it you will have to come with me. I shall look forward to that.'

She stopped, a retort on her lips, then changed her mind and continued on towards the schoolhouse without speaking. He was right; she would never be forgiven if she went against Robert's wishes and helped Rufus to escape. But if the unofficial court found him guilty, could she stand by and let them execute him? Whitely had mentioned cost; did he have any idea of what the cost to her would be if she helped him to regain his liberty? To be Robert's enemy, never to ride side by side with him or laugh with him again, was an unbearable thought, but if Robert was wrong about Captain Whitely. . .

Martin Davaco and a companion passed her, shouldering carbines, calling a cheerful '*Boa noite, senhora*. The captain will show you to your lodging.'

'Thank you,' she said and turned to watch them as they went to where Rufus was chained and marched him into the church, where she assumed he would be spending the night. He went willingly enough and she supposed he was putting his faith in her. She turned from him and saw Robert standing at the door of the schoolhouse watching her; the building behind him was in darkness.

'Where is everyone?' she asked as she approached, her voice brittle with the effort of sounding normal.

'Gone to their beds, all except the sentries and a patrol.'

'Patrol?'

'The war goes on,' he said. 'One small victory is not the end; we must be forever vigilant.'

'You include yourself in that?'

'Of course. I have joined them.'

'Why?'

'Why?' he repeated, as if asking himself the question. 'Because they asked me to and their invitation was not one I could easily refuse. And because they are doing something useful and I need to be of service. I hardly expect you to understand that.'

'I do. Of course I do. But I should have thought you could have been of greater service elsewhere.'

'Where else would I be appreciated as I am here? Where else would my past be so unimportant? Where else can I be myself?'

She took a deep breath; now was not the time to draw back. 'Where else can you hide, you mean.'

'I am not hiding. Why should I hide?'

She laughed suddenly and the old imp of mischief sounded again in her voice and reminded him of when they had first met, a few weeks, a lifetime ago. 'Had you forgotten a certain pompous colonel you hood-winked? He would love to know where you are.'

He grinned. 'He is facing the other way. He thinks he is marching on Lisbon.'

'And is he?'

'No. He will be stopped long before that.'

'By whom? By Wellington? But is Wellington expecting him? And even if he is, does he know from which direction? Does he know how big the army is he faces?'

'I fancy he does. He has reliable intelligence. . .'

'Provided by Captain Whitely, you mean?'

She was driving a hard bargain and he was not even sure what it was, but she knew how to hit where it hurt. 'No. Anything he sent would be false and, for all your defence of the man, you know, in your heart of hearts, that is true.'

'You can have no idea what is in my heart of hearts,' she said, fighting back tears. 'Or you would trust me. . .'

'My dear Olivia. . .'

'I am not your dear anything,' she put in before he could go on. 'I am not anyone's dear.'

'My apologies, ma'am.' He bowed a stiff acknowl-

edgement. 'I was about to say that I did not mistrust
you. I simply think that you are misguided and have
fallen prey to a few flattering words.'

'Who has flattered me? You never have.'

'I referred to Captain Rufus Whitely.'

'Why should I believe either of you? I am convinced
this whole situation has been caused by your rivalry
over one girl; none of it would have happened
otherwise.'

He smiled. 'You could well be right. On reflection, I
am sure you are right.'

She did not stop to ponder on why he had agreed so
readily; she had the initiative and she meant to keep it.
'And it is still going on. You are both putting your
personal feelings before the good of your country and
that simply will not do.' She paused to look into his
eyes, surprised that he had given her no argument;
there was even a twinkle of amusement in them. 'Save
your personal vendetta until after the war is won; it is
more important that Viscount Wellington has accurate
information.'

'And you have appointed yourself my conscience, is
that it? You are determined to make me feel guilty.'

'If that is what it takes to make you see sense, then
yes.'

He took her shoulders in his hands and leaned back
to look at her, laughing. 'Oh, my dear, you are
wonderful.'

Taken by surprise, she could only stare at him.

'Don't look so astonished,' he said, gently now. 'I
cannot fight you; there are no weapons against the
truth. You are right, as you so often are, but I cannot
release him.'

His nearness and the softness of his voice were
almost making her forget the cause of their dissension.
In another minute she would be in his arms and all
would be lost. 'Why not?'

He sighed. 'Have you not listened to a word I have

said? He will take the opportunity to run back to his French friends.'

'But. . .'

'We will return to the British lines if that is what you want,' he said.

'You mean it?' She could not conceal her delight.

'Yes. We go together, all three, but Rufus Whitely goes in shackles.'

'Very well,' she said, realising that she had won a minor battle if not a complete victory, and the compromise would have to serve. 'When do we start?'

'Tomorrow, at first light.' He paused. 'You know it will not be easy? We have to pass through or round the French army and there will be times when we might have to fight our way out.'

She laughed. 'When have I ever ducked a fight? Just give me a good rifle and a strong horse under me, that is all I ask. I thrive on difficulties.'

'Said like a true soldier,' he said, taking her arm and leading her towards one of the houses where lights still showed in the upper windows. 'Martin Davaco's wife has offered you a room for the night and you must not keep her from her bed.'

'What about you?'

His chuckle of amusement made her feel suddenly carefree; as if a load had been lifted from her shoulders. His anger had dissipated and, though she did not think they would ever regain their old closeness, they could at least be friends, and it was no good wishing for more.

'The idea of our sharing a room as we did in Ciudad Rodrigo would horrify the good people of São Jorge,' he said. 'They would fetch the priest from his bed to put matters right.'

'It horrified Father Peredo too.' She smiled. 'He seemed to think we should do something about it.'

'And what did you say?'

'I told him that we were companions, fellow soldiers, no more.'

'Oh.' He was silent for a moment, digesting this. 'And did that satisfy him?'

'I don't know. I did not ask.'

He stopped outside the house and turned towards her, putting a hand on her arm. 'Olivia, I have compromised you and for that I am more than sorry. If, at any time. . .if you should wish. . .'

She brushed his hand off and put her foot on the bottom step. 'There is no need for you to do that,' she said, her voice breaking with the strain. 'I can live with what I have done; I feel no guilt.' She did not wait for him to reply, but ran up the steps and knocked on the door, not daring to look behind her.

He had been about to propose to her and she had stopped him! She had had to stop him. He would have been asking for all the wrong reasons and she would have been weak enough to accept him. She had been married twice before and both times for the wrong reasons; she could not let it happen again. She would not. The spectre of the unknown Juana haunted her.

If her hostess noticed the unshed tears glistening in her eyes, she kept it to herself. She made her guest welcome and showed her into a tiny room at the back of the house which looked out on to the mountains, and left her to sleep.

Sleep was almost impossible and Olivia was up as soon as it was light enough to see without a candle, washed and dressed in her old green skirt and blouse, topped by the now more than shabby blue coat, and made her way to the kitchen. Senhora Davaco was already up and about, putting together a parcel of food and a skin of wine for their journey. Olivia breakfasted on bread and honey and goat's milk, thanked her hostess and joined the two men in the road outside the church.

They were already mounted. Robert rode Thor and

had Pegasus saddled and ready for her, with a rifle in a sling on her saddle. Rufus Whitely, she noted with relief, had been provided with a piebald horse and would not have to suffer the ignominy of riding into the British camp on a mule. He was bound with his upper arms tight to his chest, but his hands were free enough for him to hold the pommel of his saddle. Robert had the reins in his own hand. Both men seemed cheerful, as if relieved that their dilemma had been resolved, though they did not speak to each other. Robert and Olivia shook hands with those villagers who had come into the road to see them off, then turned their mounts to the south and the valley of the Mondego River.

Not wanting to overtire the horses, they did not hurry. The day was bright and, once they had left the upper slopes, warm. Olivia was pensive; she was still thinking of the night before and Robert's sudden change of plan and his equally sudden attempt to propose. Had he thought she had been asking him to marry her when she told him about Father Peredo's comment? She had not meant that at all; she had simply been pleased that he was his old self and wanted to make him smile.

They skirted round the towns because the French had left small garrisons in them in order to police the population and keep their supply lines open, but Robert had been given the names of Portuguese patriots who would shelter them and help them on their way.

Two days later, the harsh outlines of the rocky peaks receded behind them and they found themselves journeying down on to a rolling plain covered with cork oak and eucalyptus and aromatic shrubs, white cystus and rosemary, thyme and lavender, interspersed with the broom which made the landscape look as though an artist had spilled a pot of yellow paint across a canvas. There were olive groves and cherry, pear and plum orchards and here and there, on south-facing slopes, terraces of vines, but every single one had been stripped of its fruit, and many were scorched by field fires.

Once in the valley, they crossed the Mondego River, keeping a careful watch for stray French skirmishers, avoiding the main roads and using the tracks made by goatherds and shepherds when they drove their animals from the lower pastures up to the mountains in the summer and down again in the winter. But now there were no herds, no flocks and every village they came to was deserted. There were no people, no dogs, no cats, no chickens even, and all the crops had been destroyed. The countryside, which should have been teeming with abundant produce, was barren. There was nothing to sustain a company, let alone an army. Olivia was glad of the several days' food they had been provided with.

'They are fools,' Rufus mumbled, 'to do all this at the whim of a general and not even one of their own.'

'Whim?' she repeated. 'They obviously do not think it is a whim. They trust Wellington.'

'And where is he, then?'

It was a good question. Wellington had moved even further back and she began to wonder if they might, after all, have to go all the way to Lisbon to find him. The prospect was not a cheerful one. Apart from the depressing thought that he did not mean to defend the country which relied on him so totally, she was more than exasperated by the two men, who said not a word to each other and addressed all their remarks through her. Many more days of it and she would explode.

They began climbing again towards Gouveia where Robert had expected to come upon the British and Portuguese army, but they had seen no one but an ageing goatherd in the straw cloak which seemed to be the uniform of his trade; they might have been the only people in the world.

At midday, almost a week after they left São Jorge, they stopped beside a stream to eat. There was very little food left and they had been supplementing their diet with small game, but Robert was reluctant to use what little ammunition they had in case they needed it to defend themselves, and they had to make do with hard bread and goat's milk cheese. As soon as they had finished eating, he secured Rufus to a tree on the bank and picked up his rifle.

'Where are you going?' she asked. She was always apprehensive when he left, as he often did to reconnoitre, knowing he trusted her to guard their prisoner while he was gone. It was all the more difficult because she did not look on Rufus as a prisoner.

'To find the French. I need to know exactly where they are.' He looked across at Rufus. The man seemed resigned to his fate, unmoving, staring into the water as it flowed over its rocky bed. 'Keep an eye on him. The nearer we come to his friends, the more likely he is to want to join them.'

Rufus looked up at her as Robert left, and smiled. 'How can you be sure he will not be the one to leave us? He did not want to make this journey, did he?'

'You know perfectly well why that was.'

'Do I?'

'You know he was cashiered. He feels the disgrace very keenly.' She sat down a foot or two from him. 'Captain Whitely, what happened? You know, don't you?'

'Yes.'

'Tell me, please.'

He smiled and she felt a shiver of apprehension and began to wonder if she really did want to know after all.

'We were in Lisbon, waiting for orders,' he said. 'And there was this *senhorita*. . .'

'Juana.'

'Yes, Juana.' He smiled as if he could see the

beautiful Portuguese girl in his mind's eye. 'Robert and
I were rivals, always had been, right from boyhood,
though, unlike the Honourable Robert, I was not blind
to the kind of girl she was. He was besotted by her,
would not listen to a word against her. He spent every
off-duty moment with her and her family, taking them
food and clothing and buying her presents.' He paused
and grinned crookedly. 'He could afford to because,
unlike me, he comes from a wealthy family.'

Every word he spoke wrenched at her heart. That
the cool, self-possessed Robert should feel such passion
for someone else hurt her and hurt badly, but she had
to go on listening. She wanted to understand. Sitting,
with a pistol under her hand, on the banks of a stream
somewhere in the Serra da Estrela, she was transported
to the teeming city of Lisbon where, in spite of the
war, there was still a civilised social life to be had with
concerts, balls, visits to the theatre and shopping
excursions. She could see it all. She looked up suddenly
when she heard him laugh.

'When Robert was on duty, then I met the lovely
lady. . .'

'Did Robert know that?'

'Not at first. He need never have found out, but the
silly bitch told him, threw it in his face and laughed at
him.' He grinned. 'She had two brothers — rogues, they
were, but he believed them when they said they were
poor and hungry. . .'

'They were not?'

'Not they! Juana was a past master at persuading
people to give her presents and her brothers ran a very
good business selling the surplus. She was no more
than a clever little whore. . .'

'But were you not taken in too?'

'Only at the beginning. Then I caught one of the
brothers selling a brooch I knew Robert had given
Juana and taxed him with it.' His smile of self-satisfac-
tion sickened Olivia. 'He told me what they were

doing, made me an offer too good to refuse. We joined forces and built up quite a profitable enterprise.'

'From gifts?' She was astonished.

'Not entirely. Soldiers who had loot for sale found with us a ready market.' He sighed. ''Tis a pity I lost the booty in Jeanne's wagon.'

'And Robert knew nothing about it?'

'Love is blind, my dear, isn't that what they say?'

'And the army authorities, did they not know what was going on?'

'Oh, they had an idea, but it was a question of catching the culprits red-handed. Then I found out they were getting too close for comfort; I had to do something about it.' He paused, but she did not interrupt and he went on. 'One day, when I knew the brothers were going to collect a consignment of flour. . .'

'Bought and paid for by the army,' she said sharply.

'As you say. They were going to intercept it on the road. I felt it my duty to tell Captain Lynmount exactly where and when.' He laughed harshly. 'He rode out alone to stop them. I knew the chivalrous fool would not inform on them because of Juana.'

'But *you* did.' She could see it all now. Poor Robert. Poor, dear Robert.

'It was my duty. He was caught carrying one of the sacks of flour.'

'But surely he explained?'

'The prosecution said he was taking it to the brothers' wagon, while he maintained he had been removing it to return to the store. No one believed him. They knew how he felt about Juana, you see.' He paused to watch her; she was looking down at the ground, unwilling to meet his eyes, but he knew she believed him. 'He thought she knew nothing of what her brothers were about. Not until she laughed in his face and told him the truth did he realise what had happened, but he had been court-martialled by that time and was awaiting sentence.' He stopped speaking, though his words still hung in the air, tormenting her.

She felt her hand tighten on the pistol. Nothing would have given her greater satisfaction at that moment than shooting him. She lifted the weapon and weighed it in her hand.

'Would that be wise?' he asked mildly.

She looked up at him, her eyes full of a dull hate. 'What has wisdom to do with how I feel?'

'I understand,' he said. 'But don't you want to get his name cleared? I am the only one who can do that.'

'Juana?'

'In Salamanca.'

'Her brothers?'

'In gaol.'

'But you wouldn't. Would you?' There was almost a plea in her question.

'I might.'

'For what consideration?'

'I will think of something. But until then you need me alive.'

'Alive!' She laughed suddenly. 'Alive but not necessarily well. I could. . .'

'Tut, tut,' he said. 'For a lady, and an English lady at that, you sound more like one of those barbarous guerrilla friends of yours. That is the sort of thing Don Miguel Santandos would say.'

'Don Santandos?' She put the weapon on the ground beside her and noticed that her hands were trembling.

'He is an even greater threat to me than you are,' he said. 'He will not listen to reason as you do. You and Robert Lynmount are my protectors as well as my gaolers.'

'You!' she said suddenly. 'You were the one who betrayed the guerrillas to Colonel Clavier. It was you who was responsible for the death of Miguel's wife.' She stopped speaking and stared at him with loathing. The air was still, as if a storm was brewing; a cloud drifted across the sun and cast a shadow over the water. The old goatherd they had seen earlier was making his way slowly along the riverbank towards them, hobbling with the aid of a staff. 'Robert was right all along,' she said. 'You are a traitor.'

'I prefer to be on the winning side,' he said, then laughed. 'The pay was better too, especially when I produced the design of your father's rockets.'

She laughed, but her voice was cracked and it did not sound like her at all. 'They were a failure.'

'No matter. The French did not know that. And I thought what I did would please Juana, particularly after her brothers were imprisoned by the British authorities.' He sighed. 'I should have known better.'

She smiled. He had not escaped Juana's treachery either, but she could feel no sympathy for him. The sun came out from behind the cloud and their two forms were mirrored in the water again, sitting side by side as they had sat side by side on the tailboard of Jeanne's wagon. How could she have been such a fool as to believe all his lies? Everything he had ever said was a lie. 'You were never a British agent,' she said. 'There was no special assignment from Viscount Wellington. . .'

'There you are wrong,' he said blandly. 'That I was sent by Viscount Wellington was the truth.' He laughed suddenly and frightened a kingfisher hovering over the water; it abandoned its dive for fish and flew off, a flash of red and green. 'He sent me to find Captain Lynmount.'

'To find Robert?'

'Yes, ironic, isn't it? I was to fetch him back and tell him all was forgiven, his lordship needed him. You see, my dear, Robert Lynmount is one of the Peer's best scouts, and as most of the others have been killed or captured he is needed, disgrace or no disgrace.' He looked up idly at the goatherd, who was now only a few paces from them, and then down into the water. 'I do believe there is a trout down there. I could fancy a bit of fish for supper.'

'If you think I will release you on so flimsy an excuse, you are mistaken,' she said. 'Once I might have done, but not now. Whatever sympathy I felt for you has gone and I marvel at Robert's restraint in letting you live.'

'He did it for you, my dear.' He sighed melodramatically. 'The man will never learn not to trust the fair sex. He believes in their essential goodness, Juana notwithstanding.'

'And I am glad that he does.'

'Even if it means he still loves her?'

She did not want to answer that one and turned away to gaze along the path from which she expected Robert to appear. That she loved him she did not doubt, but neither did she doubt that all his thoughts and longings were tied up with the Portuguese girl, in spite of the way she had treated him. Men, she decided, could be even more perverse than women when it came to giving their affections to the wrong people.

'Look!' Whitely's voice, coming in the middle of her reverie, made her jump. She turned to see him attempting to point at the water, though his bonds made it impossible. 'There is a trout down there, under that rock. You could almost catch it with bare hands. It's a beauty too.'

Curious in spite of herself, she leaned over the bank to look. She could see nothing in the water but their two reflections and then they were joined by a third. The goatherd was standing behind them. In horrified surprise, she saw his bent form stand up straight and her mind registered how young and tall he was as he raised his staff above his head with both hands. Then there was nothing but darkness.

She came to her senses with Robert leaning over her, calling her name in what seemed something akin to panic. He had a water-soaked cloth in his hand and was bathing her forehead. She smiled weakly. 'Has he gone?'

'Yes.' He breathed a prayer of thanksgiving. 'I should never have left you alone with him.' He paused to smooth her hair from her brow with gentle fingers. 'How do you feel? You've been out cold for an age.'

She lifted a hand gingerly and winced as she felt the bump on her head. 'A little dizzy, as if I'd drunk too much champagne.'

He smiled ruefully. 'Fine chance of that.'

'I'm sorry,' she said. 'I was a fool.'

'How did he escape? Did you. . .?'

'No, I did not.' Her denial sounded more like her old, resilient, unquenchable self. 'There was a goatherd, though I do not think he was a real goatherd, after all. He seemed old at first but then he stood up straight. I saw him in the water. . .'

'He was in the river?'

'No, silly, I saw his reflection behind mine. He had a stick.'

'Why didn't you shoot him? You had a pistol.' He did not sound angry. He ought to have been furious that she had been so easily duped into relaxing her guard.

She grinned. 'You said I would be useless as a soldier, didn't you? That first day. . .'

'I did not know what I was talking about,' he said, smiling down at her in a way that made her feel even more light-headed. It was not only the blow which had shaken her wits but his obvious concern for her and the knowledge that she now knew the truth about him, knew why he had been hurt, why he behaved the way he did, why he had found it so difficult to trust her and why his claws were important to him. What she could not understand was his continuing love of Juana.

She sat up gingerly. She was still on the riverbank, the sun still shone and the water still rippled over the stones and she wondered idly if there really had been a trout. The rope which had bound Rufus lay on the grass where it had been carelessly thrown and Robert's horse cropped the grass near by. There was no sign of the piebald or her own mount. 'Pegasus?' she said.

'Gone, I'm afraid.'

She grinned suddenly. 'I hope he throws the traitorous devil.'

He laughed. 'You seem to have changed your mind about the man.'

'He told me what happened in Lisbon. I am sorry, Robert.'

'Sorry?'

'About everything. About Juana.'

'It is of no consequence.' He did not want to talk about it; no man liked to admit that he had been a fool. When he had ridden up and seen Olivia lying sprawled on the grass with her head covered in blood, he had thought she was dead and, for one awful moment, his heart had stopped. Everything else faded into insignificance as he realised what she meant to him — more than Juana, more than honour even, more than life itself. He had hurled himself from his horse and gathered her into his arms, calling her name with a voice broken by emotion. His relief on finding she was not dead had overwhelmed him, and now that she seemed to be fully restored to her senses, except for that bump on the head, he was angry. His anger was not with her, but with himself and with that coward, Rufus Whitely. She had done nothing to harm the fellow, had even defended him; it was because of her he was still alive.

But he would not live much longer. Rufus would pay with his life, but not at his hands. It was not up to him to dispense justice; Olivia had convinced him of that, though he had hardly needed convincing. He would fetch him back for trial. 'Are you well enough to go on?'

'Yes, I think so.'

He stood up to help her to her feet. She seemed to have recovered, but he knew from experience what a blow to the head could do. 'Perhaps you should rest awhile. Tomorrow. . .'

'No, Robert,' she said firmly. 'We cannot spare the time and I am quite recovered. Thor can carry us both.'

'I must get after the traitor,' he said, picking up the pistol and handing it back to her. The rope he wound round his waist. 'I must catch him before he gets back to Colonel Clavier with what he knows about the allied positions.'

'I am quite ready.'

'Not you.' He stood up beside her. 'I go alone.'

'Oh, not that old chestnut,' she said, sighing. 'Don't you know me better than that? I belong with you.'

'True,' he said smiling. 'But I need you alive and safe. We are near the British lines now and I want you to go on alone.'

'I will not.'

He smiled. 'Are you giving me an argument, Olivia?'

'Yes.'

'But if I tell you that it is vital that the Peer knows from which direction the French are coming? Judging by what I have seen, he is not expecting them from Viseu, or we would have come across the rearguard by now. My guess is he is deploying his forces to meet them much further south and east. Who is there to tell him this but you?' He could see her struggling with herself. The old Olivia who wanted to rush in and do battle with him was fighting the Olivia who knew a soldier's duty was to obey, and she saw herself as a soldier. At least, he thought she did. He smiled. 'Duty calls us in different directions, my dear.'

She smiled impishly. 'Still looking for those claws, Robert?'

'If you like. Will you go?'

She sighed. 'If I must, but I go under protest. I am not at all sure you can manage without me.'

He laughed. 'Nor I, but I shall have to try. Now, you take Thor. Keep to the byways, avoid any trouble.' He paused to grin at her, remembering her prowess with a gun. 'No sniping at anything, however easy the target, do you hear?'

'I hear.'

He handed her a rough map. 'This shows the French route and where you might expect to find Viscount Wellington. Make sure you go direct to him. No one else will do.'

She stood to attention and saluted him. 'Yes, sir!'

He laughed to cover the fact that he wanted to take her in his arms and tell her the whole idea was mad and he would not let her go, but he could see no alternative. Later, when it was all over, he would come back to her, when he had been vindicated and his father had accepted him back into the family, when he had something to offer her; then was the time to speak. He led her to his horse, where he stopped and held out his clasped hands for her foot. 'Up you go, then.'

She mounted and turned the horse, looking down into his face as if to etch it in her memory. 'Don't you do anything foolish, either,' she said, reaching out to put a hand on his shoulder. 'Claws are not important.'

He took her hand and turned it over to kiss the palm. 'Mine are.' He did not wait for her to answer, but slapped the horse's rump and set it cantering off. 'I'll see you in England,' he called after her. He watched her until she was out of sight, then he picked up his haversack and rifle, slung them over his shoulders and set off in the opposite direction.

CHAPTER TEN

OLIVIA had plenty of time to think as she rode. Walking Thor through the depopulated Portuguese countryside looking for an army was hardly a suitable occupation for a lady. But had she forfeited her right to be called a gentlewoman even before she met Robert? She tried telling herself she had not wanted to go back to Ciudad Rodrigo, that if Robert had not made that bargain with her she would have found her way home and resumed her place at her father's side, to all intents and purposes a grieving widow. But it was not fair to blame Robert; she had chosen the path she had taken and she had no one to blame but herself if he looked on her as just another of the men under his command.

She smiled wryly. That was what came of being able to ride and shoot like a trooper. Her father had been proud of her prowess with a gun and on a horse, but it was a simple delight in her accomplishments, meant to impress his friends; it did not mean he wanted her to deny her womanhood. That was what Robert had accused her of, and if it was true she could hardly blame him for treating her like a man. He did not think of Juana as anything but a woman.

She dug her heels into Thor's broad sides and put him into a gallop in an attempt to stop herself thinking of Juana. The big horse was as much as she could manage but it was some small consolation to know that Robert thought her capable of riding him. She remembered the day they had met, the day he had said Thor was more than she could handle. He had not known her then. Did he know her even now? She had to put the memories, good and bad, behind her. She had to find

229

Wellington and make sure he knew the situation and in return he would arrange for her repatriation. That was all there was to it. She doubted she would ever see Robert again, because his pursuit of Rufus Whitely would be followed by a search for Juana, and whether he succeeded or failed made no difference because he would not come back to her.

Once home, she could pretend it never happened, could expunge it from her mind and lose herself in the social whirl of London society. What a prospect! Talked about, smiled over, everyone concluding that she was in want of a husband, curious about her, appalled by her tanned face and cropped hair. Could she start a new fashion? Why not go the whole hog and dress in breeches with stock and cravat? What a stir that would cause! She leaned back in the saddle and laughed up at the sky. It was all very well to laugh, but it was not funny; especially it was not funny because inside she was as soft and feminine as any woman and she was in love. An impossible love.

She pulled the horse up to a walk. Robert had told her to take care; galloping about like a crazed woman was not taking care. It was not so much her safety as the information she carried which was important. She had better be more alert and ready for danger.

The day wore on; the horse seemed untiring, but she had a headache and she was hungry and thirsty. She stopped at a wayside inn. A bent old man came to the door and bade her enter. 'We've little enough,' he said, looking at her suspiciously. 'Some rye bread and a few olives.'

'That will do admirably.'

'You do not sound French.'

'I am not. I am English.' She looked down at the faded blue coat, which had caught his eye. 'Oh, this. I found it. I was cold and it is better than nothing.'

He conducted her to the parlour and drew out a

chair from the table. 'You are the first traveller I have
seen today.'

'Is that so?' She was surprised. 'Have there been no
troops passing through?'

'Haven't seen any, not for days.'

'But I thought Wellington was hereabouts.'

'Did you, now?' He was still doubtful about her and
unwilling to offer information.

'I have to find the British lines.' She paused, wondering if she dared trust him. 'My husband was killed and
I have lost all my belongings. . .'

'You have no money?'

'Oh, I have money, but what can money buy? You
say you have no food.' As she spoke, she delved into
her pocket and pulled out her purse which contained
the remainder of Philippe's money in a mixture of
currencies. 'I would give all of this for a good meal and
directions to where I can find the British commander-
in-chief.'

'A meal I can give you,' he said. 'And wine, but as
for the other. . .' He turned from her and went into a
back room, returning with a plate of *gabrito*, goat meat
braised in oil with tomatoes and garlic. It was not her
favourite dish but she was almost hungry enough to eat
anything. He brought her a bottle of red wine and a
glass and stood watching her eat and drink.

'How far have you come?'

'Many leagues,' she said. 'From the mountains.'

'Ahh.' He gave her a toothless smile. 'There are
mountains on all sides, *senhora*.'

'North.' She paused, wondering how much to tell
him. 'I have been with a compatriot of yours. Martin
Davaco. Do you know him?'

'I have heard of him. He is a fighter.'

'Are you not all fighters, in your own way? Even
you, here in this place all alone, would you too not like
to contribute?' She paused to look up at him. 'You are
a loyal patriot, are you not?'

He attempted to stand up straight but his crooked back prevented it. 'I am, but I am an old man. What can I do?'

'You will understand how important it is for Viscount Wellington to know exactly where the main French forces are so that they can be defeated?'

'And you have that information?'

'I do, but I need to know where his lordship is.' She tipped the contents of the purse on to the table and watched his eyes widen in surprise. 'You can have all of it for good directions.'

'The English lord was in Gouveia,' he said, avarice overcoming his doubts. 'But he rode out from there and along this road to the west a week ago. I saw him myself. He called for wine.'

'Do you know where he was going?'

He shrugged. 'To the sea, perhaps. I heard tell there were ships ready to take him and his men off. If you want to go with him, you had best make haste.'

She hoped he had not read the situation correctly. She had come to like the Portuguese people, their courage and resilience, their faith and stoicism; she did not want to see them left to Napoleon's mercy, because that tyrant would have none. They had been a thorn in his side too long. She finished her meal and rose to go. 'Portugal will be free,' she said. 'Do not doubt it.'

She retraced her route to the last crossroads and then turned westwards, alternately cantering and walking, trying not to overtire her mount, but none the less anxious to reach her destination. It seemed that time was running out, that before long the two sides who had been dodging each other for months would come together in a great clash of men and arms, and the information she carried was vital to the outcome.

She stopped only when it became too dark to go on and found an abandoned animal shelter where she lay down and tried to rest. Long before dawn she was on the road again and this time it was a proper highway.

She knew it was risky to take to the open road, even more so now because she was almost sure she would have to cross the French lines, but the extra speed she could make was worth the gamble.

She could see lights in the distance and recognised them almost at once as camp fires. She reined in. Could it be the British or even the Portuguese Cacadores, or was it the French advance guard? She approached slowly.

It was a small company of French voltigeurs sent out to reconnoitre the ground. They were camped in an olive grove, lying round their fires or leaning against the trees, still asleep. There were two sentries who should have been patrolling the perimeter, but they were standing together talking in low voices. Thankful it was not the main column, she dismounted and led her horse round them on foot, her pistol in her other hand, alert for every sound. One of the sentries laughed and Thor's head went up. She grabbed his nose and pulled it down, whispering to him to be silent. By the time it was safe to mount again, she had lost two valuable hours.

Coimbra, an old university town on the Mondego River and once the capital of Portugal, was quiet; a few students in their torn black capes pinned with the coloured ribbons of their faculty strolled about deep in conversation, as if there were no conflict, no battle about to be fought somewhere near at hand. There were citizens going about their business and soldiers from the commissariat gathering together supplies and equipment and loading them into a string of wagons, but not the great army she had hoped to find. Her heart sank. The British commander-in-chief was more elusive than a firefly and it was some time before she could establish that he had ridden north. Did he know that was where the enemy were concentrated? She was desperate for sleep and the horse was exhausted, but she could not stop now. She rode out again and two hours later she caught up with the rear of the British forces.

It took some time to convince them she was English and even longer to persuade them to take her to headquarters. 'I must speak to Lord Wellington,' she said. 'Please tell him I have news of Captain Whitely and Captain Lynmount.'

'Who are they?'

'He will know.'

The sentry who had stopped her handed her over to his sergeant who took her to his captain. She repeated her request to speak to Wellington and he echoed the sentry's question. 'Whitely and Lynmount. Who are they?'

'Scouts.'

'Where are they?'

'Behind the French lines.'

He looked at her pensively, weighing her up. She looked decidedly disreputable; her hair was a mess and, apart from splashing her face in water from a stream which was freezing cold, she had not washed. She was white-faced with fatigue, she knew, and could hardly sit upright in the saddle. 'How long have you been riding?' he asked.

'Days.' She laughed. 'Does it matter?'

'I'll take you to the women; they will look after you. . .'

'I don't want to go to the women,' she snapped. 'And I don't need looking after. Are you deaf, Captain? I asked to be taken to Viscount Wellington.'

He shrugged. 'Come with me. I'll speak to the colonel.'

The colonel was two miles ahead. On the way they passed column after column of troops, cavalry, heavy guns and wagons loaded with supplies and ammunition. The men were cheerful. After so long without confronting the enemy, they were looking forward to a scrap; they had hated the constant withdrawal. Unlike the French, they were neither half-starved nor ill-clad, though she doubted if there were as many of them as there were of the enemy.

From the colonel she was passed to an aide and then another, each time further up the road, until at last she found herself outside the wall surrounding the convent at Bussaco, which was decorated with bones and skulls designed in black and white stones. She shivered as they were challenged by a sentry and then passed through the only gate and up through a beautiful wood of maple, oak, laurel and cypress. At the door of the convent, she dismounted and waited while her latest escort went inside. He returned very quickly.

'Come with me.'

She left Thor tethered to one of the many trees which surrounded the convent and followed the aide into a narrow cork-lined cell with a brick floor and whitewashed walls. She had seen the great man in the distance before, when he had been reviewing the troops, but never close at hand, and she was surprised at how ordinary he seemed. He was not particularly handsome, but his eyes were keen and his smile set her at her ease. He rose from behind a desk and walked forward to take her hand. 'Come and sit down, ma'am.' He waved the aide away, then led her to a bench and sat down beside her. 'You have news of Captain Lynmount, I understand?'

'Yes, my lord. He sent me to tell you that the main French column is coming down through Viseu. It is about sixty-five thousand strong.' She took Robert's report from her skirt pocket and handed it to him.

He took it and smiled. 'They must have lost a few on the way.'

'Indeed, my lord, the *guerrilleros* and the Ordenanza have been very active and pick them off at every opportunity. The French are also very hungry.'

He smiled. 'I thought they might be.' He paused.

'Where is Captain Lynmount now? Why did he not return himself?'

'He has gone after Captain Whitely.'

'Gone after him? But Whitely was sent to find Robert. What happened?. Or are you too tired to tell me now?'

She was puzzled. 'But my lord, have you not more important things to do? Do you not need to give fresh orders?'

He gave a great whoop of a laugh which startled her. 'Everything is in hand, have no fear.'

'You knew all along?' she said. 'I have wasted my time and yours?'

'Not at all, my dear, it is always useful to have confirmation of intelligence and I do want to know what has happened to Captain Lynmount.'

She sat beside him and told him everything. He did not interrupt until she had finished, then he said, 'You are a very resourceful and courageous young lady, and I salute you.'

'Thank you, my lord.' Now it was all over she was almost dropping asleep where she sat.

'Go and rest now,' he said, rising and holding his hand out to her. 'Major Hamilton will escort you to the palace. They will look after you there. We will talk again tomorrow.' He raised her to her feet, then clapped his hands and the aide came back in and was instructed to take her to the palace and see she had everything she needed.

'Thank you, my lord.' She turned to go. 'Captain Lynmount's horse, I left him outside. . .'

'Thor?' he said in surprise. 'You rode that brute?'

'Yes.'

'He will be taken care of. Now go before you fall asleep on your feet.'

She was glad to obey. At the palace, once the home of King Manuel, but now appropriated for the use of the high command, she was shown into a room which

was the height of luxury. A bath was brought in and
filled with hot water and from somewhere, as if by
magic, nightclothes were found for her. Major
Hamilton was also very resourceful, she decided, as
she fell into bed. Her last thought before she fell asleep
was of Robert. Where was he? Had he found Rufus?
And if he had, what had he done with him? And
Juana? Would he find her too?

Forget! she commanded herself. Forget and think of
England, because that is where you will be going next.
Home!

But home was where the heart was, and hers was not
in England; it was wherever that enigmatic man
decided to settle.

The next day was bright and sunny though a cold
wind blew down from the mountains and made the air
chill. She rose and breakfasted and went back to the
convent. Today arrangements would be made for her
to go home; today she would turn her back on war and
death, hunger and thirst; today she would borrow some
money from one of his lordship's aides and buy herself
some clothes in Coimbra, feminine clothes, and a hat
and shoes. Concentrate on that, she told herself, not
the love you are leaving behind. It was better that way.

The convent stood on a fork in the road where the
chaussée from Viseu climbed to its highest before
dropping down to the plains of Coimbra. From just
outside its walls, Olivia had a clear view for miles
around, to the hills of the west which dipped down to
the Atlantic where the evacuation fleet stood by, and
to the east where Masséna's glittering columns could
be seen making their way towards them, mile upon
mile of foot soldiers, cavalry with coloured plumes
bobbing in the sun, horses, guns, wagons, mules and
camp followers. They could be seen winding their way
along every road, through the pine trees of the forests,
across the heather-covered hills.

'Impressive, aren't they?' She heard Wellington's barking laugh behind her.

She turned towards him. 'Yes, my lord. Frightening too.'

'Oh, there is no need for that, my dear; we shall lick them, never fear.'

'But I can see so few allied troops.'

'They are there just the same, behind that ridge, silent and waiting.' He pointed to a long hogback of a hill running north to south. 'Let Johnny Bluecoat come on, let him think we are withdrawing once again; he will learn differently tomorrow.'

'Tomorrow, my lord?'

'Yes. They will try to climb that ridge and they will be repulsed.' He laughed again, this imperturbable man who commanded the devotion of officers and men alike. 'Soult has brought up his army from the south to join Masséna and they think they have outmanoeuvred me, but they will see that I can move troops faster than they can. My southern army is in place on my flank.' He smiled at her. 'Now to our business, eh?'

'Yes, my lord.'

He took her arm and strolled with her along the paths through the wood, past streams and fountains, shrines and statues. She was aware that two of his officers followed discreetly behind them. 'I must thank you once again for bringing me news, but what I need most is Captain Robert Lynmount himself.'

'But he was cashiered, my lord, he is no longer a soldier.'

'Stuff and nonsense! Major Hamilton tells me those two men, his so-called accomplices, have been persuaded to tell the truth. The verdict of the court-martial has been reversed. But that is of little consequence.' He paused to look closely at her. She had still not recovered from her exhaustion, but no matter, she was strong. 'Now I am going to ask a great favour of you.'

'My lord?'

'Will you go back for me?'

'Back, my lord?'

'Yes, back. Take a message to that foolish man. I have work for him, urgent work, and he will listen to you.'

She doubted that and said so, which made him laugh. 'You do not know your own powers, my dear.'

'But I do not know where to find him, not exactly. He might be at São Jorge, or Villa de Fuentes, Salamanca even, anywhere at all.'

'I would wish him in Santander.'

'My lord?' She did not understand. 'I thought you wished him back here?'

'No time for that. He is to go at once to Santander and meet a courier from Rothschild in Paris. He will be given a consignment of gold. I have to pay this army of mine and without gold I cannot do it. 'Tis no good relying on London.'

She knew her mouth was hanging open, but every time she shut it he made another pronouncement which made it drop again. 'My lord, I do not understand. How can you have communication with Paris? And Santander is. . .'

'Deep in French-held Spain. I know it. Now, will you do it? I will give you sealed orders which he will not dare to disobey, but if you are caught with them on you. . .'

He did not finish; there was no need to elaborate. 'Will you go? I will send someone to go with you, someone entirely trustworthy.' He turned and beckoned to one of the men behind him. Olivia gasped aloud when she saw that it was Father Peredo. Wellington's loud laugh rang in her ears; he certainly enjoyed a joke. 'I believe you know the good father?'

'Indeed, yes.' She held out her hand to the priest as he came hurrying towards them.

'Well done, my child,' he said, grasping her hand in both his own.

'How did you get here?' she asked.

'I rode, just as you did.'

While they made their way back to the convent, he told her that he had been an agent for the British since the Battle of Vimeiro in 1808. When they had left after that, he had bided his time, gathering intelligence, convinced that they would return.

'And well it was that he did,' murmured his lordship. 'He has been invaluable.'

'I usually send messages through scouts like Robert, but this time I was afraid Robert would not get through and decided to come myself,' Father Peredo went on. 'I arrived a week ago but tomorrow I set off again for Villa de Fuentes.' He paused and looked into her face. 'If you have any love in your heart for that man of yours, you will come with me.'

'You speak of love for a man; why not love of country?'

He smiled. 'That too.'

'You will go with the father?' Wellington asked.

She nodded agreement; there was no need even to think about it, but she was not at all sure they would be able to find Robert and, if they did, whether he would be pleased to see her.

That night the British and Portuguese forces were forbidden to light fires. They ate a cold meal and lay down behind the crest of the hill in total darkness and uncanny silence, knowing that next day there would be a great battle.

Olivia, waking at dawn, rose from the massive four-poster and went to the window. The town and the surrounding hills were blanketed by fog. She washed and dressed quickly, gathered together her few belongings and went out in the chill air to the spot where the day before they had watched the approaching French columns. Now they could see nothing of either side.

Father Peredo was waiting for her, already mounted and once more dressed in clerical robes. There was someone with him, riding a small pony and holding Thor by the reins. It was Pedro.

She greeted him joyfully and sprang into the saddle. There would be no shopping in Coimbra, no voyage to London, no gossips to face, no long and lonely widowhood; she was going to find Robert. The slate had been wiped clean and he could, with honour, return to his regiment. Most of all, he must be made to see that Juana was not the woman for him, that there was someone nearer at hand, someone he had overlooked, someone whose life was not worth a farthing without him. She, who had always said he needed her, needed him with every tingling nerve, every fibre of her body, every thought in her head. Theirs had been no chance encounter; it had been ordained.

They turned their horses south to make a wide detour round the battlefield, feeling their way through the fog. Behind them the sound of gunfire told them that the skirmishers had made contact and there would be no more withdrawing. The long-awaited battle was about to begin.

'He was riding Pegasus,' Martin Davaco explained. 'He told the look-outs that he had come from you and had news for us. We thought something had happened to you and the *senhora*. . .' He paused. 'We asked him, "What has happened?", but he did not answer; instead he raised his gun and shot one of my men.' The partisan leader was still seething. 'We should have put an end to his miserable life when we first captured him. . .'

'I am sorry, that was my fault,' Robert said. After he had left Olivia he had made for a company of French cavalry he had seen earlier when reconnoitring but, after carefully skirting all round them, he had concluded Rufus had not joined them. His efforts had

not been entirely wasted because he had been able to
steal a horse from their lines, laughing as he rode away
with it. The next day he had picked up Whitely's trail
because of Pegasus—the grey was easily remembered—and after that it had been easy to follow him
back to São Jorge.

'Now he will die in torment. . .' Martin was saying.

'Why did you not kill him at the time?'

'He had friends. . .'

'French soldiers?'

'No, English deserters, about six or seven of them.
While he was talking to us, they had rounded up all the
women and children and took them to the church.
They threatened. . .' He stopped. 'The price of releas-
ing them was the loot we had taken off him and two
days' start. It was a small price to pay.' He sounded
almost apologetic.

'Which way did he go?'

The man shrugged. 'We searched for days but could
find no trace of him or his men. We think they crossed
the border into the mountains of Spain.'

Robert thanked him and rode on. Rufus Whitely was
on his way to Salamanca to join Juana, he was sure of
it. He wanted revenge. He savoured the idea as he
took the mountain roads over the border and into
Spain. Revenge would be sweet. It was because of
Rufus Whitely that he had lost his right to call himself
an officer and a gentleman. It was because of Rufus
Whitely that he had been forced to send Olivia away.
The thought of Olivia riding alone into heaven knew
what danger nearly drove him mad. But he could not
have brought her with him. He smiled wryly; she would
have spent the entire time arguing with him that what
he was doing was wrong.

Her apparent hardness was no more than a shell but
a difficult one to crack open; once or twice he had
caught a glimpse of the inner Olivia, the vulnerable,
insecure woman, and it always made him want to take

her in his arms and promise her anything, anything in the world, if only she would allow him to take care of her. But inevitably something happened to close her off from him again and most of it his fault. Her sharp manner concealed the tenderness of someone who could feel for others; she had proved that with her concern for the women and children of Villa de Fuentes and the way she had stayed to help him when all she had ever wanted was to go home.

She would be on her way home now. One day, someone somewhere would succeed in piercing that shell and reaching the soft heart of her and he envied the unknown man.

He wished they had met in different circumstances, in London perhaps, before the war, with his father beaming in pleasure and Olivia looking all woman, softly swathed in silk, her figure with a few more curves than it had now, her hair caught up at the back of her head and falling softly to her shoulders. . . No, her hair should be just as it was now—a golden halo, nothing more. He would have left her behind when he came to war, secure in the knowledge that when he returned she would be there waiting for him and she would never have known the horror of violent death, of hunger, of searing heat or freezing winds.

He stopped himself suddenly. The woman he had been describing to himself had not been Olivia, not the real Olivia; the real Olivia's character had been shaped by what she had been through and it was the real Olivia he loved, her independence, her resourcefulness, her cheerfulness, her sheer perversity. That was Olivia.

She was worth her weight in gold, worth more than a hundred Juanas, worth more than the satisfaction of a hollow revenge, more than the bringing to justice of a traitor who, when all was said and done, had failed. What was the good of winning back his claws if he could not sheath them? Claws only hurt the people you touched; better to be without them. The sound of his laughter echoed round the mountains, bouncing from peak to peak, as he turned his horse back the way he had come.

Days and days they had been travelling, Olivia, Father Peredo and Pedro, with no sign of Robert. He had stopped at São Jorge, they had established that, and he had been mounted, but then nothing. Now they were approaching Villa de Fuentes and all Olivia's hopes were pinned on finding him there. She told herself that her impatience was due to her errand, that Wellington depended on her and the courier would not stay in Santander indefinitely, all of which was true, but, more than that, she wanted to find Robert before he reached Salamanca.

They rode over the new bridge and along the village street, with all the inhabitants crowding out of their houses to welcome their priest. They did not like it when he was away; he was crucial to their lives; he stood between them and their oppressors. It was not until after everyone had eaten and drunk and given thanks for the father's safe return that they were able to ask about Robert and then they were told that nothing had been seen of him.

'The other one, we have seen,' one of the women said. 'The other Englishman. He was here two days ago with others. . .'

'Others?' queried Olivia, knowing she was referring to Rufus. 'How many?'

'Englishmen, about seven of them. He told us they were on a secret mission.'

'Which way did they go?'

She pointed into the mountains. 'That way.'

'We must get after them,' Olivia said.

'Where is Miguel Santandos?' Father Peredo asked. 'We need his help.'

'He has been away a long time,' an old man said. 'He left his command to José Gonzales, but yesterday he came back. He went after them, swearing to avenge his wife's murder.'

'Alone?' Father Peredo asked.

'He forbade anyone to follow him.'

'Get the men,' the priest ordered Pedro. 'Tell them to gather on the bridge by the monastery. I will meet them there.' He turned to Olivia. 'You wait in the village until we come back. We will resume the search for Captain Lynmount when this is done.'

Olivia did not argue, neither did she obey; she simply mounted Thor and followed him. Knowing it would be useless, he did not send her back.

They were approaching the monastery when they heard gunfire. Father Peredo dismounted and went forward on foot, dodging from tree to rock and rock to bush, with Olivia following, her rifle at the ready. A few moments later they came within sight of the building and found themselves behind Whitely and his band of desperadoes who were trying to cross the bridge to reach the safety of the high peaks and now found themselves pinned down by fire from the building. Olivia crept closer to Father Peredo.

'Is it Don Santandos?' she whispered, looking up at the stout walls. 'Could it be Robert? Or both of them?'

'No. There is only one gun and I saw a glimpse of Miguel at a window.'

'Where are our men?'

He looked towards the bridge. It was empty, almost inviting the deserters to cross. 'Pedro must have had trouble finding them. They will come.'

'We cannot wait for them,' she said, raising her rifle. 'If Rufus Whitely realises Don Santandos is alone, he will storm the monastery, and one man cannot keep so many at bay.'

He turned and grinned at her and loaded his own weapon, an ancient musket which was normally hung on the wall of his living-room as a reminder that war was an evil thing. 'Come on, then, let us join the fun.'

Coming as they did, from the rear, they forced the attackers to turn and defend themselves. They dashed from cover to cover, reloading alternately and using pistols as well as her rifle and his musket; it made it seem as if there were more than two of them. The ruse would not serve for long and Olivia found herself praying that Pedro had found the guerrillas and they were even now approaching the bridge from the other side.

A shriek told her that one of the men had been hit, though whose shot it had been she was not at all sure. In a way she hoped it had not been hers; in spite of her prowess with a gun, the idea of killing anyone was abhorrent. All she wanted to do was render them harmless. If she and Father Peredo could keep pushing forward, they could herd them all back to the building where Don Santandos was still firing.

The priest had advanced several yards. She reloaded and followed him, passing the body of the man who had been hit. It was Rufus Whitely himself. She did not want to look at him and hurried past, eyes averted.

A noise immediately behind her startled her. She swung round to see Rufus Whitely getting to his feet. He had a demoniacal grin on his face as he came towards her. She raised her rifle, but she could not fire; her finger seemed frozen to the trigger and would not move. He reached out and wrenched the gun from her hand, but instead of turning it on her he grabbed her and held her close to his chest. Don Santandos dared not fire at him for fear of hitting her.

'Thought I was dead, did you?' he said with a short laugh of derision as he marched her forward. 'Rufus Whitely is not that easy to kill.' He shouted to his men, 'I've got the girl, you get the preacher. Keep the one in the monastery covered.'

She was forced to watch as Father Peredo was surrounded and disarmed, but not before he had downed two of them. It made them angry but Rufus would not let them kill the priest, or her. 'Later,' he said. 'We need them. Fetch their horses.'

Thor proved troublesome, much to Olivia's delight, but they brought them both up at last and put them with their own mounts, a handful of bedraggled horses and a few mules—except for one. Olivia was delighted to see Pegasus, though he was in poor condition and she concluded he had been ridden hard. The sight of him put new life into her; they were not beaten yet. She remained alert for an opportunity of turning the tables on the bandits as they forced her, Father Peredo and the animals towards the bridge, using them as shields while Don Santandos watched helplessly from the monastery windows.

A shot from among the boulders on the other side of the bridge spattered into the road ahead of them. Thor reared up, snorting his terror. The man who was leading him could not hold him and he galloped over the bridge and up into the hills. His going panicked the other animals and they began to mill round in the road, rearing and whinnying. In the confusion no one noticed Olivia slip away and dash back towards the monastery. Miguel Santandos, who had seen her coming, ran down to meet her and thrust a gun into her hand. 'Who was that shooting from the other side?' he asked.

'I didn't see, probably one of your men. Father Peredo sent Pedro to find them.'

'Pick them off,' he said, firing as he spoke. 'And let's have no more of your woman's squeamishness.' He reloaded as she fired. 'Watch out for the father.'

Father Peredo, more agile than she had ever seen him, had thrown himself over the parapet of the bridge. She did not see how he could survive the dive towards the water so far below and his unthinking courage gave her the spur she needed to continue firing and reloading and firing again. The bandits, caught on the bridge, were being shot at from both sides and several of them dropped, but she did not pause to consider who had

felled them; Don Santandos was right — it was no time
to begin behaving like a woman.

Whitely's force was down to three men besides
himself before they surrendered, and not a moment
too soon; Olivia and Don Santandos were out of
ammunition. She walked forward with the guerrilla,
holding the empty gun in front of her; their adversaries
were not to know she could not fire. She almost
dropped it when she saw Robert come out from behind
a rock on the far side of the bridge and walk towards
them. He was, she noted as she cried his name, wearing
his red coat again. Held together with cross-belts, it
still had no buttons on it, but he was wearing it with
pride.

She was about to fling her weapon away and run
towards him when she heard Don Santandos chuckle
beside her. 'Now is not the time to be a woman either,
señora. Keep your place and keep your eyes open.'

Slowly, oh, so slowly, she approached the bridge,
while her head whirled. What should she say to him?
What would he say to her? She should be miles away
on the high seas on the way to England, he should be
in Salamanca with Juana. She had been searching for
him without any real hope of finding him and now he
was here, here where he had first met her. She watched
him coming nearer. His face was drawn with fatigue,
his hazel eyes clouded, the lines about his mouth a
little deeper, but he was smiling. Soon he would be
able to reach out a hand and touch her. Her body
tingled with anticipation.

Rufus Whitely, standing with the remnants of his
men, suddenly produced a pistol from his belt and
raised it to his shoulder. Olivia heard the sharp report
of a gun going off at the same instant as she hurled
herself at Robert and dragged him to the ground. They
lay sprawled together, clinging to each other, unable to
believe they were both still alive, but she could feel the
beating of his heart against her ear and he could see

the soft rise and fall of her breasts as she tried to regain her breath. Both laughed aloud with the joy of it. Only when she rolled off him and sat up did she realise it had not been Rufus Whitely who had fired but Don Santandos. The guerrilla leader had saved one bullet, knowing exactly what he meant to do with it. Rufus Whitely lay dead at his feet.

Robert scrambled to his feet and bent towards her, holding out his hand to help her to her feet. 'Of all the foolhardy things to do,' he said sharply, knowing how close she had come to being shot in the back in her effort to save him and unable to express his concern in any other way. 'You could have been killed. . .'

Still laughing, she took his proffered hand and found herself standing in his arms. 'But I was not,' she retorted. 'Robert, I. . .' The laughter suddenly turned to tears. Sobs of relief and remorse at the killing, of love and despair shook her slight frame and she could not stop them. She wept uncontrollably. 'Robert.' She could find no other words.

He held her close against him, cradling her head into his shoulder and stroking the back of it with a hand that shook. 'Don't cry, my darling, don't cry,' he murmured. It was so unlike her to burst into tears that he did not know what to do. He felt big and awkward and completely inadequate. 'It is all over now.'

She leaned back and lifted a tear-streaked face to him. 'All over,' she repeated, then suddenly laughed. 'What is all over?'

'That.' He jerked his head back towards the killing ground.

'Oh, and what about your claws?'

'I have decided I do not need claws. I will go home with you.'

'And Juana?'

'That is most decidedly over and done with. I have known that since the day I met you.' He smiled. 'There is no one quite like you and I love you more dearly than I know how to say.'

'You do?'

'Didn't you realise that?'

'How could I? You never gave so much as a hint. Come to think of it,' she added, 'you didn't have much to say at all about how you really felt. Strong and silent, that's you.'

'I did not want a put-down.'

'A put-down!' Her laughter rang out, startling the prisoners who had been tied up by Don Santandos and were morosely watching him round up the horses. 'Oh, Robert, how comical you are!'

'Being laughed at is worse than a put-down,' he said, pretending hurt.

She was immediately serious. 'Oh, my darling, I am not laughing at you, I am laughing at my own stupidity. Married twice before and still I have not learned that a man sometimes needs a push in the right direction. I longed for you to tell me you loved me.'

'You said you would not marry again, you said you had done with men.'

'That was before I met you and fell in love for the very first time.'

'But I tried to ask you to marry me and you stopped me. You would not let me go on.'

'It would have been for the wrong reason. I did not want you to marry me out of duty. I wanted you to say it was because you loved me.'

'I am saying it. Like this.' He bent his head to kiss her. They forgot where they were, forgot the prisoners watching them in sullen silence, forgot the dead Rufus and the faithless Juana, forgot Tom and Philippe, forgot everything except the pleasure of that kiss and the promise of more delights to come. He did not want to release her, afraid she would disappear on the wind that sighed down the pass and rustled the leaves of the trees.

'In truth, this will never do,' said a voice which sounded uncommonly like Father Peredo's. 'I advised you before to do something about your unholy liaison but now I really must insist on it.'

She twisted out of Robert's arms and flung herself at the priest. 'Father, you are alive! I thought. . .'

'Clung to the struts,' he said. 'Climbed down and then came up the path. Now, what is the state of the play?'

'Four dead and three prisoners,' Miguel answered him. 'And Lolita is avenged.'

'And Robert loves me,' Olivia said, laughing with the sheer joy of it.

The priest turned to her and cocked one eyebrow. 'So what's new?'

'You knew?' She was astonished.

'It seems everyone but you knew it,' he said laconically. 'Now, I think a wedding before you go on, don't you?' He paused. 'Has the good captain been told of his next assignment?'

'Next assignment?' Robert queried.

'Now, you did not suppose this young lady came all the way back from Bussaco with me just for the pleasure of being kissed, do you?'

Robert turned from the priest to Olivia; it had only just occurred to him to wonder why Olivia was in Spain when he had supposed her to be crossing the Bay of Biscay, if not actually back in England. Had he misunderstood her yet again? 'Why *did* you come back?'

She laughed. 'Father Peredo was right — for the pleasure of a kiss.' She watched the changing expressions cross his face, then added, 'And because I was asked to find you by Viscount Wellington himself. It had been Captain Whitely's mission, but he failed to complete it. I have orders for you.'

'What orders?'

'Number one.' She held up her hand with one finger pointing skywards. 'You must marry me tomorrow.'

'That is one order it will be a pleasure to obey.'

'Number two,' she went on, holding up a second finger. 'You are to proceed forthwith to Santander and there meet with a representative of Lord Rothschild who will give you gold for the army's coffers.'

He groaned. 'Just when I thought I was going back to England with you. It really is most unfair.'

'Three,' she said, ignoring his protests, 'you are to report back to his lordship to have the verdict of the court-martial rescinded and promotion to major confirmed. That is,' she added with a twinkle in her eye which warned him to be on his guard, 'that is if we come safely back from Santander with the gold. . .'

'We?' he yelled. 'We? What are you talking about, woman? If you think. . .'

'I go with you.'

'Oh, no, you do not! You will go back to England and wait for me like a good wife. God knows I do not want to part from you. . .'

'Then don't.'

'You could be killed. We both could.'

'So, in the words of the good father, what's new? It could have happened any time in the last two months and I did not hear you complaining about the danger then.' She laughed suddenly and stood on tiptoe to plant a kiss on his nose. 'I will not leave you. You know perfectly well you cannot manage without me. . .'

He sighed, knowing he had lost, but he took pleasure in the defeat. What he would have done if she had conceded, he did not know. He did not want to go anywhere without her, now or ever. She was all woman, argumentative, provocative creature that she was, and he would not have her any other way.

The other exciting

| MASQUERADE |
| *Historical* |

available this month is:

EMPIRE OF THE HEART

Jasmine Cresswell

Lady Lucinda Larkin, having accompanied her father to India, suffered the horrifying trauma of seeing him murdered before her eyes, and then spent two years captive in Afghanistan before being rescued by the Indian trader, Rashid.

Lucy's return to London was a mixed blessing, for the society of 1877 believed her to inevitably be a fallen woman. And her stepsister Penelope was in daily expectation of receiving an offer from Edward, Baron Ridgeholm – who bore a startling resemblance to Rashid! But this pompous inane man surely had nothing to do with the resourceful and courageous trader?

Look out for the two intriguing

MASQUERADE *Historical*

Romances coming in August

WHISPERING SHADOWS
Marion Carr

Despite the strides women were making in 1907, Abigail
Carter felt stifled as companion to Mrs Emilia Goodenough,
and standing in loco parentis to her sister Polly was no
sinecure!

All the ladies were roused to excitement when Emilia's
nephew, Carl Montegne, arrived to sweep them off to Italy to
help him seek the long lost family fortune. But, Carl made it
clear he really only wanted to sweep his aunt, and even the
lovely castello couldn't stop the friction between Carl and
Abigail – until the enchantment of the quest suddenly turned
into danger, and Abigail knew the extent of her feelings . . .

A MOST EXCEPTIONAL QUEST
Sarah Westleigh

'John Smith' was something of an enigma. Plainly gently
born, he had been fighting in the Peninsular War, and had
apparently lost his memory. While widowed Mrs Davinia
Darling felt sorry for him, she saw no reason why her family
should take Mr Smith to their bosom! Still less did she see
why her own services were needed to aid Mr Smith in his
search for his identity. That she was discomposed by his
effect on her, and found the undercurrent of laughter in his
voice intriguing, she would not allow to weigh with her – the
sooner he found his memory, the quicker she could return to
her safe mode of life!

Also available soon in Large Print

TWO HISTORICAL ROMANCES

MASQUERADE Historical

Witness the fight for love and honour, and experience the tradition and splendour of the past for FREE! We will send you 2 Masquerade Historical Romances PLUS a cuddly teddy and a mystery gift. Then, if you choose, go on to enjoy 4 exciting Masquerades for only £2.25 each! Return the coupon below today to:-

Mills & Boon Reader Service, FREEPOST, PO Box 236, Croydon, Surrey CR9 9EL

& TWO FREE GIFTS!

- NO STAMP REQUIRED - - - - - - - - - ✂ - - - - -

Please rush me 2 FREE Masquerade historical romances and 2 FREE gifts! Please also reserve me a Reader Service subscription, which means I can look forward to receiving 4 brand new Masquerades for only £9.00 every 2 months, postage and packing FREE. If I choose not to subscribe, I shall write to you within 10 days and still keep my FREE books and gifts. I may cancel or suspend my subscription at any time. I am over 18 years. Please write in BLOCK CAPITALS.

Ms/Mrs/Miss/Mr _____ EP 51 M

Address _____

_____

_____ Postcode _____

Signature _____

Offer closes 31st July 1993. The right is reserved to refuse an application and change the terms of this offer. One application per household. Overseas readers please write for details. Southern Africa write to B.S.I. Ltd., Box 41654, Craighall, Transvaal 2024. You may be mailed with offers from other reputable companies as a result of this application. Please tick box if you would prefer not to receive such offers. ☐

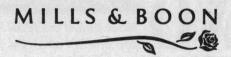

MILLS & BOON

Our ever popular historical romance series—Masquerade—will be undergoing a transformation in October 1993. The mask will be removed to reveal...

LEGACY *of* LOVE

An exciting range of 4 historical romances from mediaeval settings to the turn of the 20th century.

Every month will feature 1 much loved Regency romance along with an increasing variety of romance with historical backgrounds such as the French Revolution and the Californian Gold Rush.

All your favourite Masquerade authors and some newcomers have been brought together in 'LEGACY OF LOVE'.

From October 1993, in a new longer length. Price £2.50

Available from W.H. Smith, John Menzies, Martins, Forbuoys,
most supermarkets and other paperback stockists.
Also available from Mills & Boon Reader Service, Freepost, PO Box 236,
Thornton Road, Croydon, Surrey CR9 9EL. (UK Postage & Packing free)